THE
TROUBLESHOOTERS

A GUNS OF THE VIGILANTES WESTERN

THE TROUBLESHOOTERS

WILLIAM W. JOHNSTONE

AND J.A. JOHNSTONE

PINNACLE BOOKS
Kensington Publishing Corp.

www.kensingtonbooks.com

PINNACLE BOOKS are published by

Kensington Publishing Corp.
119 West 40th Street
New York, NY 10018

PUBLISHER'S NOTE
Following the death of William W. Johnstone, the Johnstone family is working with a carefully selected writer to organize and complete Mr. Johnstone's outlines and many unfinished manuscripts to create additional novels in all of his series like The Last Gunfighter, Mountain Man, and Eagles, among others. This novel was inspired by Mr. Johnstone's superb storytelling.

All Kensington titles, imprints, and distributed lines are available at special quantity discounts for bulk purchases for sales promotion, premiums, fund-raising, educational, or institutional use.

Special book excerpts or customized printings can also be created to fit specific needs. For details, write or phone the office of the Kensington Sales Manager: Attn.: Sales Department. Kensington Publishing Corp., 119 West 40th Street, New York, NY 10018. Phone: 1-800-221-2647.

PINNACLE BOOKS, the Pinnacle logo, and the WWJ steer head logo are Reg. U.S. Pat. & TM Off.

First Printing: October 2021

ISBN-13: 978-0-7860-4761-1

10 9 8 7 6 5 4 3 2 1

Printed in the United States of America

of buildings half-a-mile to his east across the west Texas plain, a ramshackle sprawl that gave the town the appearance of a shipwreck adrift on a shoaling green sea.

"What kind of town is that?" the man said.

"A town like any other. More prosperous than most."

"Will I be made welcome?"

"Made welcome? Yes. If your pockets chime with coin."

The woman wore a brown, cotton dress, much patched and mended. A threadbare shawl covered bowed shoulders and on her head a poke bonnet, ragged around its edges. On her feet she wore laceless, hobnailed boots, obviously castoffs. Her skin was wrinkled from the unrelenting Texas sun, and her eyes were colorless, once blue, now faded by age and cataracts.

"Grandmother, I'm looking for a woman," the horseman said. "Are there such in Broken Back?"

Thunder rumbled in the distance, and the sky threatened lightning. Gray clouds curled like sheets of lead, and the air smelled of far-off rain.

"There are women in Broken Back," the crone said. "There are respectable women and a few of the other kind. What is your preference?"

"I seek a woman who arrived in town recently," the man said. "Young, pretty, probably of the other kind."

"And what is your business with this young lady?"

"I plan to take her home."

The old lady shivered. "You make me feel afraid. All dressed in black, are you a parson . . . or are you death?"

"No, not a parson and I've been death for some, not for others," the rider said. "But not for you, grandmother. Now, what of this woman?"

"That one came into town by the Patterson stage," the woman said. "She's a whore, but I think she has a kind heart. She stopped me in the street and gave me a silver dollar."

"Do you know her name, this woman?"

"If I did, I can't remember. Say a name and maybe it will come back to me."

"Her name is Yolanda Butler."

The old woman nodded. "Yes, yes, that is her. I recollect that name . . . Yolanda."

"Where can I find her?"

"She's pretty."

"Yes, she is as I recollect."

"The prettiest whores work in the Brass Buckle saloon," the woman said.

"Who owns the place?"

"Simon Trigg is his name." The horseman nodded, and the old woman said, "Walk wide around him." She made a gun of her hand. "Pistolero. He's killed many."

"I've met his kind before," the rider said. "I'll be careful."

Rain ticked through the branches of the cottonwood, and lightning flashed, followed by a boom of thunder. The bright day had gone dark. The wind rose.

The horseman shrugged into a black slicker and then urged his mount forward. He reached into his coat pocket, leaned from the saddle, and handed a coin to the old woman. Amazed, she looked at the small gold piece in her palm and said, "Five dollars . . . for me?"

"Yes, for you. It's storming," the rider said. "Pick no more dewberries today, grandmother. Buy yourself happiness. With mirth and laughter let old wrinkles come."

As the man urged his horse forward, the woman said to his back, "Who are you?"

"My name is Frank James," the rider said. "And I often quote from Shakespeare. There are some who say it's a bad habit."

"Ha!" the old woman said. "Where is Jesse?"

"Cold in the grave this last seven years."

"Yes, now I remember," the woman said. "I'll say a prayer for him. For Jesse."

"He'd like that," Frank James said.

"Why do you gather dewberries in the rain, grandmother?"

The man sat a black horse under a lone cottonwood. He was dressed in black: black pants, frockcoat, boots, and hat. Shabby. His cartridge belt and holster were black, as were his mustache, hair, and eyes. The only color about him was the silver that adorned his saddle and the ivory handle of the Colt strapped high on his right side. A Winchester was in the boot under his left knee.

The old woman, gray and bent, showed a half-full basket of fruit to the horseman. "I trade them at the mercantile in town."

"You exchange the berries for food?" the man said.

The woman shook her head. "I trade the berries for laudanum. I'm old and I'm sick and I don't need food, but I do need laudanum. It brings moments of happiness into an unhappy life."

"What town is this?" the rider said.

"The town is called Broken Back," the old woman said. "Named for the men who built it."

The horseman's gaze slowly shifted to the collection

Chapter One

Broken Back was a Western town like any other, a wide, dusty street bookended by rows of rickety, false-fronted buildings, mostly stores of one kind or another, a bank, a couple of saloons, a two-story hotel, and a dance-hall. A couple of burned-out structures offended the eye like rotten teeth, and a livery stable stood at the end of the street near a rusty windmill. Scattered behind the buildings, scores of wood-framed tarpaper shacks and outhouses looked as though they'd wandered into the prairie and lost their way. There was no church and no school. The town's reason for existence was to provide cowboys from the surrounding ranches a place to buy what they needed and come Friday nights a haven to drink, gamble, and whore. Nothing else. Prayer and book learning didn't enter most of the inhabitants' thinking. Overall, Broken Back was a dreary, bleak, and cheerless place that had squatted for a half-dozen years on the teetering edge of nowhere.

Now as Frank James rode into town, the rain had already turned the street into a sluggish quagmire of odd, mustard-colored mud. Lightning seared the black sky, and thunder rolled. He smiled. As they so often did, a line from his beloved Shakespeare popped into his head, "When shall we three meet again, in thunder, lightning or in rain? When the hurly-burly's done, when the battle's lost and won."

Frank hoped there would be no battle. He'd ride in, do what had to be done, and ride out again.

He didn't know it then, but all too soon his hopes would be dashed.

As thunder banged, Frank James made two stops before he headed for the hotel.

The first was to the bank, a small, cramped building that smelled of wood polish. The teller was an innocuous-looking young man with thin, sandy hair parted in the middle and a trimmed mustache. A pair of mild brown eyes peered from behind round glasses with gold rims.

The teller flashed a practiced smile and said, "And what can I do for you this fine morning?"

"It's raining," Frank said.

"Ah, yes, so it is," the teller said.

"I'm here to make a deposit," Frank said. He reached into his saddlebags, pulled out a white sack, and stretched to pass it over the brass grate to the teller. "Five thousand, count it," he said.

"Right away, sir," the teller beamed, as though it was his own money. "And your name, sir?"

"Frank James."

Now the teller's jaw dropped and he swallowed hard a couple of times before he yelled, "Mr. Bradshaw!"

A door at the rear of the building opened and a stout,

bald, red-cheeked man wearing black broadcloth stepped toward the teller. He looked at Frank, didn't like what he saw, and said, "My name is John Bradshaw. I'm the bank manager. What seems to be the trouble here?"

"No trouble," Frank said. "I want to deposit the five thousand dollars your clerk holds in his hand."

Bradshaw's attitude changed, he smiled at Frank, and said to the teller, "Take the man's deposit, Tim. What's wrong with you?"

The teller looked pale, as though he'd seen a ghost. "Mr. Bradshaw . . . this . . . this man is Frank James."

"*The* Frank James?" Bradshaw said. "Jesse's brother?"

"From this day to the ending of the world, Jesse will be remembered," Frank said. "And I'll always be just his brother. Yes, I am he, but I'm here to make a deposit, not a withdrawal."

"Droll, Mr. James, very droll," Bradshaw said. He stepped out from behind the counter and said, "Let me shake the hand that shook the West." The banker pumped Frank's hand and then said, "I'm proud to have you as a depositor, Mr. James." He smiled. "Jesse's brother's money is safe in my bank. I can scarce believe it."

Frank James's second stop was to the livery stable where he put up his horse.

The livery owner was a one-armed man who had an empty left sleeve.

"Where did you get it?" Frank said.

"Gettysburg. I was in General John B. Gordon's corps. The Yankees were the hammer of God in that battle."

Thunder crashed with a sound like cannon fire.

"My name is Frank James, and we are comrades, you and I."

The man's lined face registered surprise. "Yes . . . Jesse's brother," he said.

"The very same."

"I always figured Jesse was the last casualty of the War Between the States," the man said.

"You figured right, my friend," Frank said. "The war ended, but Jesse and me, we never stopped fighting."

"The man stuck out his hand. "Name's Ed Wallace. I was a brevet major in the 60th Georgia Infantry."

Frank looked around him at the sagging barn, thin beams of sunlight streaming through every chink and hole. "You've fallen far, Major."

"The South fell far and took me with it," Wallace said. He smiled. "Broken Back is a long way from the officers' balls and beautiful belles of Richmond. So what are you doing here, Mr. James?"

"Call me Frank. I'm here to return a runaway girl to her home in Kansas. After that, I'll return to my regular job in Dallas."

"You a lawman there in Dallas?" Wallace said.

"No. I'm a shoe salesman."

Wallace laughed, something he didn't do often. "Doesn't that beat all. Major Edward Wallace of the Charleston Wallaces is shoveling dung with one hand in a jerkwater town in Texas and the famous Frank James is a shoe salesman in Dallas. Aren't we a pair?"

"Major, do you enjoy having a livery stable?" Frank said.

"It's a living."

"And so is selling shoes."

Both men laughed and shook hands again.

After arranging that his bay be rubbed down and fed oats, Frank then sought out the Palace Hotel in a downpour and signed the register with his real name.

When the desk clerk looked up at him, his face framing a question, Frank said, "Yes, I'm Jesse's brother."

"Then welcome to the Palace Hotel, Mr. James," the clerk said. "You honor us with your presence."

"Glad to hear that," Frank said. "There was a time when I wasn't always so welcome."

"Times change," the clerk said. "Forgive and forget, I say. I've given you the best room in the house, number twelve on the second floor." The youngster behind the desk grinned. "It's the bridal suite."

"Of course, it is," Frank said. "And that's why it costs so much. What is the room per night?"

"Two dollars, and that includes a complimentary bottle of champagne."

"What's room eleven cost?"

"One dollar a night," the clerk said.

"Then I'll take that for one night," Frank said.

The disappointed clerk gave him the room key. "Be careful on the stairs, Mr. James," he said.

"Young feller, I'm always careful," Frank said.

It should be noted here that when the desk clerk spread the word around town that the notorious Frank James was in town, the local newspaper, *The Broken Back Bulletin,* made it front-page news.

But the page was scrapped the following day, replaced by the much more exciting headline:

FRANK JAMES KILLS AGAIN.

A yellowed copy of that edition of the Bulletin was found among Frank's possessions after he died.

As the thunderstorm raged, Frank James retired to his room, removed his hat, boots, and gunbelt and stretched out on the bed. It had been a long ride from Dallas, and it had tired him out. He was forty-six years old that summer, not old, but no longer young, and the hard, hunted life he'd led as an outlaw had aged him.

He closed his eyes, listening to the rain drum on the window and soon sleep took him.

Sheriff Jared Wagner watched the rain runnel down the dusty panes of his office window, his face, plump cheeks traced with a drinker's broken veins, grimacing in thought. Finally, he sighed deeply and said, "Go talk with him, Dan. Ask him why he's in Broken Back."

Dan Caine smiled. "That's simple. He's here to rob the bank."

"Not funny. Hell, he deposited five thousand dollars," Wagner said. "Bank robbers withdraw money, they don't make deposits. At least, none I've known."

"Maybe he's just passing through," Dan said. "On his way to rob another town's bank."

"Dan, would you pull your lariat on that bank-robbing stuff," Wagner said. "Frank James must have a good reason for being in town. Hell, now he's retired, maybe he has a mind to settle down right here. He could put his rocker on the hotel porch and watch the world go by."

"Broken Back ain't a town that has much world going

by," Dan said. "In a six-month ol' Frank might see a drunk cowboy ride by or a stray dog or maybe a jackrabbit."

Wagner sighed again. "Talk with him, Dan."

Dan Caine rose from his chair and pulled on the official sheriff's department slicker, a yellow oilskin that began its life on the high seas and had seen better days. Dan was a tall young man that summer of 1889, built on the lanky side, with coal black hair and eyebrows that were a little too heavy for his good-looking, lean face. Under his dragoon mustache he had a wide, expressive mouth that smiled easily and often. Dan Caine looked a man right in the eye, holding nothing back, and most times he had a stillness about him, a calm, but of the uncertain sort that had the brooding potential to suddenly burst into a moment of hellfire action. In his youth, he'd spent three years in Huntsville for attempted train robbery, made friends with John Wesley Hardin, and had been straight up about it with Sheriff Wagner. The lawman had replied that he didn't give a tinker's cuss. What he needed was a gun-handy deputy, not a saint. In fact, when it came to dealing with rowdy Friday-night cowboys, the unsaintlier a lawman, the better.

Wagner watched Dan rub the ears of his little calico cat before stepping to the door and said, "You forgot your gun."

The younger man smiled. "This is a social call," he said. "Me and Frank are going to make like kissin' kinfolk."

"Don't depend on it," Wagner said. "They say he's as mean as a curly wolf."

"As far as I know, Frank hasn't committed a crime since Jesse died," Dan said.

"Maybe so," Wagner said. "But you don't take chances with a man like that." He opened a drawer and slid a small

Smith & Wesson .38 revolver across the desktop. "Carry that in the pocket of the slicker," he said. "When you and Frank are making like kissin' cousins, keep that pointed at his belly."

"Not a trusting man, are you, Jared?" He shoved the revolver into the slicker pocket.

"Live longer that way," Wagner said.

Chapter Two

Dan Caine walked through rain to the Palace Hotel and stepped to the front desk. Before he could say a word, the clerk jabbed a thumb, indicating the upper floor.

"Is he in?" Dan said.

"He's in," the clerk said. "Room eleven."

"How is he?" Dan said.

"I don't know how he is. He doesn't like champagne, I know that."

Dan mounted the stairs, annoyed that his stomach had suddenly balled up in a knot. Frank James had learned to kill during the War Between the States and afterward, and by all accounts he was mighty good at it. He stood at the door to Room 11, steeling himself, but a voice from inside said, "Well, if you aim to come in, come in. Don't stand there dawdling."

Dan swallowed hard, opened the door, and stepped inside. He smiled. "Can you see through doors, Mr. James?"

"I heard you," Frank said. Then, figuring that an explanation was called for, he added, "In the seventeen years and more I was on the scout, I never knew a good night's rest. Now I still listen for footsteps in the hallway, and

I've lost the habit of sleep." An ivory-handled Colt, the cartridge belt wrapped around its holster, lay on a table alongside a water basin and pitcher. It was close enough to be handy.

"You know my name, what's yours?" Frank said. "By the way, you're dripping water all over the rug. What in hades is that thing you're wearing?"

"It's an oilskin. Came off a whaler, I'm told," Dan said. "And my name is Dan Caine. I'm the Broken Back Deputy Sheriff."

"Oilskin?" Frank said, as though he hadn't heard. "Who wears an oilskin?"

"Mariners mostly," Dan said.

"Sailors? In that getup you look like the canary my ma kept in a cage back home in Missouri. She called it Charlotte. You look like Charlotte in that getup. I've never seen the like."

"Well, anyhow, I'm here to welcome you to Broken Back, Mr. James," Dan said.

"Call me Frank."

"Frank."

"I'm not here to rob the bank, Deputy. I'm all done with that. I've got me a regular job in Dallas and I make an honest dollar."

"Doing what?"

"I'm a shoe salesman."

If Frank James was taken aback by the yellow oilskin, Dan Caine was equally dumbfounded by the notorious outlaw's new profession.

As a smile touched Dan's lips, Frank said, "Yeah, hard to believe, isn't it?" He shrugged. "I'm good at it. I've always liked lace-up shoes. Never wore them much, but I admire the way they look . . . oxford, derby, blucher, budapester, I like them all."

"So why are you in Broken Back?" Dan said.

Frank smiled. "That's the question you came here to ask, isn't it?"

"Yeah, but in a friendly way," Dan said. "Think of me as a one-man welcome committee."

"All right, I'm here to take a runaway woman back to the James family farm in Clay County, Missouri," Frank said.

"Who is she?" Dan said.

"My wife's cousin. It was Annie who sent me here. She and Yolanda were very close."

"Yolanda? That's the name of the runaway?"

"Yeah. Yolanda Butler. She works in the Brass Buckle saloon, and maybe she's whoring. I don't know. Anyway, it doesn't matter a damn, I'm taking her home."

"How did you know she was here in Broken Back?"

"She wrote to Annie and told her where she was," Frank said. "She said she was done running."

"What's she running from?" Dan said.

"A killing."

"What kind of a killing?"

"The usual kind, when somebody ends up dead." Frank saw the question in Dan's eyes and answered it. "She shot a man in an Abilene brothel. His name was Decker, Tom Decker, the oldest son of a local cattle baron."

Dan smiled. "Seems like a catch."

"He wasn't. From what Annie told me, Yolanda knew the man was taking mercury for the pox, and when he tried to force himself on her, she pumped two balls from a derringer into his belly and snuffed out his candle."

Dan said, "She should have stayed put. If she'd stood trial, no jury would've convicted her."

"There was to be no trial. A cowboy lynch mob thought otherwise," Frank said. "She rode out of Abilene minutes ahead of the hemp posse and didn't stop running until she stumbled on Broken Back."

Dan Caine took a deep breath and then said, "Quite a story."

Frank James's black eyes glittered. "You wouldn't have any ideas, would you?"

"What kind of ideas?"

"The idea of arresting Yolanda Butler for murder."

"You say it happened in Abilene?"

"Yeah. In a brothel."

"Abilene is out of my jurisdiction and as far as I know the woman has committed no crimes in Broken Back. If she's selling it, she's welcomed by the law in this town. Every Friday night Sheriff Wagner collects a five-dollar fine from each of the girls. The money goes to pay police department expenses. Or so he says."

"I'm taking Yolanda out of the Brass Buckle tonight," Frank said. "Can you dance to that tune, Deputy?"

"Just so long as you keep it friendly," Dan said.

"It will be," Frank said. "Now let me get back to my nap."

Dan smiled. "I thought you never slept."

"I sleep with one eye open," Frank said.

"I've got a calico cat who can sleep standing up," Dan said.

"I've done that many a time back in the old days," Frank said.

"You miss Jesse?" Dan said.

"Yeah, every day of my life," Frank said.

Dan nodded. And headed to the door. "I'll let you nap," he said.

"Deputy."

"What?"

"If the hotel charges me extra for drying the rug, I'll send you the bill," Frank said. "Your damned canary coat must've dropped a gallon of water on the floor."

Chapter Three

"Frank James told me I look like a canary in this oilskin," Dan Caine said.

"He told you that?" Sheriff Jared Wagner said.

"Sure did."

"You should've shot him."

"I didn't have my gun. Only the .38 you gave me."

"A canary. That's a small yellow bird. Sings all the time, don't it?"

"I don't know."

"Well, it does. Coffee's biled. Help yourself and tell me why the hell Frank James is in Broken Back. By the way, you do look like a canary in that getup."

Dan hung the oilskin on a hook behind the door, greeted his cat, and then poured coffee into a thick white mug. He sat in the chair opposite Wagner and recounted his conversation with Frank James.

After Dan stopped speaking, the sheriff said, his florid face incredulous, "A shoe salesman?"

"That's what he said. Told me he was good at it."

Wagner shook his head, slowly, pondering the unthinkable. Finally, he said, "I think I liked him better when he was robbing banks."

"He's come down in the world," Dan said. "A big change of professions."

"And he plans to take the Yolanda Butler gal out of the Brass Buckle tonight?"

"Seems like," Dan said. "I mean, that's what he said."

"By force if necessary? Grab her by the corset and carry her out of the saloon kicking and screaming."

"Jared, I don't have a crystal ball."

"What's Simon Trigg gonna say about Frank James snatching one of his prettiest whores?" He read Dan's face and said, "Yeah, yeah, I know. You don't have a crystal ball."

"Trigg has gone to the gun before," Dan said. "Right here in Broken Back."

"Yeah, I know," Wagner said. "Some say he's killed three men, but I don't know about that. I reckon he's slick with the iron though, mighty slick."

Wagner took a sip of coffee, his shrewd brown eyes staring hard at a thought passing through his head. A man who sighed a lot, he sighed now. "All right, Dan, come dark mosey along to the Brass Buckle and keep your eyes open for trouble. You know Trigg, he's a finger looking for a trigger."

"I reckon Frank James isn't hunting trouble," Dan said. "He says he's set on his new, peaceful ways, and I don't think he'll be a problem."

"It ain't James I'm worried about, it's Trigg," the sheriff said. "Hell, it's been a six-month since he drilled Buckskin Bob Spenser. His finger must be getting itchy by now."

"That's before my time," Dan said.

"Last Christmas Eve in the Brass Buckle Trigg and Buckskin Bob got into it over a woman . . ."

"Of course, they did," Dan said, smiling.

"Buckskin Bob was no pushover," Wagner said. "He gunned Willard Burnette, the Trinity River drawfighter, over to El Paso that time. And he may have killed a couple more."

"So he was a match for Trigg," Dan said.

"It seemed that way. Bob ended the cuss fight between him and Trigg when he hauled out his gun and commenced to firing. He missed Trigg with his first two shots and didn't get a chance for a third. Nice as you please, Trigg plugged him right between the eyes and ol' Bob went down . . . dead as a doorknob before his beard hit the sawdust." Wagner shrugged. "It was a clear-cut case of self-defense, of course. You can't hang the man who shot second."

"No, I guess you can't," Dan said. "I'll pay particular mind to Trigg tonight."

"See you do, Dan," Wagner said. "He's a snake."

"I won't take my eyes off him until Frank James leaves the saloon, with or without Yolanda Butler."

Wagner, a big-bellied man, sat back in his chair and worked his left arm. "Damn, my arm feels funny, kinda numb," he said. "I must've slept on it last night."

"You should see Doc Monroe about that," Dan said.

"Hell no, I stay away from doctors," Wagner said. "They can kill you quicker'n scat. I just slept on it, that's all. I've done it before."

He rose ponderously to his feet and stepped to the window. "Rain's stopped, and the sky is clearing. Look at the damned street, mud from boardwalk to boardwalk. There's Mrs. Mulgrew going into the mercantile. Looks like she's pregnant again. How many will that make? Six? Seven?"

"Six, I believe," Dan said.

"Her husband's Tim Mulgrew. Just a little feller. Works as a teller at the bank."

"I know, I've talked with him a few times," Dan said. "He collects butterflies. Dead ones."

Wagner turned and grinned. "Yeah, I've seen him running around out there in the long grass with a net thing in his hands. He wears some kind of fancy hat with brims fore and aft."

"He says it's called a deerstalker," Dan said.

"We should get one of them to go with the oilskin," Wagner said. He held his left arm close to his body. "Keep your head dry."

"No, we shouldn't," Dan said.

"Hey, I think we got a visitor," the sheriff said. "Looks like one of them buffalo soldiers."

"Sergeant Miles Ransom, G Company, 10th Cavalry, with a dispatch from Colonel James Nesbitt," the soldier said. He was a tall, handsome black man wearing a dark blue slicker and campaign hat with an upturned brim. "It's a verbal dispatch."

"Sergeant, you look like you could use a cup of coffee," Sheriff Wagner said.

"That would be much appreciated, sir," Ransom said.

Dan Caine poured coffee and handed the cup to the soldier. "A verbal dispatch, Sergeant?" he said.

"Yes, sir, directly from Colonel Nesbitt." Ransom drank coffee with obvious relish and then said, "All right, here goes . . . the colonel wishes it to be known to all concerned that forty young Mescalero Apaches led by a war chief named Delshay have split from Geronimo's band and are already playing hob. Yesterday, half a day's ride from here three drovers were caught out in the open range and murdered. Three horses stolen along with a pair of Winchesters, a Colt's revolver, and a bowie knife. Closer to Broken Back . . ."

"How close?" Wagner said.

"Two miles to the north, no more than that," the soldier said.

"Please go on, Sergeant," Dan said.

"A peddler was tortured and killed and an unknown quantity of goods stolen from his wagon, which was then burned," Ransom said. "Colonel Nesbitt says there is every reason to believe the peddler was carrying a supply of ammunition and possibly several Winchester rifles."

"Was the peddler's name Jacob Golden?" Dan said. He looked concerned.

"As I recall, sir, that was the dead man's name," Ransom said.

"He was probably on his way here," Dan said.

"Too bad," Sheriff Wagner said. "He was a real nice feller. He sold peppermint candy that I'm right partial to, and he always had the best smoking tobacco. I recollect he had a wife and daughter up King County way." Wagner shook his head. "I'm right sorry to hear he's dead. Tortured. Apaches know how to torture a man."

"Anything else from Colonel Nesbitt?" Dan said to the soldier.

Ransom drained his cup and Dan took it from him.

"Yes, sir, there is," the sergeant said. He hesitated, head tilted back, eyes half-closed, obviously recalling something he'd memorized. Finally, he brightened and said, "Colonel Nesbitt says that though there is little chance the savages will attack Broken Back, its lawmen and citizens must stand to arms and prepare to be resolute in defense. At some future date, once the army has ended the Apache menace, the armed citizenry may return to their peacetime status. In the meantime, I urge each and every one of you, to be courageous in the face of danger, stalwart in your duty and may the good Lord help you all."

"In other words, we're on our own," Wagner said. "The army has abandoned us like last year's bird's nest."

Sergeant Ransom took some time to answer and when he did, he said, "Ah . . . that would seem to be the case, sir. But only until the 10th rounds up the hostiles." The soldier saluted and said, "Thank you for the coffee. And now I must return to my duties."

Wagner waved an irritated hand, leaving it for Dan to say, "Thank you, Sergeant."

After the soldier left, the sheriff said, spitting out the words like a string of cusses, "First Frank James and now cutthroat Apaches. What in holy hell is next?"

Sheriff Jared Wagner didn't know it then . . . but his problems were just beginning.

Chapter Four

The Brass Buckle looked like any other frontier saloon, narrow, dominated by a long mahogany bar backed by a French mirror, a scattering of tables and chairs surrounding a small dance floor, a collection of mounted deer heads on the walls and, taking pride of place above the double doors, a portrait of Robert E. Lee in his best uniform. Scowling at the famous soldier from the opposite wall, since Simon Trigg was an Englishman, was a portrait of old Queen Vic. It was Friday night, and the place had rapidly filled with cowboys from the surrounding ranches, a respectable showing of the town's businessmen, and the usual saddle tramps, hangers-on, and drifters surreptitiously thumbing the few coins in their pockets.

A haze of cigarette, cigar, and pipe smoke shrouded the room like a thin fog, and the air smelled of sweat, spilled beer, and cheap perfume.

Behind the saloon was the outhouse and three tiny line cabins each containing a cot with a blue tick mattress and a washstand with a water jug and basin. Above each cot hung a framed, painted sign that asked the question, *Have You Written to Mother?*

As places of prostitution went, Simon Trigg had spared no expense.

The *Broken Back Bulletin,* reporting on the violent events of the night, would later claim that there were four "hostesses" present, branding three of them with the unlikely names of Lily la Plant, Rocky Cox, High Timber (a lass six foot and an inch tall) . . . and the fourth was Yolanda Butler.

It had been several years since Frank James had seen the girl, and he sat at a table and looked around for several minutes before he spotted her through the smoke haze, a blue-eyed blonde as pretty as a china doll. She stood by the bar, talking and laughing with a couple of cowboys, sipping what was alleged by Simon Tripp to be a champagne flip. Frank, true to his Baptist upbringing, was straitlaced enough to be scandalized by Yolanda's outfit, an emerald green corset with black lacing, a skirt that hung low at the back but at the front was hemmed high enough to reveal black fishnet stockings and high-heeled ankle boots. Her curly hair was piled on top of her head and held in place with long pins. Her face was heavily painted, and she looked what she was . . .

A whore, Frank decided.

No matter. Annie wanted Yolanda back on the farm, and that's where she was going.

Frank rose to his feet. He was tall, but in a saloon filled with many tall men he went unnoticed . . . unnoticed that is by everyone except Dan Caine who sat in a dark corner away from the glow of the oil lamps. Dan sat straight in his chair and prepared to wait on Frank James to make his move on the unsuspecting Yolanda.

Tense, his belly tied its first of many knots.

Keep it peaceful, Frank. For God's sake keep it peaceful.

Frank James moved through the crowd civilly enough, pushing no one, once apologizing profusely when he stepped on someone's foot.

Dan nodded.

So far, so good.

Frank reached the bar and stood beside the girl. She turned and looked him up and down and then said something that Dan couldn't hear, the words lost in the clamor, especially now that Banjo Ben Tanner perched on one end of the bar and struck up a spirited rendition of "Sweet Betsy from Pike."

The girl and Frank argued back and forth and Yolanda, hanging on to a cowboy's arm, seemed to make it clear that she was going nowhere. Frank, his chin set and stubborn, seemed to make it clear that she was going somewhere . . . all the way to Clay County, Missouri.

To Dan Caine, it looked like a Mexican standoff and if he was a betting man, he'd put the odds of picking the winner at evens.

As Dan watched, Frank grabbed the girl's arm and tried to drag her away from the bar. But the two cowboys with her, obviously annoyed, pushed him away from Yolanda, and judging by their faces, harsh words were exchanged. Both young punchers carried guns on their hips . . . and so did Frank James.

The saloon patrons narrowed their field of vision to the four people arguing loudly at the bar, Yolanda, the two punchers, and Frank James.

Dan rose to his feet as his belly tied a second knot, and alarm bells clamored in his head.

This was bad . . . really, really bad. The situation had to be defused before guns were drawn and things cartwheeled out of control.

But then the real trouble that brought everything to a head came down fast.

Attracted by the commotion, a red-faced Simon Trigg elbowed his way through the crowd, his brace of British Bulldogs visible under his open gray frockcoat. Some half-drunk rooster yelled, "It's Frank James, by God!"

Finally, Banjo Ben Tanner realized something was going on, his entire audience now engrossed in the noisy confrontation between Trigg and the man who called himself Frank James. His "Sweet Betsy from Pike" choked away to a plink, plink . . . plink . . . And an excited, breath-held hush fell on the crowd.

It was time to act.

Dan tried to force his way through the throng, but men purposely stood in his way, refusing to budge. They weren't about to let the local lawman spoil their fun.

But Dan Caine, admired by many Texans for his outlaw-fighting exploits in the Sierra del Carmen Mountains, would not be denied. Using his considerable strength, he barged through the immobile bodies, shoving men aside, and made his way toward the bar.

Too late. Seconds too late.

Dan watched in horror as Simon Trigg made a play.

And Dan knew why the Englishman acted the way he did . . .

I'm the man who gunned Frank James.

It was so simple, a kill that could only enhance Trigg's reputation and perhaps elevate him to the status of a named shootist.

When men talk about the Brass Buckle gunfight, they still repeat the story that Simon Trigg and Frank James faced off across the width of the barroom, a distance of about thirty feet. That's untrue. In fact, they were only about five feet apart when Trigg drew. He used the same technique as John Wesley Hardin, arms crossed over his chest, hands reaching for his guns. His draw was fast, smooth and practiced, a grandstand play designed to kill . . . and one that had already ended the lives of five men . . . most of them drunks or frightened rubes, easy kills.

Unfortunately for Trigg, apart from the low-ranked shootist Buckskin Bob Spenser he'd never come up against a steel-nerved, lethal gunman like Frank James before.

Frank didn't have a fast gun rep and never sought one, but he was nonetheless considered a hard, dangerous pistolero. He'd used a revolver often during the war, a Colt Navy Model of 1851, and later in the course of his bank-robbing profession, a Smith & Wesson Model 3. But that night in the Brass Buckle saloon, he was armed with a Colt 1873 Single Action Army in .44-40 caliber. And that Friday evening, he was death.

Trigg's hands were on the ivory handles of his Bulldogs when Frank's first bullet hit him high in the chest, in the center of the V made by his forearms. Realizing he was hit hard, Trigg's face took on a look of horror and disbelief. His fast draw had failed him. Let the record show that Simon Trigg was good, fast on the draw . . . but he'd just met someone faster. Trigg staggered back a step but, determined to get his work in, he pulled the gun from the holster under his left arm.

"No!" Dan Caine yelled.

But Frank had already thumbed off his second bullet, a hit to Trigg's right shoulder that exited from his back in a crimson fan of blood and bone chips. Dying on his feet, the Englishman triggered a round that went nowhere and a second that burned across the back of Frank's gun hand. Frank hesitated an instant, looking for Trigg to fall, but the man was still on his feet. "Damn you to hades!" Frank James yelled. He fired the final shot of the gunfight. Hit in the chest a second time, Trigg's legs collapsed beneath him and he went down on his back.

"Boys, he's killed me," he said. And died.

Dan Caine pushed the muzzle of his hammer-back Colt into Frank's left temple. "Frank, lay the piece on the bar or I'll blow your brains all over the sawdust," he said.

"Anything you say, Deputy," Frank James said. He put his gun down and then said, "It was self-defense. He drew down on me."

"Tell that to a judge, Frank. In the meantime, you're coming with me," Dan said. His eyes moved to Yolanda Butler who stood pàle-faced and trembling, staring down at Trigg's bloody body. "And you come along as well," he said.

In an instant, the girl's face switched from a look of horror to tight-mouthed defiance. "I didn't do nothing," she said. "You can't arrest me."

"You're a witness," Dan said.

"So is everybody in the saloon," Yolanda said. "Just ask them."

"You were there from start to finish and saw the whole thing go down," Dan said.

"I won't go," the girl said, her face stubborn. "You can't make me."

"Lady, if I have to, I'll drag you out of here by the hair and I won't be as gentle as Frank," Dan said.

"He wasn't gentle. He hurt my arm. Look at the bruise."

"Go with the deputy man, Yolanda," Frank said. "Just tell him what happened. Tell him what you saw."

"I'll go, but you're not taking me back to Missouri, Frank James," Yolanda said. "I ain't living on any damn farm with a bunch of hayseeds."

"Well, that's up to you, lady," Dan said. "But in the meantime, you're coming with me."

Dan holstered his Colt and pushed Frank in front of him as the awed crowd parted, a scowling Yolanda Butler in tow. They were almost at the door when a small agitated man dressed in black broadcloth and a top hat entered and bumped into Dan. "Oh, Deputy Caine," he said. "I heard shooting."

Dan jerked a thumb over his shoulder. "He's back there, Thaddeus."

"Who is the dear departed?" the undertaker said.

"Simon Trigg."

"Oh, my lord, what a tragedy," Thaddeus Winch said. "Such a fine man. Ah . . ."

"Submit your bill to the new proprietor of the Brass Buckle, whoever he is," Dan Caine said.

Chapter Five

His reputation doing him no favors, Frank James stood behind bars, Sheriff Jared Wagner, Dan Caine, and Yolanda Butler on the other side.

"Frank James told Simon Trigg that if he had to, he'd pull me out of the Brass Buckle by force," Yolanda said. "And then Simon said he would sell me for a thousand dollars."

"And what did Frank say?" Dan said.

"He told Simon to go to hell," the girl said.

"And then what happened?" Wagner said.

"Simon called him out for a piece of Johnny Reb trash . . . and that's when Frank drew his gun and shot him," Yolanda said, her china blue eyes blinking.

"You're lying, Yolanda," Dan said. "I saw Trigg go for his guns first."

"I'm not lying. I mean I don't know. Maybe he did . . . it all happened so fast," Yolanda said. "All I do know is that when Simon said what he did about Frank being Southern trash an' all, Frank shot him."

Frank shook his head. "Hell is empty and all the devils

are here." The girl looked at him blankly, and he said, "It's Shakespeare, Yolanda."

"Never heard of him," the girl said.

"Of course, you haven't," Frank smiled.

Sheriff Wagner said, "Miss Butler, it all comes down to this . . . is my deputy right? Did Trigg go for his guns first? Take your time, young lady. Think it through."

Yolanda bit her bottom lip and after a few moments said, "I don't know for sure if he did or did not." Beads of sweat gathered in the V between her breasts. "But if I had to swear on the Bible, I'd say Frank James went for his gun first."

"Dan?" Wagner said.

"I saw what I saw, Jared," Dan said. "Trigg drew down on Frank and it was then that Frank shot him. It's self-defense, clear as day."

"Across a packed saloon thick with smoke you saw what you think you saw, Deputy," Yolanda said. "Or maybe you saw what you wanted to see."

Wagner said, "Deputy Sheriff Caine has no special regard for Frank James, young lady. To think otherwise is just wrong and offensive." The girl opened her mouth to speak, but the sheriff held up a silencing hand. "Circuit Judge Hyrum C. Spindler will arrive by the Patterson stage on the fifteenth of this month to hear other cases. Mr. James, until then you will remain in custody on suspicion of murder." He stared hard at Yolanda. "You and Deputy Caine will present your . . . conflicting . . . evidence to hizzoner then."

"Others saw it," the girl said. "Not just me."

"And they will be questioned in due course," Wagner said.

"Will Frank James get hung?" Yolanda said. She looked nervous, her eyes darting from Frank to the sheriff and back again. "I don't want him hung."

"If he's found guilty that will be up to the court to decide," Wagner said. "Now, if you'll excuse me, I'll be right back."

After the sheriff left to his unknown errand, no one spoke for a while. Then Frank James said, "I guess you can all leave. Shut the door upon me, and so give me up to the sharpest kind of justice."

Dan Caine smiled. "More of that Shakespeare feller?"

"King Lear."

"Ah . . ." Dan said. He was spared further comment by the return of Sheriff Wagner, a large glass of amber whiskey in his hand. He handed the glass to Frank and said, "After the night you've had, I guess you can use that."

Frank sipped the whiskey, smiled, and said, "It's much appreciated, Sheriff."

"Just being hospitable, Frank," Wagner said. "You'll be here for a spell . . . longer if the Apaches play hob with the Patterson stage routes."

Frank said, "Sheriff, lay in plenty of bacon and eggs and Old Crow and we'll get along just fine."

"Don't push it, Frank," Wagner said.

"Jared, it was self-defense, plain as the ears on a mule," Dan Caine said.

"That's not how Yolanda Butler saw it," Sheriff Wagner said. "You heard her."

"I know she's lying," Dan said. "She'll do or say anything not to live down on the farm in Clay County Missouri."

"Then if he's an innocent man, why is Frank James in our jail?" Wagner said.

"Because it's the safest place for him until the judge gets here and dismisses the case against him," Dan said. "There may be others who'll lie and claim Frank drew first."

"I know Judge Hyrum C. Spindler," Wagner said. "I know how he operates. He'll scare the hell out of them and get to the truth."

"Trigg wanted another notch on his gun. I believe he hankered to be known as the man who killed Frank James, just like Bob Ford did with Jesse."

"I'm aware of that too, Dan," Wagner said. "Don't you think I've met his kind in the past? It's afore your time, but right here in Broken Back we had a kid who fancied himself a shootist. His name was Bill Matthews, an orphan raised by his aunt Ella, a Godfearing Christian woman who could do nothing with him. Well, sir, Bill got hold of a Colt and he practiced his draw just about every single day of his life, becoming faster and faster. He hit what he shot at too. By the time he was eighteen, he was a nasty, arrogant little son of a bitch, and I hated his guts. Then came the day he called out a teamster by the name of Pete Tooley and the two had at it. Tooley was drunk and broke at the time so I buried him at the city's expense."

"Did you arrest him? Matthews, I mean?" Dan said. "Like I did Frank James."

"I had no call to. A dozen people were on the street

that day and they all swore Tooley was first to reach for the iron," Wagner said. "Like Trigg, the kid wanted a notch on his gun."

"And he got one," Dan said. "He's not in town, so what happened to him?"

"Well, Matthews claimed to be the cock o' the walk in Broken Back. He took to wearing two guns and began to call himself Billy the Kid and made others do the same. Now there was a man in town by the name of Smith who worked the counter in Gray's General Store who refused to call Matthews by that name. The kid didn't sit still for that, of course. He made it known that if Smith didn't call him Billy the Kid in public, out in the street on a Friday night, he'd shoot him down like a dog."

"But he picked on the wrong man, huh?" Dan said.

"I guess you could say that. On Friday morning, Smith crept up behind Billy the Kid and bashed his brains out with a hickory pickaxe handle. It happened just across the street on the boardwalk outside Gray's. It seems Matthews had stood at the store window and practiced his fast draw and twirled his guns where Smith could see him."

"What happened to Smith?" Dan said.

"A jury found that he'd acted in self-defense and he left town shortly after that. I don't know where he went."

"And the moral of the story?"

"There is no moral," Wagner said. "I'm just telling you that I've known men like Simon Trigg before. Wannabes that came to a bad end. Don't worry. Dan, I'll make sure Frank James gets a fair shake."

The sheriff rose from his desk and then, breathing hard, said, "It's getting late. I guess I'll turn in." He rubbed his left arm. "Damn arm keeps coming over numb on me. What the hell?"

"You should see the doctor, Jared," Dan said. "That ain't normal."

"Nah, it'll be fine," Wagner said. "Like I told you, I sleep on it. The Palace Hotel beds are as hard as the hubs of hell. Just ask your friends Buttons Muldoon and Red Ryan, they came in earlier with the Patterson stage. I heard Buttons complain all the way down the hallway about damn rocks in his bed."

Dan smiled. "Buttons is a man who likes his comfort."

His smile slipped and he said, "Still, go speak to Doc Monroe and let him examine you." He saw Wagner scowl and said, "I know, I know, you stay away from doctors. But recently your arm seems to be getting numb more often."

"I declare, Deputy Caine, you sound like a nagging wife," Wagner said, visibly irritated. He opened the office door. "Now, goodnight, and be damned to you and your doctors."

Dan shook his head at the stubbornness of the departing lawman, rose to his feet, and picked up the oil lamp. He carried it to his little box of a room that adjoined the cells and got ready for bed, a narrow, squealing iron cot that had seen better days. The comfort of its peace officers was of minor concern to the city fathers of Broken Back.

Dan Caine woke to darkness and a sense of unease. His eyes flew open and he lay on his back and listened into the night, ears tuned to the slightest sound. Through the thin partition that divided his room from the cells, he heard Frank James's soft snoring and from somewhere out on the prairie a pair of hunting coyotes yipped back and forth. Unease grew to a vague dread that pressed on him like a heavy weight. Cursing himself for a maiden aunt who hears a rustle in every bush, he rose to his feet and slid his Colt from the holster on the nightstand. He jammed his hat on his head and made his way to the front door of the office, padding silently on bare feet. The railroad clock on the wall above Wagner's desk showed two o'clock. Wearing only his long johns and hat, Dan stepped onto the front porch, into the murky silence of a slumbering town. There was not the slightest sound and nothing moved. Suddenly the darkness felt oppressive, weighing on him, accompanied by the same sense of apprehension that had wakened him. There was something out there . . . something threatening . . . but lost, faceless and formless, in the gloom. Finally, Dan stepped back into the office and turned the key on a door that was never locked. It took him a long time to return to sleep.

Chapter Six

The new aborning morning came in bright, clear, and clean, and swallows fluttered around the office porch as Dan Caine left the building and crossed the street, headed for breakfast at Ma's Kitchen. Gray-faced, Sheriff Jared Wagner pled a lack of appetite for his decision to remain behind his desk and make do with coffee.

By the time Dan stepped into the steamy, bacon-scented heat of the restaurant, the apprehensions of the night had left him. He dismissed them as a man shrugs off the memory of a bad dream.

As it always was in the morning, Ma's place was jam-packed with the early breakfast crowd, and Dan nodded and said his good mornings to a dozen people before he sat at a shared table and ordered scrambled eggs, toast, and coffee.

A couple of men at the table argued national politics and another toyed with the food on his plate, nursing what appeared to be the granddaddy of all hangovers.

The waitress, a pretty middle-aged woman who looked a decade younger than her years, a rare sight in Texas, brought Dan his breakfast and said, "Deputy, is it true Frank James killed a man in the Brass Buckle last night over a fallen woman?"

"More or less," Dan said. Up close, the waitress smelled of lavender water.

"As far as I know, him and his brother Jesse led a violent, sinful life, but they had a good mother," the woman said.

"I heard that too," Dan said. He picked up a slice of toast and began to spread it with butter, signaling that he was through talking.

The waitress took the hint and said, "It takes all kinds, don't it, Deputy Caine?"

"Sure does," Dan said.

The woman left and the gent with the hangover suddenly lurched to his feet, said, "I'm gonna puke," and headed for the door.

Dan chewed on toast, thinking that this was shaping up to be an interesting morning. Just how interesting was revealed a few minutes later as he picked up his last forkful of egg. The fork remained poised between plate and mouth as the restaurant door slammed open and a hysterical man yelled, "They're robbing the bank!"

An instant later a flurry of gunshots ripped apart the fabric of the morning, together with the shouts of men and the whinny of frightened horses.

Dan Caine dropped his fork, barged his way out of the restaurant, and, Colt in hand, ran into the street. He took in the situation at a glance . . . Sheriff Jared Wagner down on his back, unmoving. Seven horsemen galloping out of town, trailing a billowing dust cloud. Several men, including the bank clerk, taking ineffective pot shots. A woman sprawled on the street, and Dan recognized her as old Maggie Dunn, the berry picker.

Dan ran to Wagner and took a knee beside him. The sheriff's mouth was twisted horribly to one side and his eyes were wide and scared. "Jared, where are you hit?" Dan said.

"Ap . . . apoplexy . . . I can't . . . can't move my left arm . . . leg. After them, Dan. They've got the town's money."

"Jared . . ."

"Go. Raise a posse."

The bank clerk Tim Mulgrew, small, balding, and thoroughly frightened, ran toward Dan. "Deputy, thirty-thousand dollars gone, they cleaned us out! Mr. Bradshaw is dead, shot through the heart."

"Sheriff Wagner and old Maggie need Doctor Monroe," Dan said. "Get him."

"Maggie is dead," one of the town's respectable matrons said. "A robber's horse ran into her, knocked her down, and killed her."

Dan felt a stab of regret. She'd been a nice old lady who'd made no secret of her laudanum habit. As far as he was concerned the bank robbers were guilty of two murders, Bradshaw the bank manager and poor Maggie . . . and he would see them hang for it.

Then to the men gathered in the street. "You fellows arm yourselves and mount up. We're going after them."

* * *

Dan ran to the livery, saddled his horse, and returned to the sheriff's office. Jared Wagner had been carried to his room in the hotel and Thaddeus Winch the undertaker and his assistant were placing Maggie Dunn on a stretcher.

The morning was bright and clear, windless, still tainted by a drift of gunsmoke.

Within minutes, eighteen riders gathered in front of the sheriff's office, and Dan Caine was glad to see buckskinned, beaded old Ephraim Traynor among them. As a boy, Traynor had first ventured west in 1820 and joined the famous mountain man Joseph Walker in an illegal trapping expedition into the Spanish-controlled New Mexico Territory. In 1833, still with Walker, he took part in an expedition that bushwhacked its way from Wyoming to California across the spine of the Sierra Nevada and became one of the first white men to encounter majestic giant sequoia trees and the wonders of Yosemite Valley. Since then, he'd worked as a trapper, army scout, and wagon train master . . . and was reputed to have never lost a pilgrim in his care.

Now almost eighty years old, and still only semi-civilized, Traynor was a man who could not be stampeded and if pushed would fight like a cornered wildcat.

The rest of the posse was made up of men typical of the frontier cow town, a few booted and spurred cowboys, some businessmen and local merchants, a pair of gamblers, who for a change were out of bed before sundown, Tim Mulgrew the bank clerk, and a couple of lanky youths, grinning and eager for adventure. Big Elbert Conway, the blacksmith, had a Sharps 50 across his saddle horn and beside him was a rider Dan didn't know, a dark-haired, dark-eyed, slender man who studied him with hooded, careful eyes, assessing him, as though making up his mind about something. Caine returned the man's stare and then glanced away, dismissing him. The slender man had the look of the con artist about him that Dan had seen too many times before, a young man on the take, hoping to make his fortune on the frontier off the backs of the foolish and gullible. But why would such a man join a posse? Boredom, likely as not.

Dan took no time to ponder the question further.

"Let's go, boys," he said.

He stepped down from the porch and mounted his horse.

"Wait! Wait up!"

Dr. Duncan Monroe hurried toward him, leading a saddled, tall bay horse. "Deputy, Sheriff Wagner says you must release Frank James and include him in the posse," he said. He sounded out of breath.

"Frank is an expert on posses," a cowboy said, and the men around him laughed.

"The sheriff asked me to saddle Mr. James's horse," the doctor said. "So you can have him join you right away."

"How is Jared?" Dan said.

"Poorly," Monroe said.

"Is he still in his right mind?" Dan said.

"The sheriff told me you'd say that, and he said to remind you that five thousand dollars of the stolen money is Frank's."

Dan Caine shook his head. "Jared Wagner is the sheriff.

What he says goes. One of you men take the horse from Doc. I'll be right back."

"Hell, time we got this show on the road," Conway, the blacksmith, grumbled. He was a sour man, much given to fits of melancholy.

Dan swung out of the saddle and hurried into the office. He grabbed the keys and unlocked the cell door. "You're out of here, Frank," he said. He saw the man's look of surprise and said, "You're joining my posse. We're going after the bank robbers. Your horse is outside." Frank opened his mouth to speak, and Dan snapped, "Don't argue, Frank. Get your guns and follow me."

"No argument from me, Deputy," Frank said. "Sitting in a cell, just thinking, wears on a man. Make not your thoughts your prisons."

"Think on this . . . a big chunk of the money is yours," Dan said.

"Damn right it is," Frank James said, jumping up from his cot.

The bank robbers had headed north across the rolling plains country, and the posse followed, old Ephraim Traynor riding point. Frank James, an acknowledged expert on such matters, told Dan that the outlaws were probably headed for the Oklahoma Territory.

"After a bank robbery and a killing, they won't want to linger long in Texas," he said.

And Dan agreed. Each and every one of them faced a noose when they were caught and returned to Broken Back, and they knew it.

The pursuers were three miles into the chase when something occurred that should never have happened. It was an event so extraordinary that no one in the posse had heard of its like before.

And, tragically, it cost the lives of four of its members.

Chapter Seven

As a *Broken Back Bulletin* editorial scolded, "Mistakes were made . . ."

But there were no mistakes.

An overconfident posse, perhaps, coupled with a band of outlaws with experienced fighting men in their ranks was the most likely reason for the debacle . . . that and an old man's failing eyesight.

No dust cloud was visible in the distance, and ahead of the pursuers Ephraim Traynor had drawn rein, horse and rider distorted by a shimmering heat haze.

Dan Caine did not halt the other men but instead closed the space between his riders and the old mountain man. Afterward critics who weren't there claimed he should've halted and let Traynor come back to him.

This was rolling country, endless miles of buffalo grass, here and there stands of trees and brush. To Traynor's right stood a tree island, mostly post oak, juniper, and a few plains cottonwoods surrounded by mesquite, yucca, and other plants.

Traynor stood in the stirrups, his gaze intently fixed on the trees. Only later would Dan discover that the old man's eyesight was failing and had been getting progressively worse over the past half-dozen years . . . "a fact Deputy Caine should have known," accused the *Broken Back Bulletin*.

Frank James, once hunted, hounded, and harassed, possessed the sharp-honed instincts of a bronco Apache. To Dan, riding in front of him, he leaned forward in the saddle and said in a tense, hollow whisper, "Deputy, I don't like it. Something's not right."

In that, Frank was correct . . . but his warning came too late.

An instant later, seven horsemen burst from the trees and came on at a gallop. The riders didn't hit Dan Caine and his men head on. Rather, they charged past his right flank, pouring on a withering fire from their Winchesters. Seven men. Texans all. Experienced killers bred to the saddle and the gun, they hit the posse hard and fast, their guns hammering.

Four saddles were emptied in the first volley, and two horses went down.

Dan Caine, startled, called on the experience he'd gained in the Sierra del Carmen, recovered quickly, and drew and fired, and so did Frank James and several others.

But the outlaws were gone, galloping into the brazen day, hidden behind a rolling cloud of dust . . . and Dan and the others scored no hits.

Again, the *Broken Back Bulletin* criticized the posse's shooting skills, the editor claiming that "much powder was burned, many a bullet unraveled, but nary a mark was struck."

The reason was that the attack had been almighty sudden. There and gone. The confused tangle of falling men and horses, blasting rifles, and yelling, hurtling outlaws unsettled the posse and dangerously reduced its returned fire.

Four dead. No wounded. It was carnage. Professionals shoot to kill.

Old Ephraim Traynor rode back to Dan Caine, tears in his eyes, saying, over and over again, "I'm sorry . . . I'm sorry . . ." The man who'd guided a score of wagon trains and never lost a pilgrim, had helped lose a battle.

Dan, painfully aware of his own failure, could not bring himself to blame another. "It's not your fault, Ephraim," he said. "I led the posse, so put that saddle on me."

"I knowed there was something in the trees, but I didn't see the outlaws until it was too late," Traynor said. He looked at the four dead men laid out on the grass, the others gathered around them. "Young men, all of them. I'm sorry . . . so sorry . . ."

And they were young.

Dan had spoken with and often shared a laugh with each and every one of them . . . Tim Mulgrew, bank clerk, a pregnant wife and five children. John Porter, stock boy, just eighteen years old, unmarried, lived with his mother. Dewey Bender, butcher, a wife and one child. Paul Mullens, carpenter, an ailing wife and seven children.

Now the four men lay with their gray faces turned to the burning Texas sun and Dan Caine dreaded his meeting with three widows, a grieving mother, and thirteen orphan children.

His posse. His failure. His fault.

Chapter Eight

The posse, what was left of it, returned to Broken Back like a defeated army.

Dan Caine rode in the lead, followed by Frank James and Ephraim Traynor, then four horses, a bloody body draped over each saddle, head down, hair blowing in a rising prairie wind. Two other men shared a horse and the remaining shoulder-slumped riders took up the rear, the slender dark-eyed man Dan had noticed earlier tagging a few yards behind the rest.

A crowd gathered to watch the sad procession, and then the widows came out. Their long skirts flapping against their legs, unbound hair wild, eyes wilder, they went to their dead husbands, a fainting mother to her only son. Tears, wails, sorrow beyond sorrow, the women's cries tore at Dan Caine and he wanted to clap hands to his ears and block out the sound. But he rode, stiff-backed to the sheriff's office and drew rein . . . a strong man who, in that moment dug deep and tried his utmost to be stronger.

Dan stepped out of the saddle and walked to where

solemn men carried the hurting dead to their widow's homes. The women, comforted by young John Porter's mother, herself bereft, mourning for a lost son, followed their men.

Dan stood in the east wind, his hat in his hands. Outside the stores, hanging signs banged and their fastening chains rattled. Dust devils spun in the street, and the wind sighed around the eaves of the frame buildings as though it too grieved for the dead.

Moving closer to the women, Dan said over and over, "I'm sorry . . . I'm sorry . . ."

But the women only looked at him, looked through him . . . looked away.

And then they were gone.

"Death lies on them like an untimely frost upon the sweetest flower of all the field," a voice said behind him. When Dan turned, Frank James added, "You're not to blame, Deputy. The blame lies with the men who robbed the bank. God knows, I know all about that. Me and Jesse made more than our share of widows."

"The widows, young John Porter's mother . . . they . . . I mean, it was as though I wasn't there," Dan said. "The women didn't say a word to me."

"What was there to say?" Frank said. "Their men are dead, and they know you're not responsible."

"I was responsible for the posse and I led them right into an ambush," Dan said.

"You did everything right," Frank said. "You had an experienced scout riding point."

"Who's as blind as a fence post."

"The old man should've told you that," Frank said.

"Look, we could go around in circles about this all day and get nowhere. What you should be thinking about is what you're going to do next."

"Do next?" Dan said.

"The outlaws are still out there, Deputy," Frank said.

"After today will men still want to ride with me?" Dan said.

"Yes, they will. Now do your duty, Dan Caine," Frank said. "Don't hide behind a defeat and let your conscience beat you to death."

Dan thought about that last for a considerable time, and finally he said, "All right, I'll put together another posse and ride out tomorrow at first light."

"You can count me in," Frank said.

As he watched dispirited men head home or to the saloon, Dan said, "I'm not bringing any of that outlaw trash back to Broken Back for trial. By God, I'll kill them where I find them."

"Then you won't be leading a legal posse," Frank said. "You'll be a vigilante."

Dan nodded. "I've led vigilantes before . . ."

"In the Sierra del Carmen," Frank said. "I heard about that scrape. You done for Clay Kyle and Black-Eyed Susan Stanton and them."

Dan managed a thin smile. "You blame me for that, Frank?"

Frank James shook his head. "No blame. But Clay Kyle was a member of my former profession and a brother Freemason." He returned Dan's smile. "Feel free to deduce that my current hypocrisy has its limits. Now let me put up your horse before I do my duty and return to my cell."

Dan handed over the reins and said, "I'm going to visit Sheriff Wagner and the saloon to round up some volunteers. Frank, you ain't exactly popular in the Brass Buckle, so if you need me later, I'll be back in the office real soon."

"Can I bring you some grub from the restaurant?" Frank said.

"No, I'm not hungry. I left my appetite somewhere out there in the long grass."

Sheriff Jared Wagner lay on his hotel bed in a deep coma. Beside him, keeping vigil, sat Jane Ward, Dr. Monroe's elderly nurse, a tall, thin woman with iron gray hair and a pronounced overbite.

When Dan stepped into the room, the woman looked at him without enthusiasm and said, "He can't talk. I doubt that he'll ever talk again."

"What does Dr. Monroe say?" Dan asked.

"He says Sheriff Wagner was struck down by apoplexy and won't recover," the nurse said. "It's only a matter of time, and I'll continue with my death watch until he passes."

The words, "death watch" chilled Dan to the bone. "There's no hope for him?" he said.

A stern woman, nurse Ward said, "What did I just say to you, young man? Were you listening to a word?"

Shadows had gathered in Wagner's face. His cheeks and temples were hollow, his face a ghastly blue color. Dan swallowed hard and said, "Is there anything I can do?"

"Yes, there is. You can bury him," Jane Ward said.

* * *

Dan Caine had never been close friends with Jared Wagner, but he liked the man and he was yet to beat him at checkers, and it saddened him that he'd no longer get the chance. As he walked from the sheriff's room, farther down the hotel hallway a head popped out of an open door and Dan recognized the slender, dark-eyed man who had been a member of the posse.

"Ah, Deputy, I wanted to talk with you, if you can spare a moment," the man said, his words heavily accented. "I have something to tell you in private."

Whoever he was, the man was not a native English speaker, Dan decided. Mexican, probably.

"Sure," Dan said. "I was about to head for the saloon to recruit another posse. But I have the feeling that finding the right men is going to be an uphill battle."

"And that's what I wanted to talk about," the man said, standing in the doorway of his room. "Please, if you would care to come inside."

Dan stepped into the room and the man said, "Take the chair, Deputy Caine. I'll sit on the bed." He smiled. "It's hard enough."

After Dan sat, he said, "You were on my posse, but I never caught your name."

"It's Moretti. Luca Moretti." The man stuck out his hand. "Pleased to meet you."

Dan shook the man's hand and then said, "You from Old Mexico?"

Moretti said, "No, I'm Italian. From Rome, Italy. There are not many of us Italians west of the Mississippi. Drink?"

"I could use one," Dan said.

Moretti poured bourbon into a glass and handed it to the deputy. "Mind if I smoke?" Dan said.

"No, not at all. Please, go ahead."

As Dan built a cigarette he said, "You're the first Italian I've met. Now what can I do for you?"

"I want to join your posse," Moretti said.

"Glad to have you," Dan said.

"Do you think the bank robbers will keep heading north?" Moretti said. "Or turn south into Old Mexico?"

"Either one, but if I was them, I'd head for the Indian Territory." Dan lit his cigarette, took a deep drag, and said behind a blue cloud of exhaled smoke, "Not much law up there. Not much of anything."

Moretti thought about that and said, "If the *banditi* go north, then I will remain with the posse. But if they head for Mexico I must leave. I will not ask your permission."

"Why? North, south, what difference does it make to you?" Dan said. He found the Italian's intense brown-eyed gaze unsettling. "Mr. Moretti, I'm not catching your drift."

"It's because I am on a quest, and I believe my road leads to the north."

"Quest? You mean you're hunting somebody?"

"Or some . . . thing. Yes."

Dan smiled and shook his head. "Hell, you're a bounty hunter." Then realizing a foreigner may not have heard that term, he said, "You kill wanted men for pay."

"Yes. Something like that," Moretti said. His eyes were guarded.

The man's revolver lay on the table by the hotel window along with a yellow rag and a small can of oil. "Mighty strange looking piece you got there, Moretti," Dan said. "What kind of gun is that?"

"It's an Enfield revolver in .476 caliber. British made, and not of the highest quality, but I'm competent enough with it."

Six stubby rounds lay beside the gun, and in the fading daylight Dan peered at them hard. Finally, he said, "Can I see one of those?"

"Of course," Moretti said. He stood, stepped to the table, and handed the other man a cartridge. "Yeah, I thought so," Dan said. "It looks like the bullet is cast from silver."

"Argentum, yes. Or as you say, silver."

Then something strange . . .

Moretti refilled the cylinder, but before he thumbed a round into a chamber, he blessed all six with a sign of the cross.

Dan badly needed volunteers to man his posse, but he put a question mark next to the name Luca Moretti. That blessing thing . . . the Italian seemed three pickles short of a full barrel.

Dan sighed and rose to his feet. Beggars can't be choosers. If a man wants to shoot silver bullets, then that's his business.

"Be on the street at first light," he said.

"Depend on it," Moretti said.

Chapter Nine

Dan Caine left the hotel and his boots thudded on the boardwalk as he headed in the direction of the Brass Buckle. Discouraged by what had happened and by the deep mud in the street, he saw no one. Broken Back was in mourning, and its people grieved behind drawn curtains.

The mercantile was open and Dan stepped inside, to be met with dim light, a long counter, rounded glass display cases, and side walls lined with shelves, drawers, and bins. The store sold everything from ladies' notions to buggy whips and smelled of ground coffee, spices, tobacco, and of the molasses that had leaked from a barrel spout. At the far end of the room a potbellied stove was accompanied by a couple of chairs and between them a checkerboard on an upturned apple crate.

The proprietor, a man of middle age and middle height, named Dave Harvey greeted Dan and then said, "A bad business, Deputy. Four dead and the money gone."

"I'll get it back," Dan said. "My posse leaves at daybreak tomorrow."

Harvey leaned across the counter and whispered, "Don't you think it's too much of a coincidence that the bank is robbed the day after Frank James rides into town?"

"Frank James had five thousand dollars of his own money in the bank," Dan said.

"That proves nothing. He knew his outlaw cohorts would take it right back out again."

"Frank James was in my posse and the outlaws shot at him, just like they shot at everyone else," Dan said.

"Deputy, there's been talk," Harvey said.

"What kind of talk?" Dan said, guessing what the answer would be. He was right.

"Lynching talk."

"Who's making this kind of talk, Dave? Give me a name," Dan said.

"No names, Deputy," Harvey said. "Just general talk."

"Saloon talk?" Dan said.

"Could be. But it's general talk. Folks are mighty upset."

"We're all upset," Dan said. "But there will be no lynching in this town. I'll kill any man coming at me with a noose."

"And add to the town's already high butcher's bill?" Harvey said.

"If I have to," Dan said. "And if you hear any more general talk about a lynching you can tell the rabble-rousers so."

"Just thought you'd like to know, Deputy. Now what can I do for you?"

Dan bought a box of .44-40 cartridges and a sack of tobacco and papers.

"Dave, remember, if you hear anything about a lynching,

let me know," Dan said before he headed for the door. "Even if it's just general talk."

"I certainly will, Deputy," Harvey said.

Men were drinking hard in the Brass Buckle and few seemed to notice Yolanda Butler and the other girls as they patrolled the bar and flaunted their lace-up corsets, high-heeled ankle boots, and fishnet stockings.

And few noticed Dan Caine when he stood in the middle of the empty dance floor and called for attention. The men lining the bar turned and stared at him with empty eyes. They were men with sand, most of them, but the disastrous events of the day and the cold corpses of the dead had taken the fight out of them. Western men were not made for defeat.

"I need volunteers to form another posse," Dan said. Young, slim, strong, and with a gun rep he had not coveted, he was respected enough that men listened, even the pale gamblers Jack Fulton and Bill Kent, like prostitutes, members of a persecuted profession who had no love for the law.

"I plan on going after those murdering outlaws," Dan said. "And I aim to kill them where I find them. And for that reason, this will not be a legal posse. You'll be riding as vigilantes."

"Count me out," Ebert Conway, the blacksmith, said. "I've had enough."

"I could use your Sharps," Dan said.

"Then take it, only I won't be attached to it," Conway said.

"Goes for me too, Deputy," one of the cowboys who'd

been in the posse said. "We got whipped like a red-headed stepchild today, and I won't let it happen a second time. Besides, I'd no money in the damned bank."

Several men said nothing but turned their backs on Dan, movements more eloquent than words.

"They got my money," Bill Kent said. "I needed that cash to quit this hick town."

"And head where, Bill?" a man asked through a laugh.

"Anywhere but here," Kent said to more laughter.

"Be on the street at sunup, Bill," Dan said. "Anybody else?"

"You can count on me, Deputy," Ephraim Traynor said. He spoke hesitantly, almost timidly. Fearful of the response.

"I need you as a tracker, Ephraim," Dan said, smiling. "Be on the street tomorrow morning. Anybody else?"

There was a deal of cussin' and discussin' among the men at the bar that lasted for several minutes, but finally Dan snagged four volunteers, a lanky cowboy with a huge cavalry mustache named Red Lawson, his small, stocky sidekick Jake Roberts who was something of a pugilist, John Brooks who owned a rod and gun store and had lost money to the robbers, and last, and least, Sam "Sly Eye" Barnes, a slender, ragged barfly and sometimes chicken thief who had no visible means of support and worse . . . no horse and no gun. He didn't even own a hat.

Dan took the man to much derisive jeering and laughter because he was desperate . . . and hoped that he would have no cause to regret it. Blue Jones's Livery and Horse Rental would supply a mount, and Dan figured to arm the man with a rifle from the sheriff's office gun rack.

Standing in the center of the dance floor, telling himself he sounded like a politicking congressman, Dan said, "You volunteers assemble outside the sheriff's office at first light."

"What about supplies?" John Brooks said. "I can supply ammunition, but if it's a long trail, we got to eat."

"I'll take care of that," Dan said, wondering where the hell he was going to find the money.

"And don't forget the whiskey!" someone at the bar yelled.

The man was almost invisible in the smoke gloom, and Dan wanted to shoot him. Then, to Sam Barnes he said, "Sly, you come with me."

Once outside, Dan grabbed the little man by his skinny upper arm and said, "When did you last eat?"

Barnes shrugged. "I don't know. It's been a spell."

"Are you feeling gant?" Dan said.

"Have you any whiskey, your worship?"

"You need grub," Dan said. "I won't have a hungry man ride with me."

"Well, I could eat, that's for sure," Barnes said.

Dan pushed the skinny arm forward. "Let's go," he said.

Dan Caine first stopped at the livery stable. He spoke to Ed Wallace and told him he needed a pack mule and a horse, "The horse is for him," he said, jerking a thumb at Barnes.

Wallace could be cranky at times. He'd lost his left arm at Gettysburg but managed just fine with his right. He looked at Barnes and said, "Sly Barnes, when you stepped through the door, I was more than inclined to grab my scattergun and guard my watermelon patch."

"He's reformed, Ed," Dan said. "He's joining my posse to go after the bank robbers."

"Then God help us all," Wallace said. And then to Barnes, "Can you even ride a hoss?"

The little man grinned and said, "I stole enough of them in my day, but that all came to a stop a couple of years ago when I almost got hung up El Paso way. A Texas Ranger saved my skin and after that I quit the profession."

"And became a chicken thief," Wallace said.

Barnes looked offended. "I steal other things beside chickens."

"I know," Dan said. "You've written your name on the cell wall seventeen times. One night when I was bored, I counted them."

Wallace shook his head said, "It's a wonder Sheriff Wagner hasn't hanged you fer a public nuisance."

"He was getting around to that way of thinking," Dan said. "Now about the horse?"

"I've got a little buckskin mare in the stall over yonder that will take you there and back," Wallace said. "And a Missouri mule that will carry anything you want."

"He'll need a saddle and bridle, Ed," Dan said.

"Got that too," Wallace said.

"We're heading to Ma's for a bite to eat," Dan said. "Then to the mercantile for supplies. I'll be back after that to load the mule."

Wallace studied Sly Barnes again. "You feeding him at Ma's?"

"Yeah."

"Waste of good grub if you ask me," Ed Wallace said.

Dan Caine ordered steak and eggs for two and as he ate, he watched, fascinated, as Sly Barnes devoured his food with all the good manners of a hungry bloodhound. After he'd eaten, Barnes looked at the meager leftovers on Dan's plate and said, "Ain't you gonna finish that?"

Dan shook his head.

Barnes's fork dived on the plate like a striking rattler. He was still chewing fat when the waitress came by and said, "Anything else? More coffee?"

His voice muffled by a full mouth, Barnes said, "What kind of pie you got?"

"We have apple pie and peach cobbler," the waitress said.

"I'll try both," Barnes said.

"Sly," Dan said, "you're pushing your luck."

Dan left Sly Barnes to pick up the buckskin and pack mule in the morning and then made his way to the mercantile where he loaded up on bacon, flour, salt, coffee, and other supplies.

"There's been no further talk of a lynching," Dave Harvey said. "Well, a couple of hot heads tried to stir things up in the saloon, but nobody listened."

"I'm glad to hear it. There's been enough death in this

town," Dan said. "Charge the supplies to the bank, Dave. It's their money we're going after."

After he packed the mule, ready for the morning, Dan told the same thing to Ed Wallace. "Charge the rentals to the bank," he said.

"Those robbers got the nest egg I was keeping for my retirement and maybe getting wedded someday," Wallace said. "Bring the money back and the horse and mule rental is free of charge."

It was fully dark and a hazy horned moon nudged aside the stars. The east wind blowing off the prairie had cooled the air, and one by one the store oil lamps that had made their windows rectangles of yellow light went dark, and the street shadows grew and probed the hidden places like black, skeletal fingers.

Dan Caine stopped and stood perfectly still in the gloom.

He listened into the night, clutched by the same feeling of unease that had wakened him from sleep the night before. The gray wolves were close to town, howling, keeping the pack together. Knowing how relentlessly hunted the wolves were, Dan had never before known them to venture this near to the humans they feared.

Something . . . out there . . . had scared them.

A cougar perhaps?

Dan immediately discounted that possibility. The big cats were solitary animals and wolves travel in packs and they could, and sometimes did, kill an adult cougar. Something had boogered them all right, but it wasn't a catamount. The animal had never been seen around Broken Back.

Then what?

The howling intensified. Closer now. His disquiet increasing, Dan's hand dropped to his Colt, the familiar feel of steel and walnut comforting him.

A woman emerged from the gloom and hurried toward him, a plump matron with sacks of sugar and flour in her arms, a late shopper who'd kept the mercantile open past closing time. She stood square in front of Dan and said, "Deputy, are we all going to be devoured in our beds?"

Dan smiled. "The wolves sound a little agitated, but they'll soon move on."

"A little agitated!" the woman said, her round, rosy cheeks getting redder. "They're right on our doorstep!" She glared at Dan. "Well, Deputy, what are you going to do about it?" She snorted through her nose. "They are wolves after all."

"I know," Dan said. "If they don't shut up soon, I'll get rid of them."

"And I should think so," the matron said. "What are we paying you for?" Her eyes were slitted slightly from the fullness of her face, but overall, Dan thought her quite pretty. "First the bank is robbed and if you include that awful Simon Trigg person, five men are dead in this town and now this, packs of ravening wolves prowling around our doorstep. Oh yes, and the Apaches are out. Deputy, it's a bad omen I tell you. It's as though Broken Back is under a curse."

Dan said, "You're quite safe, I'll see to that, Mrs. . . ."

"Blankenship, Theodora Blankenship. My husband

is bedridden with the rheumatisms, and I'm quite defenseless"—she freed an arm of its sugar sack and waved it in the direction of the prairie—"against those . . . those demons."

"Don't worry, I'll make sure no harm comes to you," Dan said. He smiled. "Listen. The wolves are already moving away."

"Maybe so," the woman said. "But it's an omen, I tell you, Deputy. An evil omen."

She gathered up her skirt, swung around and left, and was soon swallowed by darkness.

Dan watched the woman go, and his unease went with her. The wolves had moved away and their howls grew more distant. The stars seemed brighter, the night less shadowed.

But Dan Caine wasn't finished with wolves, not quite.

As he passed the Palace Hotel, he was hailed from the front porch by Luca Moretti. The man was a dark silhouette, the glowing cigar in his mouth a crimson point of light in the gloom.

"She wolves are the worst, Deputy Caine," he said, his words hollow in the gloom. "They're more savage than the males."

"They've gone now," Dan said, his voice sounding unnaturally loud in the stillness of a grieving town.

"They're afraid," Moretti said.

"Of what? Apaches?" Dan said.

"No, not Apaches."

"Then what?"

"One day you may find out," Moretti said. His cigar arced scarlet in the darkness and hit the muddy street in a shower of sparks. "Sleep well, Deputy," he said. "I'll see you again come morning."

The Italian turned on his heel and reentered the hotel, leaving Dan to ponder the man's strangeness.

"Well, it takes all kinds," he said to himself.

And the night seemed darker again.

Frank James was in his cell, reading the newspaper when Dan Caine returned to the sheriff's office.

"Seems like I'm the lesser of two evils," Frank said. "The *Bulletin* says Simon Trigg drew first. Listen to this . . .

"'Trigg, a practiced gunman, drew his murderous revolvers and said to Mr. James, "I've got ye now. You'll soon be shaking hands with Jesse." At this juncture, Mr. James, quick as a flash produced his own weapon and declared, "Be damned to ye, you British braggart." Both men walked off ten paces and then turned and fired. Trigg, as fast on the trigger as always, discharged both his revolvers but in the smoky, dark hell of the saloon, he did no execution. Mr. James, cool as a cucumber, then fired and his unerring ball struck Trigg in the chest and killed him at one stroke. Trigg, a tavern owner and pimp, was a well-known figure in Broken Back. He was said to have killed several men in the past and the Bulletin's obituary for the man is simply this . . . Good Riddance!'"

Frank laid the paper on his knee and said, "'Be damned to ye, you British braggart.' It's certainly got a ring to it, don't you think?"

"Except that's not how the scrape happened," Dan said.

"I know," Frank said. "But you must allow them at least a little poetic license."

Dam smiled. "I've got some interesting news, Frank."

"Then speak," Frank said.

"Dave Harvey over to the mercantile says he heard that certain parties wanted to hang you."

"Hang me? Why?"

"For being in cahoots with the bank robbers."

Frank shook his head. "I wondered when some ranny would try to make that connection. I had nothing at all to do with it, and if ever I was tempted to take up the profession again, I'd rob my own banks."

"The whole thing blew over," Dan said. "I think a lynching was the last thing on most folks' minds."

"I'm glad I didn't know," Frank said. "If I had, it would've been the first thing on my mind."

"All's well that ends well," Dan said. "Did your Shakespeare feller coin that?"

"No, he borrowed it," Frank said.

"Well, I'm to my bed," Dan said.

"Me too," Frank said. "Make sure you lock the door."

Chapter Ten

At first light, Dan Caine led his eight-man posse out of Broken Back. There was no one around to see them off and wish them well. The men who mattered, Frank James, the cowboys Lawson and Roberts, the gambler Bill Kent, and John Brooks were of the same mind as himself . . . they were vigilantes and no prisoners would be taken. The others, the man of mystery Luca Moretti, Sly Barnes, and old Ephraim Traynor, were considered to be of no account, unless and until they proved themselves otherwise.

Dan held out little hope that this would be the case.

When they rode out into the buffalo grass under a gold and lapis sky, Red Lawson took point and Ephraim Traynor was just a little behind him, casting around for tracks. Sly Eye Barnes rode drag with the pack mule.

At noon, as the sun burned a hole in the flawless blue sky, Traynor rode back and drew rein next to Dan. "They turned and headed north, Deputy," he said.

"Ephraim, are you sure?" Dan said.

The old mountain man nodded. "Sure, I'm sure. It's a guaranteed natural fact." Then by way of explanation.

"Far away, my eyes are no good. Close up, I can see just fine."

Dan shook his head, irritated for no real reason. "Where the heck could they be headed?" he said.

"North? Up that way, south of the high plains country, there's Fort Worth and Abilene and half a dozen smaller settlements. Take your pick," Traynor said. "There's plenty of whiskey and women in all of them burgs for a man with a good time on his mind and money to burn."

"They'll swing west and head for Fort Worth," gambler Bill Kent said. "That's a lead pipe cinch. It's a wide-open town where bank robbers can spend money in saloons, bawdy houses, and dancehalls and no questions asked."

"You been there, Bill?" Dan asked.

"Yes, I was and I was on a roll and doing just fine. But then I had to kill a man, and I left town in a hurry." Kent looked pensive. "Strange that. I mean how Jim Courtright, the city marshal, took a set against me over that shooting. It was a fair fight. The man came at me with a knife, said he'd cut my heart out, so I drilled him."

"Who was the man?" Frank James said. "Anybody I might know?"

"I doubt it. His name was Long Shot Murphy, and he was a gambler who was always broke. It was when I asked him to give me back the fifty dollars I'd loaned him that he came at me with a pig sticker. Long Shot was sociable enough when he was sober, but quarrelsome and dangerous in drink. But Courtright didn't want to hear that."

"There's just no accounting for lawmen," Dan said. "Especially when they get a notion to study on things." Then to Traynor, "How far are they ahead of us, Ephraim?"

"Hard to tell on grass, but a fair piece. Deputy, I'd say we got some riding to do."

"Any sign of Apaches?" Kent said.

Traynor shook his head. "No. But that don't mean they ain't out there."

"Ephraim, go back to tracking," Dan said. "Holler to Red Lawson to stay out there at point and tell him to keep his eyes skinned."

Traynor nodded, swung his horse away, and Dan watched him go. Then he said to Kent, "If they head for the Indian Territory, we'll never find them."

"Then we have to run them down before they reach the border," the gambler said.

"That's about the size of it, but easier said than done."

Frank said, "Those boys now have six killings on their back trail and the cards are all faceup on the table. They know they'll get hung if they're caught. My guess is the Territory. They'll split up the money there and then go their separate ways."

"Like you and Jesse would've done," cowboy Jake Roberts said. He had a broken, flattened nose that whistled slightly when he talked.

"Me and Jesse wouldn't have robbed the Broken Back bank in the first place." Frank said. "The country around the town is way too open."

"So how come we don't see them bank robbers?" Roberts said.

"Too far ahead of us, my friend," Frank said.

"So what do we do?" Roberts said.

"We close the distance," Frank said. "That's what we do. And then, when we find them, we shoot them where they stand and take back our money."

"Sounds simple," Roberts said.

Frank shook his head. "No, it's not simple. Simple truth is often miscalled simplicity."

"Huh?" Roberts said.

"I'm misquoting Shakespeare," Frank said.

"Huh?" Roberts said.

"Let's ride on," Dan said. He angled a look at Frank. "Enough with the Shakespeare. You buffalo the boys with that kind of talk and that includes me."

Frank sighed. "How sharper than a serpent's tooth it is to have a thankless child."

Dan Caine shook his head. "Frank, how come you lived this long without getting shot?"

They camped that night in a stand of post oak and mesquite about two acres in extent, and Ephraim made a fire for the coffee and bacon. Dan, wary now of a sudden surprise attack, had the men take it in turns to stand sentry during the night.

The following morning just after daybreak Red Lawson topped a low, grassy rise where here and there scarlet paintbrush bloomed among outcroppings of limestone rock. He drew rein and studied the terrain around him, rolling country that stretched to the horizon under a lemon-colored sky. But what caught his attention was a wagon road about a hundred yards away that cut across the prairie like a saber scar. The narrow track came in from the east, curved around another low rock formation, and then straightened up again. As far as Lawson could tell, before it was lost in the distance, the road continued north, straight as the crow flies for the Indian Territory.

Lawson stood in the stirrups and waved and hollered, hoping that if Ephraim Traynor couldn't see him, he could at least hear him.

The old man looked up, saw the cowboy signaling, and came on at a fast trot.

"What did you see, sonny?" Traynor said.

"A wagon road," Lawson said. He pointed. "Can you see it."

Traynor peered into the distance and said, "Yeah, I see it. Let's go take a closer look."

"For sure, the bank robbers will be on that road," Lawson said, his young face earnest.

"That would be my guess," the old man said. He kneed his horse forward.

Ahead of the two riders a large gray wolf loped across the wagon road, stopped, and turned its head toward them. It studied the two men closely for a long moment before running again and was soon lost among the long grass.

Grunting, Ephraim Traynor dismounted and scouted a stretch of the road.

"Riders passed this way, no longer than two, maybe three days ago," he said.

"The bank robbers you reckon?" Lawson said.

"Well, there are shod and unshod pony tracks," Ephraim said. "Maybe the bank robbers, maybe cavalry soldiers, but definitely some were made by them bronco Apaches. Hey, over there, what's that?"

Lawson kneed his horse over to the east side of the road and said, "It's a signpost. And it looks like two riders left the road right here and headed east."

Ephraim led his horse to the sign and then bent over to study the tracks. It took him a long while, parting grass, studying the underlying dirt, before he straightened and said, "Yeah two men riding shod horses. They're following the sign."

The old scout mounted again and said, "You set a while here on point, sonny, and smoke your pipe. I'm heading back to the deputy to tell him what we seen."

Lawson studied his back trail and said, "The posse ain't even in sight, so don't be long bringing them here. Hell, I didn't cotton to the size of that damned wolf that fixed his eyeballs on us."

"Then keep your rifle handy," Ephraim said. He cackled. "And never trust a wolf till he's been skun."

Ephraim Traynor rode up on the posse at a fast trot.

He drew rein beside Dan Caine and said, "Seen something, me and the cowboy."

"Then wring it out," Dan said.

"The cowboy came up on an old wagon road," Ephraim said. "It doesn't seem to get used much, maybe now and again by the army and the occasional wagon, but I seen fresh tracks that could've been made by both white men and Apaches."

"You think the white men were the bank robbers?" Dan said.

"Maybe cavalry sodjers, but bank robbers would be my guess," Ephraim said. "A wagon road makes for easy travel in this country. But here's the thing, not so long ago two riders split from the rest of the bunch, left the road and headed east." Then to hammer home his point, he pointed, "Thataway."

"What the hell?" Dan said. "But that doesn't mean

they were robbers. Could be it's only a couple of drovers riding the grub line."

Jake Roberts said, "I know of a few ranches out this way but there's a heap of long-riding miles between them. A man would starve to death just getting from one spread to another."

"Ephraim, if they are two of the robbers, where would they be headed?" Dan said.

"Well, they're too far south for it to be Abilene," Ephraim said. "Unless there's a burg closer that I don't know about. But . . ."

"Jake, what do you think?" Dan said.

Ephraim snapped, "Damn it, Deputy, let a man talk."

"All right, air your mind, Ephraim," Dan said.

"I was trying to say that there's a marker where them boys turned off," Traynor said.

"What kind of marker?" Dan said.

"The wooden kind of marker."

"What does it say?"

"Read it fer yourself, Deputy," Traynor said. "It ain't such a fur piece, you know."

The marker was a wooden board nailed to a stake driven into the ground, with crude lettering that read:

FRANK'S FARM

"Seems like they're a couple of sodbusters," Dan Caine said.

"There are no farms around these parts, Deputy," Jake Roberts said. "You can't plow an inch of soil on top of bedrock."

Ephraim said, "Deputy, I'd say it's a hog farm, a place a fallen woman lands when she can fall no further." He raised a bristly eyebrow. "Led a sheltered life, ain't you?"

"A brothel? Out here in the middle of nowhere?" Dan said, ignoring Ephraim's last remark.

"In the middle of nowhere is usually where you find a hog farm," Roberts said. "But since it's near a road, I reckon there's enough soldier and passing wagon trade to keep it going. Cowboys too, now and again, if truth be told."

"The two riders that left the road could be anybody," Bill Kent said. "There's nothing to say they're bank robbers."

"I know, but I aim to find out for sure," Dan said.

"Take a big chunk of our time," Frank James said. "We could go off on a wild goose chase to the hog farm and lose them boys entirely."

"I'm going alone," Dan said. "Frank, you'll lead the posse until I get back. Just keep pressing the robbers close." He answered the question on Frank's face and said, "I'll catch up."

"Take Brooks with you," Kent said. "I hear he's pretty good with a rifle."

"You heard right, gambling man," John Brooks said.

Dan shook his head. "No, I don't want to weaken the posse that much. You might need Brooks's rifle. The outlaws could take it into their heads to attack us again." He smiled. "Don't worry, Frank. I'll make this a short detour."

"You won't catch up on that two-bit nag you're riding," Frank said. "Take my black. He's fast enough to eat up the miles and there's no quit in him."

Dan said, "I don't want to . . ."

"I don't argue with bull-headed lawmen," Frank said.

He swung out of the saddle and held up the reins. "Here, Deputy Dan, take the damn horse."

Dan dismounted and then stepped into the saddle of the big American stud.

"A horse, a horse! My kingdom for a horse," he said. He looked at the surprise on Frank James's face, grinned, and said, "You're not the only one who can quote Shakespeare."

Chapter Eleven

The long grass had not yet erased the tracks of the two riders and Dan Caine reckoned they'd passed this way only a couple of days before. He'd been no more than three hours on their trail when he saw the roof of a cabin in the distance overshadowed by a pair of tall cotton-woods. As he rode closer, since there was no waterwheel in sight, it looked like the cabin sat in a shallow hollow by a stream, a place isolated in the middle of a vast, windy ocean of rippling grass.

When he was a hundred yards away, Dan drew rein and studied the place.

The cabin was long and low with a swaybacked roof and tilted badly to one side. Several slanted wooden beams, one end driven into the ground, supported its weight and stopped the whole rickety structure from collapsing. A pole corral to the right of the cabin held half-a-dozen horses, four of them nags as swaybacked as the roof, but two of the animals were of good quality and a pair of saddles that straddled the top fence pole carried a flashy amount of silver, more silver than a forty-a-month puncher could afford.

Expensive horses and saddles . . . were the men inside two of the bank robbers?

Dan Caine listened to what his gut was telling him . . . he was damned sure the pair inside were two of the outlaws he was after.

Dan rode closer. The usual collection of outbuildings surrounded the cabin, an outhouse, a ramshackle tool shed, a smokehouse, and a small barn. But what caught his attention was the woman who emerged from the creek that ran behind the property. She stood on the bank, naked as a seal, water dripping from the long black hair streaked with gray that fell lank and straight over her shoulders, and she was thin, her rib cage showing.

The woman picked up a scrap of white towel and applied it to her left armpit and said, "Go right in, cowboy. No need to knock."

Dan stepped out of the saddle and led his horse closer to the woman. "Who are the two gents inside?" he said.

"You the law?" the woman said. She dried her other armpit.

"Something like that," Dan said.

"The one with eyes like a snake is Whitey Church. The other with him is Arizona Charlie Fisher. They're both pure pizen. Mr. Something Like That, take my advice. Get back on your horse and ride away."

"I have business with those gentlemen," Dan said. "I'll go talk with them."

"What's your favorite go-to-prayer-meeting hymn, mister?" the woman said.

Dan smiled. "I don't know, and I can't rightly say that I've ever been to a prayer meeting. Why do you ask?"

"I've a fair to middling singing voice. I figured I'd sing

a hymn at your funeral." The woman pulled a stained red dress over her head and then wriggled it into place. She looked down as she buttoned the bodice and said, "Don't fret it none, I'll sing 'Rock of Ages.' That covers the music for most dead folks."

Dan thought that funny and laughed. But as he loped the black to the hitching rail outside the cabin, he felt that old, familiar knot in his belly. Not fear, he told himself. But mighty close.

"Hey, mister!"

Dan stopped and turned.

"Take my word for it, the worst of them inside is Frank Austin," the woman said. "It's his place and he's the meanest pimp west of The Big Muddy. You don't believe me, take a look." The woman pulled up her dress and turned. Her lower back and hips were covered in vicious red welts. She dropped the dress again and said, "Frank is a hand with a riding crop."

"Doesn't take much of a man to abuse a woman," Dan said.

"Even a two-dollar whore like me?"

"Any woman."

"Well, Frank ain't too much of a man, but he's sneaky, so be careful," the woman said. Then after a pause. "Lawman."

Dan Caine stepped from the glaring heat of the day into the dank heat of the cabin. The place was small and cramped and stank of sweat, piss, cheap perfume, and raw whiskey. A plank of rough-cut timber rested on two saw-horses and served as a bar. On a shelf behind the bar a barrel rested, apparently dispensing the rotgut that passed as whiskey, the only available beverage. Above that, a sign tacked askew on the wall read, *No spitting. No cursing,* and beside that a bill of fare chalkboard advertised the specialty of the house with the single word, STEW.

Two men stood at the bar, each with a woman on his arm. Like the one outside, the whores were very thin, pale, plain women, graduates of the line, unlike their painted and corseted sisters who worked the saloons in the big cattle towns. These prostitutes had been around, and as soon as Dan Caine walked through the door, they sensed trouble and stepped away from the men, holding their bodies stiff and wary.

Whitey Church was easy to pick out, a medium-sized man in his late twenties with prematurely gray hair and green, reptilian eyes. The other man was taller, bigger, probably tougher, with a wide, rough-hewn face, a black beard growing from just under his massive cheekbones to the top of his chest. Just visible was a bright yellow bandana knotted around his hairy throat. Both men wore a gun, shabby range clothes, and, despite the heat, suitcoats.

The pockets of the bigger man's coat bulged . . . a thing Dan noticed.

His spurs chiming, he stepped to the bar and said, "Howdy, boys."

No answer.

The bigger man looked at the newcomer as though he was something that had just crawled out from under a rock, and he hawked and spat close to the toes of Dan's boots. His slow gaze snail-slimed from Dan to the woman who'd just deserted him. "Come here, you slut," he said. "Don't walk away from me again."

The whore stayed where she was. She looked tense, frightened.

"You must be Arizona Charlie Fisher," Dan said. "You sure got a way with the ladies, Charlie."

The big man was taken aback at such affrontery. Now he looked closer at Dan, six-foot tall, slender, and in that moment relaxed and relevant. It gave Fisher pause. Young Texas draw fighters were all the rage, and this could be one of them.

"What the hell do you want, mister?" Fisher said. "State your intentions."

"I'll give it to you quick and simple enough so even you can understand, Charlie," Dan said. "I'm looking for the men who robbed the Broken Back bank, shot the manager, and trampled and killed an old lady as they made their getaway. Have you seen such, recent?"

Church and Fisher exchanged a glance, and then the bigger man said, "Naw, I ain't seen nobody like that."

Dan smiled. "And what about you, Whitey?"

The man's snake eyes narrowed, and he said, "I ain't seen nobody either."

Dan said, "Seems like you boys got to get around more, meet people."

"You're pushing it, feller," Whitey said. His hand was close to his gun. "Don't push it any further."

"What we have here is a stalemate," Dan said. "Now somebody has to give a little, and it ain't going to be me."

Dan let a few moments of silence pass, then he said, "All right, Charlie, empty your pockets onto the bar. Let's see what you're holding."

"You go to hell," Fisher said.

He went for his gun and opened the ball.

Speak to a dozen historians about how fast Dan Caine was with a gun and you'll get a dozen different answers. And no, Wes Hardin didn't teach him to shoot since they met in Huntsville when both were prisoners. But all agree that at the Frank Austin hog farm, he was a sight faster than either Whitey Church or Charlie Fisher, at that time both gunmen with confirmed kills.

Fisher did clear leather, but Dan's first shot took him high in the chest, an inch under the bottom of his beard. The bullet staggered Fisher and for a moment took him out of the fight. Whitey Church got his work in quickly, but he hurried the shot and his bullet grazed the meat of Dan's left bicep. Dan fired at Whitey, a solid hit to the belly, that dropped the man and plunged him into a world of hurt. Fisher, still on his feet but probably aware that he was already a dead man, two-fisted his Colt to eye level, trying for an aimed shot. But the play took too long. Dan put another bullet into him and Charlie joined his shadow on the floor, dead before he hit the timber.

Gunsmoke hung around Dan like a gray fog as he lowered his gun to his side and looked at the men at his feet. His eyes wild, Whitey Church held on for a few more seconds and then gasped loudly and died.

Dan felt no regrets. He'd pledged to shoot down the bank robbers where they stood, and that fate had just befallen a couple of them.

BLAM!

The shot came from behind Dan Caine.

He spun around, his gun coming up fast.

A tall, thin man stood on tiptoe, his face stricken, and

the shotgun in his hands clattered to the floor. He stood like that for long moments, on his toes, as though trying to touch the ceiling with the top of his head.

BLAM! BLAM!

Two more shots ripped through him from back to front and the spent rounds thumped into the wall behind Dan. Then slowly, like a toppling oak, the man fell flat on his face.

The woman Dan had met at the creek stood with a smoking Colt in her hands. She looked at Dan and said, "Frank Austin. A rutting pig among the sows."

"He was about to kill me," Dan said. "Lady, you saved my life."

"Think nothing of it," the woman said. She straddled Austin's body and fired three more shots into his back. Again her eyes lifted to Dan. "Right now, he's already burning in hell."

"Not one to hold a grudge, are you?"

"You don't know the half of it, lawman," the woman said.

The two other women in the room stepped to Austin's body and prodded it with their toes. "He's dead," one of them said. "Good riddance."

The woman with the Colt said, "Those your bank robbers?"

"Two of them at least," Dan said. "The big one . . ."

"Fisher," the woman said.

"Yeah, Fisher. His pockets look like they're stuffed with the bank's money."

"Let me take a look," the woman said. "I've never seen a big pile of money, stolen or otherwise."

"Go ahead," Dan said. "Put it right there on the bar."

As the other whores crowded closer to take a look, the woman kneeled beside the bloody corpse, her face revealing not the slightest revulsion. She dug her hand into the dead man's coat pocket and an instant later, she did show emotion . . . shocked surprise.

"There's no money. Lawman, I think you shot the wrong men," she said.

It was Dan's turn to be startled. "What do you mean?" he said.

The woman withdrew her hand from the pocket, waved a bright red bandana at him, and said, "This and . . . see for yourself."

Dan dropped to a knee and shoved his hands into the pocket. He came up with a wad of crumpled paper, a pocketknife, and a sack of tobacco. Desperately now, he tried the other pocket . . . another bandana, this time blue and folded, a steel fire starter, a tintype of a near naked woman, identified as *Lili La Plant, Denver, Colorado*, and a sheaf of newspaper clippings.

"The money's got to be here," Dan said. "Whitey must be carrying it."

He rifled through the pants' pockets of both men and found nothing but five dollars and thirty-five cents that he laid on the bar.

One of the women kicked Fisher's body and said, "That's all the money you brung, you damned skinflint. We don't come that cheap, bandana man."

"Their saddlebags!" Dan said. "Did they have saddlebags?"

He was answered by blank stares.

"The corral!" Dan said.

He rose to his feet, hurried outside, and ran to the two

silver saddles. There was no sign of saddlebags, or of anything else that would hold money. As he stood there defeated, the woman in the red dress stepped behind him.

"I already told you, lawman, you shot the wrong outlaws," she said. She'd smoothed out the crumpled paper that had been in Fisher's pocket. "It's a wanted dodger." Now she held it in both hands and read, "Proclamation. One-thousand-dollar reward. Wanted Dead or Alive. Whitey Church and Charlie Fisher. For murder, rape, robbery and disturbing the peace." The woman turned the dodger so that Dan could see. "Got their likenesses and everything right there. So you killed the wrong men but did the right thing."

Dan angrily shook his head. "I did the wrong thing. I don't give a damn what those two did in other towns. They weren't in Broken Back when the bank was robbed."

The woman sighed and said, "Helluva old world, ain't it? Shooting men by mistake an' all. Oops, I'm sorry I killed you. It was all a misunderstanding."

Dan stared at the woman and said nothing.

She smiled and said, "There's five dollars and thirty-five cents on the bar inside." The woman thumbed her chest. "That'll buy you some time with the gray mare if you have a mind. It will relax you and make you feel better."

It wasn't the whore's fault that he'd shot the wrong men, and Dan decided to be gracious. "Thank you, thank you kindly," he said. "But I got to catch up with my posse. Use the money to bury the dead men."

"Hell, we'll bury them three for no charge," the woman said.

"If the Rangers pass this way maybe you could claim the reward for Whitey and Charlie," Dan said.

"Have to dig 'em up again," the woman said. "I don't think Rangers will be willing to do that."

Dan smiled. "Probably not. What will you do now?"

"We've nowhere to go, so we'll stay where we are," the woman said. "Frank was a tightwad and I'm sure he has money stashed around here somewhere. We'll find it. And we can sell the horses and saddles. When the peddler comes by, we can buy the stuff we need."

"The Apaches are out," Dan said. "Or did you know that already?"

The wind blew a strand of hair across the woman's face, and she pushed it away with a forefinger. The day was still hot. "Mister, Apaches can't hold a candle to some of the trash we've had here. I guess we can take care of ourselves."

"I guess you can," Dan said. "I saw that today."

"Just so you know, I didn't kill a man," the woman said. "I killed a thing much less than a man."

"Some men need killing," Dan said. "You saved my life, and I don't even know your name."

"Julia Paul."

"Dan Caine. I'm a deputy sheriff from Broken Back."

The two other women walked from the cabin and one of them said, "Julia, we need help to drag the bodies out of the cabin. They're already stinking up the place."

"I'll help you," Dan said.

"No, you won't," Julia said. "It's our problem. Go attend to your own business. Find your bank robbers."

Dan dug into his pants pocket and produced a coin. "I want you to have this. It's a British gold sovereign, given to me down the Sierra del Carmen Mountains way by an Arab sheik. Keep it, but spend it if you ever find yourself down to your last chip."

The woman took the coin and looked at it gleam in the palm of her hand. "A present?" she said. She looked shocked.

"Yeah," Dan said, "it's a present."

"I've never had a present before."

"Well, you have one now," Dan said. "It's the least I can do."

Then, impulsively, he kissed the woman called Julia on her cheek, walked to his horse, and swung into the saddle.

As he rode away, Julia called after him, "Hey, lawman, what's an Arab sheik?"

"I've no idea," Dan said, grinning.

Chapter Twelve

Dan Caine followed the posse's well-defined trail for the rest of that day, through the moonlit night and caught up in the early morning as Frank James and the rest prepared breakfast. The morning air smelled of frying bacon and coffee.

As he rode in under a red dawn sky, Dan saw rifles lowered as he was recognized.

Weary, hungry, and with a story to tell, he climbed out of the saddle and on slightly unsteady legs stood and stared into the fire.

Always belligerent, Jake Roberts said, "Well? What the hell happened?"

"Hold on," Frank James said. "Let the man get some coffee into him before you start asking him conundrums."

Without looking up, Dan said, "I killed two men . . . the wrong men."

Frank handed him a tin cup filled to the brim with steaming coffee and said, "Drink that. Then tell us."

Dan carefully put the cup at his feet, built and lit a cigarette, and then picked the coffee up again. When the cup was down to half-full, he finished his cigarette, and then smoked another. Finally, he said, "I shot two outlaws, but they were the wrong ones. They'd nothing to do with the bank robbery."

Frank James saw the tear and smear of blood on the arm of Dan's shirt and said, "One of them winged you, Deputy."

"They both got their work in," Dan said. Then a reluctant eulogy, "They were game."

"How do you know they were outlaws?" gun-store owner John Brooks said.

"One of them had a dodger in his pocket offering a thousand-dollar reward for both of them dead or alive," Dan said. "Seems they were wanted for murder, rape, and robbery."

"Hell, Deputy, you should've taken their bodies to Broken Back and claimed the reward," Roberts said.

"That would've made him mighty popular," Bill Kent said.

"Chasing a reward is not what I'm here to do," Dan said. "I made one mistake. I don't want to make another."

"Who were those men?" Frank said. "I sure hope they weren't friends of mine."

"Their names were Whitey Church and Charlie Fisher," Dan said.

"Never heard of them," Frank said. "I know most of the men who are still in the bank-robbing business." His lip twisted under his mustache. "Must've been a couple of hicks. It's their kind that gives professional outlaws a bad name."

Ephraim Traynor handed Dan a sandwich of pan bread wrapped around a couple slices of fried bacon and as he ate, he asked the old man how far the robbers were ahead of them.

"Two days, I reckon," Traynor said. He bit his lip as though he was unwilling to talk further.

"Out with it, Ephraim. Cut the deck a little deeper," Dan said.

The old scout didn't answer but he called Red Lawson over and then said, "Red, tell the deputy what we're seeing out there."

The cowboy brushed coffee from his mustache and stayed silent. But his eyes were shifty, a man concealing something.

"Let me hear it, Red," Dan said.

"It's the darndest thing," the cowboy said.

"Then say it for God's sake," Dan said, tired and slightly irritated.

But it was Ephraim who spoke up. "Deputy, we keep coming across wolf tracks. One lobo, but a mighty big one."

"Gray wolf," Dan said. "There's still plenty of them around."

"Deputy, out on the range I've seen a heap of gray wolves, but none of them was big enough to leave the tracks we saw," Lawson said.

"Grass can make tracks look bigger," Dan said.

"The tracks were left in mud no later than yesterday at a playa that's now to the south of us," Lawson said. "Those were the prints of a big animal."

"How big is big?" This from Luca Moretti. The man looked concerned.

Lawson stamped a booted foot down hard into the grass. "Take a look. That's how big," he said.

The Italian shook his head. "I don't like this," he said. "The wolf worries me."

"Leave a wolf the hell alone and he'll do you no harm," Dan said. He was worn out and cranky and all this talk about a big wolf only added to his annoyance. "Now finish up here and we'll hit the trail."

But Moretti would not be silenced.

"It could be a lycanthrope," he said. His brown eyes were haunted, full of fright.

Dan snapped, "Damn it all, as though a wolf wasn't bad enough, now we got ourselves a ly . . . lycan . . . whatever the hell it is you said, Moretti."

"Lycanthrope," the man said. "It's a creature half-human, half-wolf, but it's a loner. It runs with neither humans nor wolves."

"Here, I've heard of them," Ephraim said. He chewed on bacon and was having a hard time of it. "The Navajo call them skin-walkers and they scare the hell out of everybody."

"Shape-shifters, yes," Moretti said. "The Navajo believe there are witches who can turn themselves into any animal they choose. But they are not lycanthropes. The lycanthrope can't change shape. It is an evil, demonic creature that fears only one thing on heaven or earth . . . the werewolf."

"Hell, another kind of wolf to keep me looking over my shoulder when I'm riding point," Lawson said. "What the heck is a werewolf?"

"A werewolf is a cursed human being that can shape-shift into a massive wolf," Moretti said. "Usually, the transformation only takes place once a month, under a full moon."

"I've known some ladies like that," Ephraim said.

"And I've heard enough about wolves," Dan said. He angled a look at Ephraim. "We're here to catch bank robbers, remember?"

"I'm all in favor of that," John Brooks said. "Me, I've shot a lot of wolves in my day, and a wolf is a wolf, nothing more."

"Of course, it is," Dan said. "Now saddle up, we've got some riding to do."

Sly Barnes, his eyes round, uneasy, said, "Anybody else want to take the drag with the pack mule?"

Chapter Thirteen

There was no more talk of wolves, but Lucan Moretti was oddly silent and Sly Barnes rode closer with the pack mule. Yesterday's shooting lay heavily on Dan Caine and he rode alone with his thoughts.

Finally, Frank James rode alongside him and said, "You still fretting about those men you gunned?"

"I made a bad mistake, Frank," Dan said. "Suppose they'd been just a couple of ordinary punchers out for a good time?"

"Ordinary punchers wouldn't have drawn down on you," Frank said. He thought about what he'd just said and added, "Well, it ain't likely."

"Fisher's pockets were stuffed with bandanas," Dan said.

"You told me that," Frank said.

"He liked bandanas," Dan said.

"Deputy, listen up," Frank said. "Those two were killers and they'd have killed again and again. How many lives did you save by punching their tickets?"

"I'll never know," Dan said.

"That's right you'll never know. But study on it when you feel bad about those two pieces of trash."

"You're right, Frank. I'll take your advice," Dan said.

"Of course, don't make any more mistakes like that," Frank said. "Shooting the wrong folks ain't exactly true blue."

The day was far gone, the sun a brassy ball in a sky the color of faded denim when they smelled their first dead Apache.

Ephraim Traynor and Red Lawson stood beside the body when the posse rode up.

"Found him just lying there," Lawson said. "Looks like he was killed by other Indians."

The man lay face-down in the long grass, three arrows sticking out of his back. He'd been scalped.

Dan Caine and Frank James dismounted to take a closer look while the others stood guard, ill at ease even though the featureless prairie rolled away from them for miles on all sides and there was no sound and nothing moved.

"I'd say he's been dead for a couple of days at least," Frank said. "A straggler killed by other Indians."

"There are no other Indians," Dan said. "He was killed and scalped by his own kind, Apaches." He called out to Ephraim and told him to come take a look. When the old mountain man stood by his side, he said, "Tell us what the story is here, Ephraim."

The old timer scouted the ground on either side of the corpse, then, his face puzzled, he tried to pull an arrow out of the dead man's back but it was stuck fast and refused to budge. Ephraim grunted, took a knee and bent over to take a closer look, and studied the arrow for a long time. Finally, he said, "What this ain't is Apache. And I don't know of any tribe that paints their shafts black. I'm willing to bet it's got a barbed steel head that was made at a white man's forge."

"You saying white men killed this Indian?" Frank said.

Ephraim shook his head. "Nope, I ain't saying that. All I'm saying is that the arrows in the Apache's back weren't put there by other Indians."

"What else can you tell us, Ephraim?" Dan said.

"He was a straggler right enough, and he was killed in a running fight," the old man said. He pointed behind him. "Look way over there how the grass is trampled flat. I'd say twenty, thirty horses, and it looks to me that their riders made a sport of it. Hell, they could've killed him anytime, but they ran him for a spell. He was arrowed off his horse and then he dragged himself here and this is where they scalped him. Damned Indian must've crawled a hundred yards afore he died."

"Apache bucks are tough," Frank said. "As Shakespeare said, 'He made death proud to take him.'"

Luca Moretti dismounted and led his horse to the body that he studied for a long time before he said, "Mr. Traynor, I heard you say twenty or thirty riders?"

"That would be my guess," the old scout said. "Took a passel of hooves to flatten the grass back yonder."

Moretti crossed himself with a trembling hand and whispered, "Oh, my God, preserve and protect us."

Tiredness catching up with him again, Dan said, "Hell, not your wolves again?"

"Of a kind, perhaps, but much worse. Much more

deadly and fiercer than any wolf," Moretti said. He took a string of black rosary beads from his pocket, kissed the cross, and held them tight in his hand. "Deputy Sheriff Caine, I greatly fear that recovering the bank's stolen money will soon be the least of your problems."

Frank James grinned and said, "Mister, you're one spooky feller. I bet you're mighty fond of sitting in the dark scaring folks with talk about ghosts and ha'ants and such."

"No, Mr. James, not ghosts," Moretti said. "The haunting dead can't hurt you, only the living can do that."

"All right, tell me what I'm facing here," Dan said.

"Not now, Deputy. Wait until I'm sure," Moretti said. "In the meantime, we must all be on our guard."

"Well, we know for sure there are Apaches out there," Ephraim said. "That's enough to worry about for now, I reckon."

Dan looked around him at the rolling grasslands that were now shadowed by the coming night. "Apaches . . . and I don't see a thing," he said.

"That's the trouble with Apaches and the Utes as well, when you do see them it's too late," Ephraim said.

"Don't trouble yourself over Apaches," Moretti said. "If we're facing what I think we're facing, they'll come straight at us."

"Moretti, you're starting to grate on my nerves," Frank said. "Say it straight out, who or what are we facing?"

Moretti shook his head. "When the time is right, I'll tell you. In the meantime, I'll spend some time in prayer."

"Say an extry one for me," Ephraim said. "I could sure use the help."

* * *

That night there was a tension in the camp that hadn't been there before, an unease so palpable that Dan produced a bottle of whiskey and insisted every man take a share. Bill Kent, Ephraim Traynor, and Jake Roberts agreed to take turns keeping watch through the night under a bright moon and an infinity of stars.

When Dan Caine finally sought his blankets, he dreamed of wolves and galloping, wild-maned horses.

Chapter Fourteen

The next morning brought the smell of death to the crystal-clear air and more corpses in the long grass.

Seven young Apaches lay sprawled in death around the gray ashes of a cold campfire. All were scalped. Their tongues were silenced, but they had a story to tell.

And Ephraim Traynor told it for them.

"The whiskey was left for them by the side of the wagon road where they would find it," the old scout said. "Their killers knew in what direction the Indians were headed." He shook his head. "Smart, very smart. Them young bucks couldn't resist a free jug of rotgut."

"Could it be the bank robbers?" Sly Barnes said. He sat his nag and held the lead rope of the pack mule.

"Nah, them boys are still running," Ephraim said. "They don't want any truck with Apaches."

"And they sure as hell wouldn't shoot black arrows into them," Dan Caine said.

Luca Moretti had dismounted again. He let the reins trail and looked at the face of every corpse. "These young men weren't only drunk, they were terrified."

"Of what?" Dan said. "It takes a lot to scare an Apache."

"And don't say wolves, mister," Ephraim said. "The Apaches are partial to wolves. The Mescaleros sing a war song that goes, 'Let me be powerful like the wolf.' One time I heard that song my ownself up in the Arizona Territory and I wished to hell I hadn't."

"It wasn't wolves killed these Indians," Moretti said.

Irritated again, Dan said, "Damn it, we know it wasn't wolves. Whoever it was took all their weapons, even their knives. Wolves don't do that."

Ephraim had wandered off, poking among the surrounding grass. When he returned, he said to Dan, "They came on them bucks in a rush, probably from the darkness. A lot of horses. Like I said afore, twenty or thirty riders, but I'd bet on the thirty. Somebody took a hit though." He showed Dan a blade of grama with a rusty stain. "That's blood, but human or horse I can't tell."

Bill Kent picked up the small whiskey barrel and shook it. "Empty," the gambler said. "Those boys were good and drunk when they got attacked."

"Didn't know what hit them," Ephraim said.

"They knew enough to be scared," Moretti said.

"What the hell would booger an Apache?" Dan said.

Moretti opened his mouth to speak, thought better of it, then said, "I have no idea."

The Italian surprised Dan and everyone else when he stood in the midst of the dead Apaches, raised his hand, and made the sign of a cross, his lips moving silently.

Me and Mr. Moretti are going to have another talk, Dan thought . . . not yet prepared to voice the thought.

Instead, he said to Ephraim, "Where are the horsemen that did this headed?"

The old man bladed his hand and chopped it to the north. "Thataway."

"The Indian Territory?" John Brooks said.

"Could be," Dan said. "Just so long as it's well away from us."

"Do you still want me to ride point, Deputy?" Red Lawson said. His huge mustache needed trimming.

"Yeah, I want you out well ahead of us, Red," Dan said. "Keep your eyes skinned and your rifle handy." He turned in the saddle and said to Barnes, "And yes, Sly, you ride drag with that damned cantankerous mule."

"Molly's all right once you get to know her," Barnes said.

"I don't want to get to know her," Dan said. Then, "Hey, Mr. Moretti, you about finished with those Apaches?"

The man nodded. "I am, but God isn't."

"Then mount up and let's ride," Dan said. "We must be getting close to the robbers."

"I calculate we're still two days behind," Ephraim said. "If we don't catch up soon on this wagon road, we'll lose them in the Territory, especially if they head north and get into the badlands."

"I don't think those boys will head north," Bill Kent said. "You can't spend your ill-gotten money in a wilderness where two sod cabins and a general store qualify as a town. Deputy, they put the crawl on your first posse so they've no idea they're being chased. My guess is they'll soon turn east and head for Fort Worth or Dallas where the whiskey and whores are at."

"Then we'll press them closer," Dan said. "It means long days in the saddle, but by God, we're going to corral them."

"And we'll hope we don't meet up with the Black Arrow gang," Sly Barnes said.

Old Ephraim Traynor cackled. "Truer words was never spoke, mule man," he said.

For an hour, the vigilantes rode in silence under the blue arch of a cloudless sky until Ephraim, a talking man, said, "Frank, what did they call your gang? I can't seem to recollect."

Frank smiled. "That's because Jesse and me never had a gang. We had associates who came and went."

"One of them was Bob Ford, huh?" Ephraim said.

"You can call him one of the bad associates," Frank said.

"There were others?" Ephraim said.

"Ephraim, maybe the man doesn't want to talk about the old days," John Brooks said.

"I don't mind," Frank said. "It passes the time." He looked at Ephraim. "I reckon the worst we ever had was a kid from a place called Sandy Ridge up Arizona way. His name was Vernon Decker and he was a bully and a blowhard and so downright mean and stupid he called Jesse out one day."

"How did that come about?" Ephraim said. "If'n you don't mind the tellin' of it."

"Well, first off he killed a man in camp. That was after Jesse and me and five others, Decker, Dick Liddel, Bill Ryan, Woodson Hite, and an older man who went by the name of Denver Smith, robbed a train in Jackson County, Missouri. That night in camp, Decker boasted that he was destined to do great things and that robbing trains was only a start. He said he aimed to be a more famous outlaw than Jesse himself, get his name and likeness in all the newspapers and the prettiest whores would call him Vern."

"And on wanted dodgers," Ephraim said.

Frank said, "Denver Smith, and a sour, bitter man he was, listened to all this and got madder and madder, but the kid wouldn't quit talking."

"You bet I'd have gotten mad too," Ephraim said.

Frank said, "Jesse told Decker to sit quiet and finish his coffee, but the kid wouldn't stay quiet, and things came to a head when he said he wanted to be known as the King of the Outlaws."

"Stupid thing to call himself," Ephraim said.

"Well, Denver Smith stood up and told Decker to shut the hell up, that he was sick and tired of listening to his boasting, and he accused him of being a big talker, little doer. Decker then says, 'Make me shut up, old man. Go ahead, try and make me.'"

"And then what happened?" Ephraim said.

"Smith said, 'I'll make you, by God,' and he went for his gun," Frank said. "I'll never forget the look on Decker's face, satisfaction and joy, like there was something happening that he badly wanted to happen. Of course, he drew and put two bullets into Smith's belly before the man cleared leather." Frank shook his head. "By my watch, it took Denver Smith three and a half hours to die, and him crying out in mortal agony the whole time and cursing Decker. I wanted to put Smith out of his misery, but Jesse said no, that it was bad luck to shoot a dying man. Later it turned out that Smith was the feller's real name and he'd been a preacher who'd fallen on hard times and took to outlawry. Ephraim, there's just no accounting for people."

"So, what happened to Vernon Decker?" Brooks said, interested despite himself.

"In 1881, Jesse moved his family into a house in St. Joseph, Missouri," Frank said. "He planned to live a peaceful life with his wife and young 'uns, robbing the odd bank only now and again, nothing regular. Now Vernon Decker objected to this and told Jesse that he was taking over the gang, as he called our group of associates. Jesse thought this was funny and laughed in the kid's face."

"I know what happened," Ephraim said. "And then Decker called Jesse out."

"Yes, he did," Frank said. "He stood outside Jesse's house and called him out. Only there was a problem. That day Jesse was suffering from a bad head cold and he asked me if I could handle things. I said I could, and I would tell Decker that Jesse was unwell and maybe he should drop the whole thing and dip his hot head in the rain barrel."

"I guess he didn't take your advice," Ephraim said.

Frank waved a fly away from his face and said, "As things turned out, Vern Decker was not an advice-taking man. I took my revolver from the holster, at that time I carried a .44-40 Remington, and stepped onto the porch. I had the gun down by my right leg where it couldn't be seen. Vern said, 'I don't want you, Frank. I want Jesse.' I told him that my brother was indisposed and that he should cool his hot head in the rain barrel at the side of his horse. Well, he ignored that and said, 'I'll see for myself if he's indisposed or not.' And then I told him if he wanted to see Jesse, he'd have to go through me. 'I don't want to kill you, Frank,' Vern said. 'I'll need you in the gang.'"

"He was some kind of stupid, that kid," Ephraim said.

"And a tad overconfident," Frank said. "He'd never seen me do up close shooting. Vern had been notified and had ignored me and now I said, 'Set foot on this porch and I'll kill you.'"

"And then . . ." Ephraim said.

"And then he went for his gun," Frank said. "I was on the porch, higher than Vern was, so I put a bullet in his brain pan, killed him as dead as a rotten stump."

"Served him right, I say," Ephraim said.

"There's a moral to this story," Frank said. "After that shooting, I vowed to never kill another human being. And I never did, until Simon Trigg drew down on me in the Brass Buckle saloon. I'd broken my vow and that's the main reason I joined this posse. A broken promise is like a broken mirror, it can't be put together again. And now, if I have to, I'm free to kill once more."

"I'm right glad to hear that," Ephraim said.

Dan Caine turned in the saddle and said, "Frank, don't make any other vows until the bank's money is in Broken Back and in the safe."

"I won't," Frank said. "I have a feeling I'd break it again right quick."

Chapter Fifteen

Silent lightning flashed across the night sky, shimmered on the shifting grassland, and for fleeting moments forged each blade into steel. The cool air smelled clean, fragile as glass, waiting for the first thunderclap to shatter it into shards.

But the thunder never came. Only the heat lightning persisted, dazzling the eye.

Dan Caine and his vigilantes were wide awake, each fixed gaze scanning the darkness. The guttering fire still burned, and the odor of simmering coffee offered comfort to men on edge.

Something was out there . . . waiting . . . watching. They could feel it.

Ephraim Traynor moved to the edge of the firelight and listened into the night, standing still as a marble statue on a plinth. By the fire, Luca Moretti clicked rosary beads through his fingers, his lips moving, chanting prayers no one else heard. Dan kicked his blankets aside and stood beside Ephraim.

"See anything?" he said.

"I heard a horse whinny, but that was earlier," the old

scout said. "Maybe I saw something in a lightning flash, but far out my eyes are not so good. So who knows?"

"What do you think you saw?" Dan said.

"I'm as old as a rock, Deputy," Ephraim said. "What does an old man know about anything?"

"What did you see in the lightning flash, Ephraim?" Dan persisted. The edge on his voice betrayed the tension he felt.

Ephraim turned his head and looked at the deputy. His misted eyes gleamed in the firelight. "You don't want to know."

Frank James stepped beside the old man. "Tell him, Ephraim," he said.

"I'm a crazy old coot," Traynor said.

"I know," Frank said. "But tell him anyway."

"I saw . . ."

"Out with it, Ephraim," Dan said.

"All right, I'll say it. I saw a wolf on a hoss."

Silence from Dan. A look of utter disbelief from Frank.

"Did he just say what I think he said?" This from Red Lawson.

Finally, Dan found his tongue. "Ephraim, you saw what?"

"You heard me," the old man said.

"You said you saw a wolf on a horse," Dan said.

"Yup, that's what I said. Tol' you I was a crazy old coot."

"You saw something that scared you Ephraim," Dan said. "Didn't you?"

"Sure it scared me, and it would've scared you too, sonny."

Dan stared into the darkness for a long time and then made up his mind about something.

He strode to the fire, took hold of a burning mesquite branch, and held it aloft in his left hand. In his right he held his drawn Colt. He looked at the others and said, "If you men see me come in running and hollering, shoot whatever is chasing me," he said. "Especially if it's a wolf on a hoss."

"What do we shoot, Deputy?" Bill Kent said, grinning. "The wolf or the hoss?"

"Both of them damnit," Dan said.

He stepped past the surprised Frank and Traynor, crossed the wagon road, and walked into the darkness, melting into the gloom until only the bobbing, fiery mesquite branch was visible.

Dan Caine walked about twenty yards and then stopped, his eyes skinning the night. But ahead of him he saw only a solid wall of darkness.

Then the soundless lightning flashed.

For one shimmering fraction of a second earth and sky stood still. Frozen in place and time. And what Dan saw in that instant scared him like the wrath of God. A fleeting moment went by, then an arrow zipped past his makeshift torch, so close to the flame that a shower of sparks stung his hand and the left side of his face. The archer's mark was the burning branch! Dan tossed it away and then thumbed off a shot, firing blind into the darkness. The Colt's flash blinded him further and he stepped quickly to the side, fearing an arrow aimed at the gun flare.

Now Frank James and the others stood around him, all of them shooting at phantoms.

"Hold your fire," Dan yelled. Then as the shooting

faltered to a halt, he listened into the darkness . . . only to realize his ears were ringing from the gunfire and he was temporarily deaf as a cow skull.

A moment later Sly Barnes, with a sneak thief's keen hearing, picked up the sound of hooves receding into the gloom and said, "He's gone."

"Deputy, what the hell was that?" cowboy Jake Roberts said.

Before Dan could reply, Frank James said, "Did you see anything?"

It was a while before Dan answered and when he did, he said, "Yeah. I saw a wolf on a hoss."

Luca Moretti was concerned. He took Dan aside and said, "Deputy, what did you really see?"

"I don't know what I saw," Dan said. "It was dark out there." He was on edge, seeking his blankets and disinclined to be sociable.

"You said you saw a wolf on a horse."

"Did I say that?"

"Yes, you did."

"Then that's what I saw."

"What did the wolf look like?" Moretti said.

"I only got a glimpse when the lightning flashed," Dan said. "Maybe it wasn't a wolf. Maybe it was a man with long hair who only looked like a wolf. I don't know."

Moretti fell silent, thinking, and then said, "Do you want a piece of advice?"

"No."

"I'll give it to you anyway," the Italian said. "Give up this chase and return to Broken Back. From this point on, your life and the lives of the men around you are in mortal danger."

Dan nodded. "Thanks for the advice. I'll study on it."

"Tell me when you reach a conclusion," Moretti said.

"Sure," Dan said, smiling slightly. "You'll be the first to know."

At dawn the following morning Ephraim Traynor walked into the grassland where Dan Caine had been the night before. He scouted the ground and around the base of a single post oak that stood stiffly about twenty yards away.

Dan saw Ephraim and joined him. "Learn anything?" he said.

"Nothing we don't know already," Ephraim said. "Just the tracks of one horse, probably unshod."

"An Apache?" Dan said.

"Could be."

Dan looked around him at the sea of grass restlessly moving in the wind. He saw nothing human or animal, just a vast emptiness under a pale morning sky.

Dan glanced over his shoulder, making sure no one was around before he said, "What did we see last night, Ephraim?"

"I don't know," the old man said. "But wolves don't ride horses. They eat them, mind, but they don't ride them."

"Somebody dressed up to look like a wolf?" Dan said.

Ephraim thought that through, then said, "An Injun wearing a wolf pelt? In the dark it was hard to tell."

"That sounds about right," Dan said.

"Deputy, I found the arrow that just missed your head," Ephraim said. "It's black with a barbed steel head."

"Like the ones that killed the Apaches," Dan said.

"The very same. I don't think the ranny who shot that arrow at you was another Apache."

"Then who was he?" Dan said.

"I don't know."

"That makes two of us," Dan said.

"I can tell you who might know," Ephraim said. "Luca Moretti. He's a strange one."

"I'll ask him, but not yet," Dan said. "If I spoke to him now, I'd only get some vague answers about us all being in mortal danger."

"Not something you'd want the boys to hear," Ephraim said. "They're spooked enough already."

Chapter Sixteen

For the next couple of days Frank James, the cowboys, and old Ephraim Traynor stood up well to the rigors of the long trail and made good progress on the wagon road. Luca Moretti seemed to be an enduring man. No one listened to Sly Barnes. But Bill Kent and John Brooks were tiring and that made them irritable. They began to find fault with everything, from the coffee to the slurping noises Ephraim Traynor made when he ate and Brooks several times threatened to leave the posse.

Matters came to a head on the second night after Dan Caine's brush with the mysterious bowman when Kent and Brooks got into a heated political argument that escalated into fists raised and threats made. Dan quickly intervened, stepped between the antagonists, and ordered handshakes all around.

But Brooks rode out the next morning, saying that he would no longer share a campfire with a Democrat.

Kent watched him leave and said to Dan, "I always took Brooks for a damned Yankee Republican. Good riddance."

"There's nothing good about it," Dan said. "We're

down a crack-shot rifleman, a man we could ill afford to lose."

"Deputy," Frank James said, "Brooks's heart wasn't in it from the git-go. He was too worried about his pretty wife and young 'uns, and I saw fear in his eyes when you had your brush with the wolf on a hoss."

"I don't know that it was a wolf," Dan said absently, his mind still on Brooks's departure.

"Then your brush with whatever it was on a hoss," Frank said.

"When the ball opened, Brooks would have stood," Dan said. "He had sand."

"Maybe," Frank said. "A devoted family man like that . . . well you just can't tell."

Dan was irritated. "Well now we'll never know, will we?" he said.

"This posse was mighty small to begin with," Ephraim Traynor said. "We can't afford to lose any more folks."

"We have enough," Dan said. "We can still handle the bank robbers."

Frank said, "What else are we facing, Deputy? Wolves on hosses?"

"He was an Apache on a horse," Dan said. "Just a bronco looking to cause trouble."

"And he sure did play hob," Frank said. "He nearly took your head off with an arrow."

"He hasn't been back," Dan said. "By now he's probably rejoined Delshay's band."

"Deputy Caine, you didn't encounter an Apache," Luca Moretti said. "You met up with something else, what we Italians call a *nemico pericoloso,* a dangerous enemy."

"What kind of enemy?" Dan said.

"I'm not yet certain," Moretti said.

"Can you give us a hint at least?" Ephraim said.

Moretti's smile was gossamer thin. "Look for a wolf on a horse," he said.

The relentless sun hammered the plains into submission, and around the posse nothing moved in the gasping heat, even the small music of the field crickets in the long grass had stilled. And for that reason, Red Lawson's revolver shot shattered the silence like a rock thrown through a window.

"The cowboy's in trouble, sounds like," Frank James said.

In the distance Lawson sat his horse, the gun in his hand raised over his head. Ephraim Traynor was already cantering toward him.

"Let's go talk with the man," Dan Caine said.

He kneed his horse into motion, and the others followed at a gallop, Sly Barnes bringing up the rear with the balky pack mule.

"Two things, Deputy," Lawson said when Dan drew rein beside him. "The bandits made their turn east right here." Then seeing the annoyed look on Dan's face caused by an unnecessary pistol shot, he added quickly, "And riders coming." He pointed. "You can just see them."

Dan squinted into the distance and saw three riders emerge from the far-off heat shimmer. "What do you make of them, Frank?" he said.

"Looks like white men but only three of them," Frank said. "It can't be the robbers."

"Drovers?" Dan said.

"Could be," Frank said.

"What do you think, Red?" he asked Lawson.

"Maybe hands looking for strays," the cowboy said. "But that's unlikely so far out this way."

"They don't seem to be in any hurry, so they're not running from something," Dan said.

Ephraim had scouted the robbers' tracks, and now he said, "Deputy, a horse dung pile over yonder by that clump of daisies is dry and most of the grass has stood back up. I'd say them boys are still two days ahead of us, and we ain't gaining on them none."

"Damn!" Dan said, meaning it. Then, "Frank, let's go talk with the three riders. Maybe they've seen something."

"Sure," Frank James said. "But keep your gun handy. They may not be friendly."

"The rest of you men stay on guard," Dan said. "If you see Frank and me come flapping our chaps, you know what to do."

"You can depend on us," Ephraim said.

Chapter Seventeen

When they were within hailing distance of the three riders, Dan Caine and Frank James slowed their mounts to a walk, hoping to show that they harbored no evil intent.

But the three were apparently not the trusting type. They sat their horses, rifles at the ready, and waited.

The day was exceptionally hot, and Dan felt sweat trickle down his back as he drew rein ten yards from the riders and raised his right hand in the peace sign.

Frank, less inclined to be sociable, glowered, summing up the three men as middle-aged deer hunters at best, lawmen at the worst. What they didn't look like was bank robbers. The three looked like townsmen, two of them dressed in frayed ditto suits, the other in a black vest and a collarless white shirt.

The riders rode closer, three abreast. They did not seem happy to see strangers.

"Howdy," Dan said.

The men made no answer.

"I'm Deputy Sheriff Dan Caine out of Broken Back town," Dan said. "In close pursuit of a bunch of bank robbers. This here feller is Frank James, a member of my posse."

The men seemed to be taken aback, and the one in the middle, a tall, stringy man with a graying beard and bleak eyes, said, "*The* Frank James?"

"Better known as Jesse's brother. Yes, I am he. If you do love my brother, hate not me; I am his brother and I love him well."

A couple of seconds passed as each word of the Shakespeare quote dropped like rocks into a bucket. But then the stringy man surprised the hell out of everybody when he urged his horse forward and smiling, said, "Allow me to shake the hand of my old comrade in arms. We both fought for a glorious cause that was lost, you for Captain Quantrill and me for Captain William T. Anderson, known to the Yankees as Bloody Bill." He shook Frank's hand. "Sir, this is indeed a great honor."

"Likewise," Frank said. "But the cause of southern freedom against tyranny lives on. Only the battles were lost. Now, what is your name, sir, my old confederate, we few, we happy few, we band of brothers."

"My name, sir, is Virgil Curry and my companions are Mike Cooley and Ira Kirk," the stringy man said. "We're from a settlement, if such it can be called, that lies three miles behind us, merely a mercantile that also acts as a saloon and hotel, a blacksmith's shop, and a livery. I own the mercantile, Mr. Kirk the livery, and Mr. Cooley is the blacksmith. Up until sometime early this morning, twelve souls lived there . . . now there are only ten."

"What happened?" Dan said.

"You come upon me at an unfortunate time, Mr. James. My heart, it is heavy." Curry swallowed hard, his prominent

Adam's apple bobbing. "My two daughters have been took," Curry said. "One sixteen, the other a year older. Pretty girls."

"Were seven rough-looking men responsible?" Dan said. "Well armed, riding good horses."

"Indeed, the men you describe were in the settlement two days ago," Curry said. "One of the horses had cast a shoe and while Mike reshod the animal, they came into my store and bought tobacco and coffee and paid their score. And then they rode out of town. It was not them who stole my daughters."

"They headed east?" Dan said.

"Yes, east. In the direction of Fort Worth, I'd say."

"Frank, we'd better get after them," Dan said. Then to Curry, his interest in the man's plight now waning, "If we find your daughters, we'll be sure to send them home."

But Frank James, perhaps because Curry was on old Reb like himself, wouldn't let it go. "Mr. Curry, have you any idea who took your daughters?" he said. His impatient horse tugged at the bit, anxious for the trail.

"I know who took them," Curry said. Kirk and Cooley nodded in agreement. "It was two women who lured them away."

"Two women?" Dan said, interested despite himself.

Curry nodded. "Two women who wanted a room for the night. Strange looking women."

"How strange?" Dan said. He was aware of the posse riding toward him, probably to find out what the hell all the parleying was about.

"Short skirts, knee-high moccasins and scarlet corsets strange," Ira Kirk said. "And each wore a pair of Colts on their hips."

"And top hats with dark goggles on the brim agin the sun glare," Curry said. "And they both wore ankle-length dusters. Their hair was long and fell over their shoulders, with sections pinned up on each side of their heads like . . ."

"Ears," Kirk said.

"What kind of ears?" Frank said, smiling.

"Kinda pointed . . ." Kirk said.

Hating himself for saying it, Dan said, "Wolf ears?"

Kirk's face lit up. "Yeah, that was it . . . like wolf ears. How did you guess?"

"I don't know," Dan said. "Strange ladies indeed."

"And even stranger," Curry said. "Only one of them was white. The other looked Mexican or maybe even Indian."

"Did they talk to your daughters?" Frank said.

"Oh yeah, it seems the four of them were talking all the time," Curry said. "Cora and Elsie don't get to meet many strangers around here but I try to keep them busy, bringing water from the creek and rearranging the store's shelves an' sich. But it ain't much of a life for teenage girls who dream about being sparked by lively young fellers and go dancing and picnicking and whatever it is young folks do nowadays."

Luca Moretti had drawn rein beside Dan and over-heard that last. Now he said, "Tell me what happened."

Curry's tired cheerless eyes fixed on Moretti's face. "Hell, mister, I just did."

Dan said, "This here is Virgil Curry. His teenaged daughters were taken by two women." He said to Curry, "When?"

"When I went to wake them for their chores, it was just

at sunup," Curry said. "They were gone, and their beds hadn't been slept in."

"No signs of violence?" Moretti said.

"None. They'd each packed a bag and it seems to me they went willingly," Curry said. "Unless it was at gunpoint."

"Describe the two women," Moretti said.

A look of exasperation settled in Curry's thin face, but Dan said, "They wore top hats, corsets, moccasins, and six-guns under long dusters. And the hair on each side of their heads was pinned up in . . ."

"Wolf ears," Moretti said.

Curry looked surprised, "Yeah, that's right."

The Italian was stricken. He sighed and then said, "Then I fear the worst," he said. He stared hard at Curry. "You're looking for your lost children. How did you lose track of the women who enticed them?"

Dan gave Moretti a sidelong look. "Enticed them" was a strange way to put things.

"We followed the tracks of two horses heading west, then lost them on rocky ground in the low hill country back yonder," Curry said. "We're not scouts. We haven't been able to pick up the tracks again."

"Two horses. They're riding double," Moretti said. "Seems like your daughters went willingly enough, Mr. Curry."

"I don't know what those two women said to my daughters, but they promised them something," Curry said.

"Did you ever beat your daughters, Mr. Curry?" Moretti said.

"Not too often, and only when they needed it," Curry said.

"Then the She Wolves promised them a better life, free of beatings and full of adventure," Moretti said.

"She Wolves?" Curry said. "What the hell . . ."

"That's what the women call themselves," Moretti said. "And that's what they are. For now at least, your daughters are in no danger."

Dan glanced at the position of the sun and spoke into the tense silence that followed. "We got to be riding. Good luck with your search, Mr. Curry."

Curry stared at Ephraim Traynor, at his beaded buckskin shirt and the eagle feather in his hat brim, and said, "You've got a scout, Deputy Caine. Join in our search and help us find my daughters."

"Sorry, Mr. Curry, but my first obligation is to the town of Broken Back and the stolen money of its citizens," Dan said. "After we deal with the bank robbers, we'll ride this way again."

Curry sat back in the saddle, anger in his face. "That's a hard, pitiless thing to say to a man whose children have been took," he said. "Those two women, She Wolves as you call them, have a debt to pay to me, the father of my lost children."

"And by God, when we find them, they'll pay it in blood," Ira Kirk said.

"Mr. Curry, be assured of this . . . I'll return and help you recover your daughters," Moretti said.

For a few moments Curry stared at Moretti, small, slender, and dark, and then swung his horse away. "Let us continue the search," he said. "We'll get no help here."

He momentarily turned his attention to Frank James, nodded, and then he and the others rode away.

Dan's mouth hardened. "Let's ride," he said.

"We should make a stop at Curry's mercantile and stock up on supplies," Frank said. "Everything we got, especially flour and coffee, is running low."

Dan nodded. "I've no objection to that. I need the makings anyhow."

Fran Cooley, the blacksmith's wife, was behind the counter at Curry's store when Dan Caine and the posse stopped to replenish their supplies. While Frank James and the others filled the counter with slabs of bacon, flour, coffee, and beef jerky, Dan bought a sack of tobacco and papers and as he built a cigarette he said, "I met Virgil Curry on the trail."

The woman said, "Then you also met my husband. My name is Fran Cooley and I'm watching over the store while Virgil Curry is away." She smiled faintly. "Not that he expected any customers."

"Well, now you have us," Dan said. He thumbed a lucifer into flame, lit his cigarette, and from behind a cloud of blue smoke said, "Curry told me about his daughters. That's too bad."

"Too bad for whom?" Fran said. She was a thin, worn blonde who looked middle-aged but could've been decades younger. Hard work, isolation, and the Texas sun aged a woman. "Bad for Cora and Elsie or bad for Virgil?"

"For all three, I guess," Dan said, surprised by Fran's response.

"Yes, Virgil lost his slave labor, and the girls"—she waved a hand, taking in the store—"lost all this."

For a moment Dan searched his brain for the right words, but Luca Moretti had been standing close, and now he said, "Mrs. Cooley, did you speak to the women who took the girls?" He held a half-drunk bottle of lime green soda pop in his hand.

"Yes, I talked with them," Fran said. "But they didn't take Cora and Elsie. The girls went of their own free will. I would've gone with them too, but they didn't want me in their pack. I'm too old and too damned worn out, I guess."

"In their pack?" Moretti said.

"That's what they call the women who've joined them," Fran said. "They live in a pack."

"Where do they find these women?" Moretti said. "It can't be easy on the frontier."

"Spoken like a man wearing the usual blinders," Fran said. "Mister, they can find young women all over the frontier who live lives of soul-destroying desperation with abusive or indifferent husbands. In Kansas, farm wives are known to step out of their cabin, stare at the empty, never-ending prairie that surrounds them . . . and do you know what they do? They scream. And scream and scream and never stop screaming. Those women, their minds break, shattering into a million, million pieces that can never be made whole again. Apparently the She Wolves save them from that terrible fate, so I say more power to them."

"The She Wolves offer freedom, a life of high adventure, wild suffragettes free of the tyranny of men and their only law is the law of the wolf pack," Moretti said. "Am I right?"

"Yes, you are," Fran said. "And I wish to God I was with them. This store, the livery stable, and the blacksmith's forge are my entire world. How narrow and impenetrable are my high fences."

"Mrs. Cooley, where are the She Wolves taking the Curry girls?" Moretti said.

The woman smiled. "I think you know the answer to that question."

"Black Mesa in the Oklahoma Territory. That's what I've been told."

"Yes, maybe there or to some other place. Find out for yourself," Fran said.

"Cigars?" Frank James said, leaning across the counter.

"Virgil has a humidor in the back," Fran said. "Come with me and I'll show you his selection." She looked at Moretti, a fleeting glance and said, "Let the Curry girls go. Let them enjoy their freedom and their youth."

After the woman left, Dan said to Moretti, "How come you know so much about these women who call themselves She Wolves?"

"Because it's my job to know," the Italian said. "I did the research, Deputy Caine."

Dan shook his head. "Mister, you and I are going to have a talk."

"I look forward to it," Moretti said. "You have more to learn and much to fear."

Chapter Eighteen

"What does a full bottle of whiskey standing upright on the trail mean?" Dan Caine said. "Enlighten me."

"I can tell you three things, Deputy," Ephraim Traynor said. "One, the robbers camped here last night. Two, we're gaining on them. And three, they know we're tracking them."

Dan picked up the pint of Old Crow. "And this?"

Ephraim grinned. "Why, it's a present, Deputy," he said. "I reckon those boys bought it in Curry's store and left it here for you as a good joke."

"Probably poisoned," Dan said.

He made to toss the bottle away, but Frank James intervened. "No, let me have that," he said. "I would give all of my fame for a pot of ale." Frank grinned. "Shakespeare didn't have bourbon, you see." He studied the bottle. "Good, the cork hasn't been pulled. So let's give her a try."

Ephraim anxiously watched Frank take a generous pull from the bottle, licked his lips, and said, "How is it?"

"Tastes like Old Crow," Frank said. He passed the

bottle to the old man and said to the others, "Line up, boys. Take a swig."

Everyone drank except Luca Moretti.

Dan was the last to drink and he drained what little was left of the bourbon and threw away the empty bottle and said, "Tracks are clearer, Ephraim."

"Yup, due east toward Fort Worth, sure enough," Traynor said.

"The robbers know they're being followed," Frank said. "I don't think a bushwhack is out of the question."

"I was thinking that same thing," Dan said. He looked around him, at the grassland dozing under the sun glare. "Hillier country ahead of us. If I was planning to lay in ambush, that's where I'd do it."

Red Lawson looked concerned, and Traynor said, "Don't you worry none, cowboy. The point man never gets shot, ruins the bushwhack."

"How about the drag?" Sly Barnes said.

"He's usually one of the first to take a bullet," Ephraim said.

Barnes gulped like a man trying to swallow a peach pit but said nothing.

"Deputy, you want me to ride up front with Red?" Jake Roberts said. "In that hill country, two pairs of eyes are better than one."

"Ephraim, what do you think?" Dan said.

"The young feller has it right," the old scout said. "We need to keep a sharp lookout from now until we catch up with that robbing bunch."

"The question is, do we really want to catch up with them?" Bill Kent said. The gambler smiled, but it was an empty facial grimace devoid of humor.

"What do you mean?" Dan said.

"Gunfight," Kent said. "I mean gunfight, Deputy Caine. We lost John Brooks. Are the rest of us up to out-shooting a bunch of gun-handy outlaws? I look around and figure we don't stack up to much."

Dan opened his mouth to speak, but Kent held up a silencing hand. He said, "And tell me this . . . after the smoke clears how many of us will still be standing?"

Jake Roberts, always belligerent, scowled and said, "Gambling man, all of a sudden you're showing a yellow streak."

Kent took no offense. "Cowboy, I know how to die standing up," he said. "But is a bank's money worth dying for?"

"Bill, you didn't think that way when you signed on for this posse," Dan said. "What changed your mind?"

"Hell, we ain't even a legal posse," Kent said. "We're vigilantes, and we already executed two men by mistake."

"I did that, not we," Dan said. "And I'm the one who'll live with it. Bill, it's not the bank's money, it's the people of Broken Back's money and if we don't recover it, a lot of hard-working folks will be ruined. There was a heap of life savings in that thirty thousand because people from miles around trusted the bank and made it one of the biggest in Texas."

"Small town, big bank," Frank James said. "That's why it was robbed."

"You make a good speech, Deputy," Kent said. "But I'm a gambler and I figure the odds and right now I reckon we're up against a stacked deck and it's time for me to pick up my chips and call it a day."

"You're quitting on me?" Dan said.

"That's about the size of it," Kent said. "I bought supplies at Curry's store, enough to get me back." He looked around. "Enough for two if anyone cares to join me." Kent got no takers, but Roberts said, "You didn't figure the odds, but you figured you were too damn yellow to go on. I should put a bullet in you right now fer a yellow-bellied coward."

"No, Jake," Dan said. "A man's got a right to do whatever he feels is right. I won't have him ride with me against his will."

Kent swung his horse away and then drew rein. "Sorry," he said.

"Sorry don't cut it, Bill," Dan said.

"No, I guess it don't," Kent said.

"If we meet each other in the street, just walk on by," Dan said.

Kent nodded. He couldn't find any words.

He rode away at a canter and soon vanished into the distance.

Dan Caine peered across the grassland and his eyes narrowed, watching the distant rider with deep and abiding interest. Finally, he said to Frank James, "Well, what do you make of him?"

"Been keeping pace with us for the past hour," Frank said. "And he has a partner on the other side. But I can't get a fix on either of them in the heat shimmer. But they're watching us, depend on that."

The sun was lower in the sky but the day was still hot and the shirts of Dan and the others were dark with sweat. Around them the air smelled of buffalo grass, prairie sage, and the faint honey fragrance of drop seed, overlaid by the constant odor of dust and horses.

"Yeah, the robbers are keeping track on us," Dan said. "We're getting too close for comfort, I reckon." He shook his head. "This is when I miss John Brooks and his long-reaching rifle."

Ephraim Traynor cackled. "Ol' Brooks could blow that son of a gun out of the saddle, fer damn sure."

Up ahead, Red Lawson and Jake Roberts had drawn rein and had their heads together, conferring.

"Looks like those boys might give it a try," Frank said.

Luca Moretti kneed his horse alongside Dan's mount and passed him a brass ship's telescope. "Use this," he said. "You're in for a surprise, Deputy."

It took Dan a few moments before he focused on the rider. When he spoke, there was wonder in his voice. "I'm sure that's a woman. Here, Frank, take a look. What do you think?"

After a while Frank lowered the glass and said, "It's a gal all right. Long black hair, a corset, and naked thighs." He smiled. "It sure ain't a feller."

"The other one looks exactly the same," Moretti said. "They could be sisters. In fact, they are sisters, all the She Wolves.

She's using field glasses," Moretti continued. "Observing us, studying us, summing us up. As far as we're concerned, she's not yet made up her mind. Should she ignore us or become a beast of prey?"

"What do you think she'll do?" Dan said.

"She Wolves can be ferocious predators," Moretti said. "But I don't know if they will be. Perhaps they will agree to let us live."

"Well, I'm not going to hang around until they make up their minds," Dan said. He slid the Winchester from the boot under his knee and said, "Me and that little lady are about to have some harsh words."

"Deputy, no!" Moretti yelled. But Dan had already kicked his horse into motion and galloped toward the woman.

Frank smiled at the Italian. "I reckon Dan can handle her."

Moretti was appalled. "He's no match for her," he said. "A She Wolf is a wounded, bitter, and angry creature and she can inflict terrible harm on a man. She's the most dangerous human on earth, a predator fiercer than the wolf itself."

His eyes fixed on Dan, Frank didn't turn his head as he said, "Who are you, mister? No forget that . . . what the hell are you?"

"A man who could save your life one day," Moretti said.

"Look, the deputy's shooting," Frank said. "Go get her, Dan."

The woman rode bareback on a spectacular leopard appaloosa, a wooden recurve bow in her right hand and a sheaf of arrows in a leather quiver on her back. She slowed to a walk as Dan galloped closer, her face turned to him. A mane of glossy black hair cascaded to her shoulders and she wore a short tan-colored tunic with beading on the front, a scarlet corset, and knee-high moccasins. At first Dan took her for an Apache, but her face, a white blur at a distance, told him otherwise.

"You! Hold up there!" Dan yelled. "I'm Deputy Sheriff Dan Caine and I want to talk with you."

Now at a trot, the woman let her field glass hang from a strap around her neck and nocked an arrow, drew the bow-string to her ear, and let fly. The arrow whirred a foot above Dan's head, close enough that he let out a startled, "Hey!"

A second shaft followed, this time close enough to the side of Dan's neck that he was sure he felt the tickle of the flight feathers.

In 1907 Dan Caine described what followed to a reporter for the *El Paso Herald:*

> I quickly ascertained that the woman's third arrow would find its mark and I threw my Winchester to my shoulder and fired. As far as I could tell, the ball did no execution. But it had the effect of convincing my adversary that I was a resolute man and not to be taken lightly, for she immediately set heels to her pony and galloped away. I at once set off in pursuit, firing my rifle at the run, but the woman had a better steed than my own and ere I could get close enough for an aimed shot, she left me in her dust. Thus ended my first encounter with an enemy more savage and dangerous than any I have ever encountered.

"She lit a shuck and I took some pots and missed," Dan said, answering the question on Frank James's face. "But a couple of her arrows came mighty close."

Frank smiled and held out a black-shafted arrow. "This was one of them. Ephraim pulled it out of the ground."

Dan grabbed the arrow, stared at it for a moment, and then tossed it away. "Damn thing almost took my head off," he said. Then, "Frank, something is troubling me."

"Then split it right down the middle. I'm listening."

"The woman at Curry's store led me to believe that the She Wolves . . . damn stupid name . . . hang out at a place called Black Mesa up in the Oklahoma Territory."

"All right, I savvy that," Frank said.

"Well, here's the thing, we ain't even on their home range, so how come they're so all-fired determined to punch our tickets?"

"Like they did the Apaches?" Frank said.

"Yeah, just like they did the Apaches."

"They're raiding south for some reason."

"What reason?"

"Ain't Fort Sill up that way?" Frank said. "Maybe the army chased them out of the Black Mesa country."

"Maybe," Dan said. "The Apaches are out, so it could be that the army got the She . . . women . . . and the Mescaleros confused. At a distance, easy enough to do."

"Then there's your answer," Frank said. "The She Wolves . . ."

"Hell, don't call them that," Dan said. "They're only some loco women on horses."

"All righty then, up Oklahoma way the loco women on horses got pressure from the army and hightailed it into Texas," Frank said. He chewed thoughtfully on a bite of jerky and added, "Seems we came on the scene at a bad time, huh?"

"Yeah, we did, but only because the women are a

distraction we don't need," Dan said. "From now on we concentrate on catching up with the robbers and taking back the money."

"They still outnumber us," Frank said. "But if we're lucky, maybe the loco women on horses will whittle them down to size."

Dan grimaced. "All right, call them She Wolves for heaven's sake."

Frank grinned. "I wondered how long it would take."

As he would relate in his later years, that night when the moon came up was the strangest and eeriest that Frank James had ever experienced in his eventful life. A man of some learning, he said that out in the green sea of grass siren songs began that tried to lure Luca Moretti to his doom.

Chapter Nineteen

By Dan Caine's watch, it was one in the morning when the sirens began their strange song. Around the camp, the moon cast an opalescent glow on the prairie, and the unceasing wind was still, the only sound the soft breathing of sleeping men, the occasional stomp of a horse's hoof, and the crackle of the mesquite fire.

"Luca . . ."

A woman's voice from the pearly darkness.

"Come to us, Lucaaa . . ."

Everyone rousted themselves from their blankets, and Jake Roberts held his rifle at the ready, his mouth tight.

"Lucaaa . . . we'll be nice to you . . ."

"What the hell?" Frank James said.

"She Wolves," Luca Moretti whispered. "They know I'm here."

"I could've worked that out for myself," Frank said. He sounded on edge.

"Who sent you . . . Lucaaa . . . ?"

The woman's voice had a singsong quality, taunting, menacing, and spine-chilling.

Another voice, the same mocking tone. "Did the Pope send you . . . Lucaaa . . ."

Then another. "Or was it the murderer Cardinal Ahren von Recke? Tell us . . . Lucaaa . . ."

"We'll be nice to you . . . Lucaaa . . ."

"Lucaaa . . . you'd like that, wouldn't you . . . ?"

"All the women you want . . . Lucaaa . . ."

"Drink the cup of forgetfulness . . . Luca . . . lay aside your vow of chastity . . ."

"Come to us . . . Luca . . . come to us . . ."

"We're waiting . . . Lucaaa . . ."

Roberts raised his rifle and said, "Hell, I'm gonna dust them gals."

"No!" Moretti said. "Let them be. I'll talk with them."

Unarmed, his .476 Enfield still by his blankets, he stepped away from the fire to the edge of the darkness. After a few moments, he yelled, "You know why I am here. The murders of four holy monks by the lycanthrope lies black as mortal sin on all your consciences."

Then a woman's voice, "Come closer . . . Luca . . . talk to us . . ."

Then another, "Closer . . . Lucaaa . . . closer . . ."

Moretti took a few more steps into the gloom. The night began to close around him.

Jake Roberts was nearest to him.

"Jake! Get him!" Dan shouted. "Bring him down."

The cowboy dropped his rifle and dived at Moretti's legs, dropping the man as though he'd been poleaxed, an instant before an arrow split the air where the Italian had been standing. The arrow vanished into the darkness at the other side of the camp.

As a woman shrieked in anger and frustration, Moretti

struggled. "Let me up!" he yelled to Roberts. "I have to talk with them."

"Stay right where you are, pardner," Roberts said. "There's some mighty mean people shooting arrows at you."

"Damn you, let me up," Moretti said. On his back, he aimed a punch at Roberts's cheek that the pugilist shrugged off, countering with a short, chopping right to the Italian's chin that laid him out as cold as a wedge.

"Lucaaa . . ."

A woman's voice from the moon-splashed night.

"He's feeling right poorly ma'am," Dan yelled. "Now be off with you."

But Moretti was up on one elbow, groggy, rubbing his chin.

"Luca . . . can you hear me . . . Lucaaa?"

"I can hear you," Moretti said.

"Luca . . . turn around . . . Lucaaa . . ."

Another voice, deeper. Authoritative. More menacing. Shouting.

"Go back . . . Luca . . . go back and kiss Cardinal von Recke's feet . . ."

"You go to hell, She Wolf," Moretti yelled. "You harbor a demon in your midst and you must let me destroy it."

The same woman's voice. Tight with anger.

"Luca . . . when we meet, I'll tear your guts out . . ."

"Get thee behind me, Satan," Moretti yelled.

A derisive laugh from the night.

Then a shower of arrows.

Ephraim looked in horror at the arrow sticking out of the ground between his feet and yelled, "The hell with this!" He cut loose with his rifle, firing blind into the shadows, and then everyone was firing, Frank James triggering his Colt with a speed that Dan thought hardly possible.

After a minute of firing, the night flickering silver and black from the gun flashes, Dan yelled, "Cease fire. We're wasting lead."

Old Ephraim fired off one more shot and said, "I hope we hit somebody. Serve those ladies right for being so downright unsociable."

After the ringing racket of the gunfire, as gunsmoke drifted across the prairie like a mist, a solemn hush descended on the night. Then the sound of running horses faded into the far distance.

"Right!" Dan Caine said. He drew his Colt and pointed it, hammer back, at Luca Moretti. "Who are you, mister?" he said. "And why are those wild women so fixed on cutting your suspenders?"

"They know I want to destroy the lycanthrope they protect," Moretti said.

"Yeah, I heard that earlier," Dan said. "Now, what are you?"

"I can't tell you," Moretti said. "Not yet."

Frank James said, "Who the hell is Cardinal von Recke?"

"My boss. A Prussian, and a holy and prayerful man."

Dan said, "And this critter, this lycan . . . lycan . . ."

"Lycanthrope," Moretti said.

"What the hell is it?" Dan said.

"It's a shape-shifter. It can change from man to wolf and back again at will. It's the most dangerous creature on earth."

"But you can kill it?" Frank said.

"Yes, with a bullet made from argentum."

"You mean silver?" Dan said. "I saw you load your gun with those."

"Yes . . . silver bullets."

"Lead could kill it just as quick," Dan said.

"No, you don't understand," Moretti said. "When the bullet enters the lycanthrope's body, silver sulfide lifts from its surface and travels through the creature's bloodstream, blocking off blood vessels and poisoning its cells. It is silver sulfide that kills the lycanthrope, not the bullet."

"Hey, what the hell is a cell?" Ephraim said.

Frank James said, "Ephraim, have you heard of Robert Hooke?"

"Can't say as I have," the old mountain man said.

"He was a scientist and I read about him in a book that my brother Jesse gave me the day the war began. Anyhow, back in 1665 Hooke discovered that all living things are made up of cells."

"I know nothing about that stuff," Ephraim said. "But what I do know is this . . . them crazy gals have caught themselves a wolfer and tamed him. I mind, oh, maybe twenty years back, I wintered up on the Platte with a wolfer by the name of Sam McLean. Likable enough was ol' Sam but mean in drink and sometimes best left alone. Anyhow, that son of the devil was so hairy, big yeller beard and shaggy hair, fur coat and hat, he looked more like a wolf than a wolf does. Ate his meat raw most of the time and was right partial to cougar's liver." The old man spoke directly to Moretti. "That's what you got silver bullets for, sonny . . . a tamed wolfer. Who knows?

Maybe it's ol' Sam McLean his ownself. He was always a one for the ladies, you know."

"I doubt that Sam McLean would have torn apart four holy Franciscan monks sent to the Indian Territory to convert the heathen Indians," Moretti said. "There were five, but one escaped to bring the news of his brothers' terrible martyrdom."

"Ol' Sam could've done it if he'd been drinking," Ephraim said. "But I doubt it."

"That's why you're here, Moretti, because of the dead monks?" Dan said. "Jake, throw some more wood on the fire. It's getting darker around here."

"Yes. And the monks are the reason I joined your posse. The Apaches were on the warpath, and Deputy Caine, you were a God-sent opportunity to make at least part of my journey north with some protection."

Dan holstered his Colt. "If I didn't need your gun, I'd send you on your way right now," he said. "You've put all of us in greater danger. You . . ."

Frank interrupted. "Hey, Moretti, the She Wolves know you're with us and . . . how did they recognize you?"

It took a while before Moretti answered, and when he did, his tone was bitter. "There was a Franciscan nun . . ."

"Huh?" Frank said.

"You wanted to know how I was recognized, and now I'm trying to tell you," Moretti said, irritated.

"Go ahead, Moretti," Dan said. "We all want to know."

"There was a German nun, Sister Maria von Erbach, who was given leave from her convent to work for Cardinal Ahren von Recke at the Vatican," Moretti said. "Like the cardinal, she was from a noble family and, of course, she and Cardinal von Recke spoke the same language."

"Cut a long story short, Moretti," Frank said in some exasperation. "It's time for my blankets."

"It's highly secret, but Cardinal von Recke is in charge of the Vatican's Department of Demonology and Witchery, and since I also worked there as a hunter, Sister Maria and I came in contact quite often. But for what doctors now call a port-wine stain on her right cheek in the shape of a scarlet wolf's head, she was a beautiful woman, but arrogant and selfish, and she never spoke a kind word to me."

"Damn it all, sonny, is that what you do, chase demons and witches?" Ephraim Traynor said. "The Navajo call witches *yenaldooshi,* women who wear coyote skins and only travel at night. Kinda like them She Wolves of your'n."

A falling star blazed across the dark sky and Moretti watched it before he said, "Sister Maria's fall from grace was swift. She was accused of having a love affair with a young female kitchen maid named Adriana Ricci and also of stealing Vatican funds that she used to buy the girl trinkets. The maid was dismissed, and three weeks later she drowned herself in the Tiber. Cardinal Ahren von Recke exiled Sister Maria to Switzerland, there to spend five years behind convent walls, but she escaped after six months and made her way to France and then to the United States."

"How come you know she's the same lady?" Dan said.

"The monks were murdered last winter and the survivor described one of the She Wolves as a beautiful woman with a scarlet wolf's head on her cheek," Moretti said. "Starting early in the spring of this year, after one of the hardest winters in living memory you'll remember, the She Wolves began raiding south for supplies. They clashed with the army a couple of times and reports describe their leader as having red warpaint in the shape of a wolf on her face. Of course, Washington called them Apache raids. We can't have our boys in dirty shirt blue fighting women."

"It sounds like the same woman, all right," Dan said. "And she sure is after your hide, Moretti."

"Yes, she knows I'm hunting her, and her lycanthrope," Moretti said. "And I'll tell you why later, but for now just let me say that Sister Maria has a deep and abiding hatred of men in general and the clergy in particular."

Frank James shook his head. "Mister, I've known some mighty strange fellers in my time, but you take the blue ribbon for downright weirdness."

"It gets worse," Moretti said.

"I don't reckon that's possible," Frank said.

"Me neither," Sly Barnes said. He looked at Moretti as though he was some kind of bizarre, outlandish visitor from not just a foreign country but another planet.

"I'm Padre Luca Moretti," the Italian said.

"You're what?" Dan said.

"I'm an ordained Catholic priest," Moretti said.

"I seen you with them beads in your hand and figured you for some kinda kneeler," Ephraim Traynor said. He slapped his thigh and hooted. "We got us a pulpit pounder on this here posse."

"No, we don't," Dan said. "We got a man with a gun on this posse. Moretti, when we come into contact with the bank robbers, can I count on you?"

"Yes, Deputy, you can," Moretti said. "In the past, I've faced much worse evils."

"Good, then it's settled," Dan said. "Time we all hit the blankets. Tomorrow could be a busy day."

"Busy is one way of putting it, I guess," Frank said after a last, lingering look at Moretti.

Chapter Twenty

The sun was at its highest point in the sky, glaring over the heat-hammered land, when cowboy Red Lawson drew rein. He turned his horse broadside to the posse behind him and raised his rifle in a signal for the others to join him.

When Dan Caine reached Lawson he said, "What do you see, Red?"

The big cowboy pointed with his rifle. "Yonder in the grass. From here it looks like more dead men."

Frank James reached into his saddlebags and grabbed his telescope. After scanning the area where the bodies lay, he said, "It's hard to tell. I see some movement so it could be wounded men or some kind of animal."

"You others stay alert," Dan said. "Red and I will go take a looksee."

"Be careful, Deputy," Frank James said. "It could be an ambush."

Dan nodded, slid out his Winchester from the boot under his knee, and said to Lawson, "Red. Let's go."

He kneed his horse forward at a trot and he and the

cowboy closed the distance between them and the figures on the ground.

"It's men and they're moving all right," Lawson said. "Are they all shot up and can't stand?"

Dan didn't answer, but then a startled oath of surprise escaped his lips when seven men came in view. All of them were alive, hog tied in a circle with coils of rope, and they begged for help in two languages, English and Spanish.

"What in God's name are you?" Red Lawson said.

"Seven gentlemen in great distress," one of the men said. He was white bearded and eyebrowed and his skin was beet red from the sun.

"We can see that," Ephraim Traynor said. He'd followed Dan, anticipating that his tracking skills might be needed. "But we ain't got time to stay here and shoot the breeze, so we'll be on our way on account of we got things to do, bandits to catch."

"Hold on, Ephraim," Dan said. "We can't just leave these men here."

"Why not?" the old scout said.

"Because, my dear sir, it isn't decent," the white-bearded man said. "We were waylaid by strumpets on horses, our riding mules taken along with our three burros with all our supplies, tents, and tools."

They were an unlikely-looking bunch, Dan decided. A sorry group of pilgrims.

The three white men wore tan-colored coats with multiple pockets and pants of the same color. Brown, lace-up boots and pith helmets with dark goggles on the brims completed their attire. The other four were young Mexicans dressed in their traditional white cotton shirts and baggy trousers, rope sandals on their feet, their heads protected from the sun by wide sombreros. Judging by the angles of the hats, they'd been dropped onto their heads after they were trussed up.

Dan said, "Ephraim, cut them loose," and then to the white-bearded man, "Who are you, and don't you know that the Apaches are out?"

The man watched the progress of Ephraim's huge bowie knife from sheath to rope and apparently decided that he wasn't going to get his throat cut. He said, "Our expedition started out from Austin three months ago, and thus we didn't know the savages were on the warpath. As far as who we are, my name is Professor Samuel Claringbold of the New York Institute of Natural History. The tall, red-haired gentleman who just stood is Professor Angus McPhee of the Edinburgh Explorer Society, and the third gentleman, staring in some distress at your friend's knife, is Doctor Ivan Goncharov of the Moscow Institute of Paleontology. The Mexicans porters' names are Luis, Jose, Manuel, and Ricardo. Now, before I say another word, can we all have a drink of water? We've been sitting out here like trussed chickens since yesterday afternoon and the sun has a most dehydrating effect."

"My name is Dan Caine and I'm a deputy sheriff." Dan dismounted, took his canteen from the saddle horn, and offered it to McPhee, a middle-aged man with a red beard and fierce black eyes. The Scotsman passed it to Goncharov, stocky and blunt featured, who gave it in turn to Professor Claringbold, tall, thin, his huge muttonchop sideburns framing a sensitive Semitic face. Claringbold let the Mexicans drink before he took a swig himself and then passed the canteen back to Dan. "Thank you," he said. "That was most kind."

"What are you doing out here, Perfesser?" Ephraim said. "If'n it's polite to ask."

Claringbold said, "We're bone hunters, my antiquated friend."

"Buffler bones, you mean," Ephraim said.

"No sir. My colleagues and I look for the petrified bones of the dinosaur, the gigantic thunder lizard that stalked this plain millions of years ago."

"Find any?" the old scout said.

"So far, our expedition has not been a success," Claringbold said. "And now, after what happened, it's become a disaster of monumental proportions."

"Professor, I know nothing about giant lizards, but I do know that you were attacked by women who call themselves She Wolves," Dan said. "You're mighty lucky to be alive."

"Is that what they were?" McPhee said. "Over her head and shoulders one of them wore the skull and shoulders of a wolf, and she had a red mark on her cheek in the shape of a wolf's head. Ach, she was a fine-looking woman, but a fearsome creature and no mistake. I thought we were all doomed."

"Dan, why didn't she kill them?" Frank said.

"I think she's trying to slow us down," Dan said. "We were getting too close."

Frank said, "Yeah, that makes sense. Now we're saddled with seven men without horses and no supplies and that means we'll be dragging anchor. But why don't they just attack us?"

"My guess is that the She Wolves don't feel strong

enough to attack us. I think they've sent for more help and now they're waiting until it arrives."

"Is it only us, or do the bank robbers figure?" Frank said.

"Both, I'd say," Dan said. "The robbers have good horses and guns. Those women are like Apaches, they won't turn up their noses at such valuable plunder."

Frank smiled. "To say nothing of thirty thousand dollars in cash."

"They don't know about that yet," Dan said. Then after a pause, "I hope."

"Deputy Caine, do I take it that you plan to arrest the women who robbed us and handled my colleagues and I so roughly?" Claringbold said.

"No," Dan said. "If I can, I'll try my best to avoid them. My only interest is in seven men who robbed the Broken Back bank and killed two people in the process."

"And if you can't avoid them?" the professor said. He looked worried.

"I'm not going to build houses on a bridge I haven't crossed yet," Dan said.

"But you will fight?" Claringbold said.

"Yes, if I have to," Dan said. "But let's hope I don't have to."

Doctor Ivan Goncharov sighed in true Slavic fashion and said, "Professor Claringbold, I fear we jump out of frying pan into cooking pot."

The Russian was prone to fits of melancholia, and Professor McPhee put his arm around the man's shoulder. "All will be well, Ivan. Dinna trouble yourself, laddie."

"We'll do the fighting, Ivan," Ephraim said, grinning.

"If the bullets start flying just you hug the ground and don't move until it's over."

"Nyet!" Goncharov said. He thumped his chest with a massive fist, tears in his eyes. "I Rooshian man. I fight."

"Right glad to hear that, Ivan," Ephraim said.

The day was still young and Dan Caine was anxious to press on. Professor Claringbold got up behind Jake Roberts, the Russian doctor rode tandem with Frank James, and Luca Moretti took Angus McPhee. The four Mexicans elected to walk with Sly Barnes and the pack mule.

The tracks of the fleeing robbers through the buffalo grass were fresher, their horse dung moister, and Ephraim Traynor confidently predicted they were now only hours ahead.

"We'll catch them no-good varmints no later than tomorrow morning," he told Dan. "Depend on it."

But as it turned out, the bank robbers had a completely different idea.

Chapter Twenty-one

The sun had dropped, and the sky was tinged with a pink blush when rifle shots racketed through the late afternoon quiet.

Up ahead on point, Red Lawson sat his horse, steadily firing his Winchester at three riders in the distance. Apparently figuring he didn't like the odds, the cowboy swung his mount around and kicked the startled horse into a mane-flying gallop towards the posse.

"Frank! Everybody! Get ready, it's coming," Dan yelled. "Dismount and take up a firing position."

The professors, including the fighting Russian, jumped off the back of the horses with considerable alacrity and, as Ephraim had advised, made close friends with the dirt. Sly rode up with the pack horse and the Mexicans and dismounted, joining the others on the firing line.

Red Lawson jumped off his still-running horse and hit the ground hard on his back. His rifle in his hands, he scrambled to his feet and yelled, "White men and only three of them. Where are the other four?"

"Sly, watch our backs," Dan said. "The other four may try to get behind us."

But the riders had drawn rein and sat their horses just within rifle range, staring at the posse, possibly counting heads.

"What in hades are they doing?" Frank James said. "Are they just going to sit there and look at us?"

"They're studying us," Dan said, "gauging our strength."

"Estimating our firepower," Moretti said.

"Oh, God save us all," Professor Claringbold said, his face buried in the long grass.

The standoff lasted for several minutes and then one of the riders raised his rifle to his shoulder and cranked off a shot that kicked up a startled V of dirt twenty feet in front of the kneeling posse men.

"Don't shoot," Dan said. "Let's keep 'em guessing."

Old Ephraim Traynor giggled and then said, "Them boys are dumber than a snubbin' post, and I'm gonna give them a little eddication." He lay on his belly and pushed his .44 Henry in front of him.

"Old man, you can't even see those boys from here," Frank said. "They're a right smart piece away."

"Shows what you know, sonny," Ephraim said. "I'm not a farsighted man, but I can pick up the sights on this here rifle just fine."

Dan turned his head, looked down at the old scout, and said, "Ephraim, Frank's right. You know you can't see that far. When you miss, they'll take it as a sign of weakness, so save your shooting for a closer target."

Red Lawson smiled. "Old timer, I've watched you out on point, and you're as blind as a roll of bobbed wire."

Ephraim said, "What does old Ephraim see? He sees three rannies made blurry by distance. Has he made such a difficult shot afore, maybe during the Rogue River Wars, you say? By golly, I say, yes he has."

Ephraim sighted the rifle, taking his time. He took a deep breath, let some of the air out, and pressed the trigger.

BLAM!

Ephraim fired and immediately one of the three riders threw up his arms and tumbled out of the saddle.

The old man jumped to his feet, danced a little jig, and said, "Told you I could do it."

"The other two are skedaddling," Lawson said. "Ephraim, you put the fear of God into them."

"Good shooting, Ephraim," Frank said.

"Tol' you I could make the shot with the Henry," the old scout said. "Believing is better than seeing."

"Mount up, we'll go take a look at who you hit," Dan said.

Frank took his telescope from his eye. "Whoever he is, he hasn't moved. I hope he isn't a friend of mine." He caught Dan's disapproving look and added, "Slim chance of that though, Deputy. All my friends have been shot, hung, or they're counting the rats running around their cells in Yuma."

"Friend or foe, a forty-four can put a hurtin' on a man," Ephraim said. "I guarantee he's as dead as a doorknob."

The man was dead . . . and Frank James didn't know him.

Frank sat his horse and stared at the body. "He was new to the profession and wasn't prospering before he signed up for the bank robbery," he said. "Look at his hands, he was a laboring man for a spell and hard labor at that." He shook his head. "He was probably the least of them . . . and fortune's fool."

"He could fire a rifle," Dan said.

"Oh, he was dangerous all right," Frank said. "Like Bob Ford," he spat, "the least of them always has something to prove."

"Kinda like me," Sly Barnes said.

Frank smiled. "Yup, Sly, kinda like you."

"I still can't understand why they only sent three and didn't come all together," Jake Roberts said. "It don't make sense."

"It makes sense if they underestimated us," Dan said. "You don't send men to do a boy's job. Now we've burned them, they'll be more careful next time."

"Next time they'll send the best of the gun handlers, probably all six that are left," Frank said.

"The odds are near even. We'll burn them again," Dan said. "And then take back the money."

The vigilantes made camp that night near a rock shelf that excited the professors. Samuel Claringbold said, and the others agreed, that the limestone outcropping contained the fossils of mollusks, seashells, sharks' teeth, urchins, and ammonites. "Those are coiled shell relatives of the octopus and squid," he proclaimed. "Three hundred million years ago, a great sea covered these plains and all the animals I've mentioned swam in its warm waters."

Forgoing the dubious comfort of horse blankets, Professors McPhee and Goncharov declared themselves too excited to sleep and agreed that they would join Professor Claringbold and their four Mexican helpers in an exploration of the shelf by moonlight.

"There will be no slumber for my colleagues and I tonight," Claringbold said. "There are exciting scientific discoveries to be made."

The professor was right. No one would sleep that night . . . but because of gunfire and the violent deaths of men and women . . . not science.

Chapter Twenty-two

Gunfire rolled across the plains with a sound of distant thunder, and muzzle flashes seared the darkness like heat lightning.

Dan Caine tossed aside his blankets, grabbed his gunbelt, and sprang to his feet.

Frank James, Colt in hand, stood beside him. "What in hades is that?" he said.

Everyone was awake, armed and standing, their eyes fixed on the far-off conflict.

"I'd say the bank robbers and the She Wolves are having at it," Dan said.

"Could be Apaches," Ephraim Traynor said.

"Could be, but I doubt it," Dan said. "Apaches will fight at night if they're pressed, but they're not keen on it."

"What do we do, Deputy?" Jake Roberts said. Nervous breath whistled loudly through his oft broken nose.

"Do?" Dan said. "We do nothing except prepare ourselves for an attack. Where the heck are the professors and the Mexicans?"

"I'll get them," Roberts said. He disappeared into the

dark and returned with the three academics, all of them thoroughly frightened. "Is it a war?" Claringbold said.

"Mighty close," Frank said. "Lead could be flying here soon, so you and your friends keep your heads down."

"This is an outrage," Claringbold said.

"Truer words was never spoke, Perfesser," old Ephraim said. "And I reckon things are gonna get even more out-rageouser."

Dan kicked apart the embers of the small fire and plunged the camp into darkness. Only the moon and the stars were bright.

The gunfire had become more desultory as dead or wounded men, and probably women, dropped out of the firing lines. Then the firing stopped altogether . . . and after a pause, three widely spaced shots rang out.

"They're killing the wounded," Frank said.

"Who's they?" Dan said.

"Bandits or banshees, take your pick," Frank said.

Dan smiled. "You have a way with words, Frank."

"And a little education wouldn't hurt you any, Deputy," Frank said.

"I wasn't much of a hand at book learning," Dan said.

"Just as well, since we've got all the professors we need," Frank said. "What we need right now is your gun learning."

"I wasn't much of a hand at that, either," Dan said.

"You could've fooled me, gunfighter," Frank said.

"Listen!"

Sly Barnes's head was tilted back, his face intent.

"What do you hear, Sly?" Dan said.

"Listen!"

Then Dan heard it, borne on the night breeze, a howling

coming from many female throats. The howls were not those of the wolf hunting pack, but softer, a haunting, plaintive paean of grief and loss. The lament rose and fell in cascades of sound, howling as hollow as blown glass . . . the sigh of the wind through tree limbs . . . the soulful mourning of the stricken She Wolves.

Then. Abruptly. Silence.

Every man present listened into the echoing quiet of the plains. The soundless stars glittered, the uncaring moon shed its silver light on the grass.

"What just happened?" Luca Moretti said.

"A massacree is what just happened, Padre," Ephraim Traynor said.

"And then She Wolves mourned their own dead," Dan Caine said.

"In all my born days I never heard howling like that," Ephraim said. "Even big ol' gray wolves don't make that much of a racket."

"I found it to be quite beautiful," Moretti said. "A plain-song for the dead."

Frank James coughed politely and then said, "Shakespeare says that he who dies pays all debts. Well, I reckon the bank robbers are dead, so who pays back the thirty thousand?"

"The money!" Dan said. "Where's the money?"

"Yes, Deputy, where's the money," Frank said. "Now who's got it?"

"Them She Wolves don't need money," Ephraim said.

"Yes, they do," Moretti said. "Sister Maria can't steal

everything she needs, so she has to buy supplies now and then like everyone else."

"Now we have a problem," Dan said. "I can't say it any other way."

"If the women took the money, we got a barrel full of problems," Frank said.

"Maybe they didn't take it," Ephraim said. "Maybe it's lying there in the long grass jest a-waitin' to be picked up."

"Maybe the women didn't see the money sacks in the dark," Red Lawson said.

"And maybe pigs can fly," Frank said. "The sacks are white, isn't that right, Dan?"

"Yeah, they're white," Dan said. "It's easy to see white sacks in moonlight. One way or another, we'll know come first light."

"And if they took the money?" Frank said.

"I'll deal with that problem when we come to it," Dan said.

"Now that is gonna be interesting," Frank said. "Since we've already come to it."

Sly Barnes said timidly, "And it could have been Apaches that got killed."

"I just don't see it that way," Dan said. "We know the She Wolves and the robbers were in the same vicinity. They were bound to clash sometime."

"We can go around and around about this," Frank James said. "All will be made crystal clear come sunup."

"I sure hope so," Dan said. "I'm starting to have a bad feeling about this."

Chapter Twenty-three

Six dead men lay sprawled on the grass, shot to pieces.

Frank James dismounted and studied the gray face of each corpse.

He called over Dan Caine and prodded a body with the toe of his boot. "Rudy McIntyre. So his luck finally ran out."

"You knew him?" Dan said.

"Met him a few times," Frank said. "A towheaded Kansan who ran with that Bill Bonney kid and them for a spell and then him and Clell Miller tried their hand at stage robbery. But after Clell was killed at Northfield, Rudy dropped out of sight."

"Until now," Dan said.

"Yeah, until now," Frank said. "Looks like he died game. A man should look death in the face and spit in his eye, even a no account like Rudy McIntyre."

"The money isn't here, Deputy," Jake Roberts said. "Me and Red and the padre searched high and low, and it just ain't to be found."

"Damn it, if by the padre you mean Moretti, call him

Moretti," Dan said, irritated to the point of anger. "Riding with a Bible pounder is always bad luck."

"Dan, Jake didn't mean anything by it," Frank said. "He's been listening to old Ephraim who calls Moretti padre every chance he gets because if he turns up his toes on this trip, he's tickled to have a holy man close."

Dan looked at the cowboy. "Sorry, Jake, I'm on edge, I guess."

"We're all on edge, Deputy," Roberts said.

"We can't bury these men, but at least we should take the arrows out of their bodies," Dan said. "Hell of a thing to leave white men looking like that."

"Like porkypines," Sly Barnes said, his face ashen.

A few minutes later Ephraim Traynor came in from his scout.

"The She Wolves came in at the gallop from the dark," he said. "I guess the robbers were asleep and didn't know what hit them at first, but then they fought back. By the blood on the grass, I reckon at least four or five of the women were shot, maybe more."

"Any sign of the money?" Dan said, expecting a negative answer.

He got it. "Nope, not even a dollar bill in sight."

"Well, Deputy Caine, do we follow the money and die in a blaze of glory?" Frank said.

"We're here to get the thirty thousand back, not die," Dan said. "But I can't figure the odds. Ephraim, how many women were involved in this attack?"

"The grass talks to me and it says no more than a dozen, and they've lost a few."

"You sure about that?"

"Nope."

"In other words, you're buffaloed," Frank said.

"You could say that," Ephraim said.

"So you don't know how many?" Dan said.

"At least a dozen."

"Show me."

Ephraim led Dan to a trampled area of grass to the east of the outlaws' camp. And after a while he said, "So, how many, Deputy?"

Dan shook his head. "At least a dozen."

"Told you so," Ephraim said. He looked beyond Dan. "The boys are waiting for you, Deputy," he said. "I reckon it's time to state your intentions."

"My intentions? Ephraim, right now I'm trapped in a box canyon looking for a way out," Dan said.

"Seems like, sonny," the old scout said.

To his joy, Frank James discovered a full coffeepot, still upright, still warm, on the embers of the fire and he and the others drank from dead men's cups as Dan stepped toward them.

"What have you decided, Deputy?" Frank said. He handed Dan a cup of coffee. "It's still hot," he said. "Well, it ain't cold."

The sun had climbed higher in a blue sky and the morning grew warmer. In the distance a small herd of pronghorns stopped and intently studied the humans, sensed no danger, and moved on at a stately walk. The smell of sage was in the air and the ever-present odor of man sweat and horses. And the iodine tang of blood. A lot of blood.

Professor Samuel Claringbold stood in front of Dan and said, "My colleagues and I are deeply concerned, Deputy Caine, and our Mexicans are most unhappy. It seems we have fallen in with men of violence and I can assure you that the New York Institute of Natural History will be most distressed to hear of our plight. In the light of what has happened, what have you decided?"

"I haven't decided anything yet," Dan said. "But I'm open to suggestions."

Claringbold shook his head. "I have none."

"And I say we forget the whole thing and go home," Frank said.

"And the Broken Back bank goes bust, the town dies, and the people die with it," Dan said.

"He sure didn't like that one, Frank," Ephraim said. "You got another?"

"All right, suggestion two . . . we go after the She Wolves and take the money from them by force," Frank said.

"And we all die," Red Lawsokn said. "Every last one of us."

"There's always that possibility," Dan said. "Any other suggestions?"

"That's it, Dan," Frank said. "We go or we stay. There ain't no more to say than that."

"Then nothing is decided," Dan said.

"Not yet, it isn't," Frank said. "I say we put it to a vote, majority carries."

"It's my job to stay," Dan said.

"Then that's one vote for staying," Frank said. "Red?"

"Go."

"Jake?"

"Go."

"Ephraim?"

"Stay."

"Sly, even you get a vote," Frank said.

"Stay," Sly said, surprising everybody.

"Moretti?"

"I'll stay. Like the deputy, it's my job."

"And what's your vote, Frank?" Dan said.

"Since I've got money in this, I'll stay," Frank said. "Red, Jake, it seems that you're outvoted."

Red Lawson said, "Outvoted or not, me and Jake are leaving. We've had enough."

"Ahem," Professor Claringbold said. "Don't we three get a vote? And the Mexicans?"

The four Mexicans looked like they didn't care one way or another. They'd accept any fate that was headed their way.

Ephraim said, "No, Perfesser, none of you get a vote on account of how you ain't bona fide members of this posse. Your perfessership, you can come and go as you please."

"Red and Jake can ride out of here with no hard feelings," Dan said. "You helped us get this far, and for that I'm grateful. You've got no stake in this and no call to risk your lives further."

The two cowboys exchanged glances, and Jake said, "Sorry, Deputy Caine, but we just don't feel like bucking the odds. All I want to say more is, come back with us. Nobody in Broken Back is gonna blame you for calling it quits. You're braver than most men I know, and if anybody says you showed yeller, I'll punch him right in the mouth."

Dan smiled. "Thanks, Jake, I appreciate the thought, but I reckon it's my duty to stick it out to the end, whatever that end might be."

Red said, "I feel bad about this, Dan, real bad. I got nothing else to say."

"I understand, Red," Dan said. "It was no safe or easy thing to ride point. We'll give you the grub we can spare and you can buy more supplies at Curry's mercantile. Do you have money?"

"No, we're flat broke," Red said.

"We're always flat broke," Jake said.

Frank James dug into his pocket and came up with a five-dollar coin that he gave to Jake. "Buy more grub with that," he said. "You can pay me when we meet again in Broken Back."

Red Lawson looked embarrassed. "Mr. James, I want you to know that I ain't no coward like Bob Ford."

"I didn't think you were," Frank said. His smile was meagre, unamused. "Just don't say that name around me again."

"I won't say that name again, ever," Lawson said. "It leaves a bad taste in my mouth." Then to Claringbold, "You and your friends can come with us."

"The Apaches are on the warpath and nine men and two horses is not a good situation," the professor said. "We just conferred on this, and reluctant as I am to say it, we'll take our chances with Deputy Caine and Mr. James, both bold and determined men who might see us through." He looked at Dan. "Is that all right with you, Deputy?"

"Sets fine with me," Dan said. "You've made your choice, Professor, now you live with it."

"Or die with it," old Ephraim crowed.

"Red, Jake, you boys ride," Dan said. "I'm not one

for long farewells. And if you see Fran Cooley at the mercantile, tell her we haven't seen the Curry girls yet."

Red Lawson and Jake Roberts rode away without looking back . . . and Dan Caine felt the loss deeply.

Chapter Twenty-four

An hour later, after Dan Caine and the others had laid out the bloodstained dead and took to the trail again, Sly Barnes said, "Rider ahead."

"I see her," Dan said.

"Under a flag of truce, no less," Frank said.

"Draw rein, let her come," Dan said.

The rider rode closer and Frank said, "Well, would you look at that. She's wearing a wolfskin."

"I seen Indians do that," Ephraim Traynor said. "If she didn't have a wolf skull on her head, she might be real purty."

The woman sat bareback on a paint pony, a white rag attached to the Henry rifle she carried upright, the butt on her naked thigh. She wore a short, homespun tunic without sleeves, dyed gray, and Apache knee-high moccasins. From a rawhide thong around her neck hung a large, silver cross and there was a gold wedding ring on her left hand. Her eyes were large, brown, and lustrous and her brows were plucked into a natural arch. She used no other beauty enhancements.

From both sides of her pony's bridle hung a black scalp, probably Apache.

The woman drew rein and said, "I come in peace."

Dan nodded. "Peace it is. Now state your intentions."

"My name is Sister Sophia, a nun of the Order of the She Wolf." The woman's accent was deeply Southern. "Our founder and mother superior is Maria von Erbach, daughter of Baron Dieter von Erbach, and it is from Mother Maria that I bring a message."

"And that is?" Dan said.

"How are you called?" the woman said.

"Deputy Sheriff Dan Caine."

"Caine, you harbor in your midst the murderous priest Luca Moretti, a hunter here on the orders of the man of blood Cardinal Ahren von Recke," the woman said. "Give Moretti to us and the rest of you can go in peace. You will suffer no harm from the She Wolves."

Moretti dismounted and stepped toward Sister Sophia, but Dan blocked him with his horse. "Not a chance in hell, lady," Dan said. "I formed this posse to go after bank robbers and if the word spread that I betrayed one of its members, I would never be trusted to form another. Tell your Mother Maria that my answer is no. Luca Moretti stays with us."

"Then you are all willing to die for the man of blood," the woman said.

"We're not willing to die for him, but we're willing to fight for him," Dan said.

Professor Claringbold took an angry leap forward. "Now see here, young lady, listen to me. You're . . ."

The Henry leveled and the woman said, "Not another step."

"Perfesser, get back here!" Ephraim said. He grabbed Claringbold by the tail of his coat and pulled. "She'll blow your dang fool head off, an' it full of brains too."

"Lady, you're here under a flag of truce," Dan said.

"Then tell the graybeard to back off," the woman said.

"Keep out of this, Professor," Dan said. And then to the She Wolf, "I reckon we've said all there is to say."

"One thing more," the woman said. She frowned. "The priest Luca Moretti is here to kill Baron Dieter von Erbach because he destroyed four monks sent by the Vatican to spread their filth and lies among the Apaches. That was enough to declare him a man possessed by a demon. To kill a demon, Rome sends a demon hunter."

Moretti dodged around Dan's horse and yelled at the She Wolf, "Dieter Von Erbach is a lycanthrope. He tore the holy monks' throats out and ran around on all fours, blood in his fangs. Deny that if you can."

The woman smiled. "The monk who escaped was a bigger liar than most of them," she said. "The baron is a man like any other."

"He's a shape-shifter," Moretti said. "And Sister Maria is a thrice-damned, unnatural witch. I want them both dead."

"Caine, ask this demented priest to tell you about Lithuania," the woman said. "Ask him how many lycanthropes and witches he murdered with his silver bullets who were neither."

"Where is Lithuania, your worship?" Ephraim said to

Moretti, again revealing his respect for the clergy. "Is that up Montana way?"

"No, it's a nation in eastern Europe, many leagues from here," the She Wolf said before Moretti could answer. "Padre Luca Moretti and his fellow priests descended on its isolated peasant villages like the hammer of Thor. Mother Maria read the report Moretti sent to Cardinal von Recke, and he claimed to have burned or shot one hundred and sixteen men and women who had deserted the faith."

"All of them demonic, ravening lycanthropes and evil witches," Moretti said.

"All of them ignorant peasants, blamed for a series of bad harvests and every unsolved murder for miles around," the woman said. Her paint became restive and she fought to settle it down.

"Sweet Jesu!" Moretti yelled. He tore open his shirt and said, "Tell Maria von Erbach that I bare my breast to her. She can slay me, but only after I kill her satanic father."

"Moretti! Git back here," Dan said. "You're all done speechifying for the day."

For the first time since they'd left Broken Back, he realized that he had a raving lunatic on his hands.

"I'll give Mother Maria your message," the She Wolf said.

She was about to swing her horse away, but Ephraim's voice stopped her.

"Beggin' your pardon, ma'am, but did you happen to find money when you . . . um . . . when you done what you done?"

"Why?" the woman said.

"Because we'd admire to have it returned," Ephraim said. "It was stolen from a bank in the town of Broken Back."

The She Wolf stared at him for long moments and then swung her horse away. She left at a canter, laughing, her head tilted back and the wolf pelt on her shoulders rippled, as though the animal was still alive.

Chapter Twenty-five

The Thompson and Butler stage out of San Angelo, bound for El Paso, topped a shallow rise, and the few remaining hairs on the head of the driver, Ezra "Baldy" Sutter, stood on end.

"Apaches!" Sutter said.

"I see them," Bill Fisk, his laconic messenger, said.

"Thousands of them," Sutter said. "Mescalero, Chiricahua, maybe some Utes."

"At least a hundred, I'd say," Fisk said. Then, after some consideration, "Damned unusual."

Dave Anderson, a gambler and shootist of reputation, stuck his head out of the coach window and said, "Driver, do you see those Indians?"

"See them?" Sutter said. "I can't take my eyes off them."

"Keep the team at a walk," Anderson said, a lean, sallow-faced man with a neatly trimmed Imperial mustache and beard. "Don't get them excited."

"Sutter turned to his shotgun guard. "Should we try to outrun them, Bill?"

"Walk or run," Fisk said. "Either way, we're dead. Save the last bullet for yourself."

Sutter nodded. "Then we'll do what the gambler said. We'll walk right past them."

Anderson spoke from the window again. "Driver, they're not showing any hostile intent, as though they're not interested in us."

"In all my born days I never knew Apaches to act like this," Sutter said. "It's mighty strange. It just ain't natural."

The Indians, Anderson calculated eighty to a hundred, sat in a large circle, chanting, their horse herd grazing nearby. All had their weapons close to hand and as far as Anderson could tell, all were painted for war.

Then one of the Apaches left the circle and walked closer. He stared intently at the stage, his black eyes glittering.

Sutter and Fisk looked straight ahead and if a one and a quarter ton Concord coach, a six-horse team, and a big American stud on a lead rope could tiptoe, they did that day.

Finally, the stage was past the Apaches, and the warrior who'd watched it so closely returned to the circle.

"Well, don't that beat all," Sutter said. He took off his hat and ran a bright red bandana over his sweaty bald head. "I thought we were goners fer sure."

"Fer sure," Fisk said.

"I can't explain it."

"Me neither."

"But Apaches are notional," Sutter said.

"Seems like," Fisk said.

"I'd admire to know what's going on in their heads," Sutter said.

"Killing," Fisk said.

Sutter nodded. "When that many gather in the same place at the same time, they're set on killing somebody."

"Just so long as it ain't us," Fisk said.

Sutter had pushed the team to a distance-eating lope and he leaned over in the seat and above the rumble of the wheels yelled, "Mr. Anderson!" The gambler stuck his head out the window, and the driver said, "Jay Warren's stage station coming up. He serves good grub."

Anderson waved in reply and sat back in his seat. After the Apache scare, he hoped the rest of his trip to El Paso would be uneventful.

But as fate, in the shape of the Harper brothers, would have it, his hopes would soon be dashed.

Warren's station wasn't much, a flat-roofed sod cabin, a corral, a barn, and, something of a wonder in West Texas, a three-holer outhouse that was Jay Warren's pride and joy. He'd painted it blue.

The stage rattled to a halt outside the cabin, and Sutter greeted Warren with news of the Apache gathering just a couple of miles away from the man's front door.

"Darndest thing I ever seen," he said. "We was lucky to escape with our scalps."

Normally Warren would've been scorched speechless by the news, but he seemed to take it in stride. A tall, thin, joyless man, his bearded face was unusually grim.

"Ezra, drive down to the corral and we'll change the team and water the big American stud you got tied up at the back," he said. Then he said to Anderson, "Is he yours?"

"He sure is," the gambler said. "I won him in a poker game."

"A fine animal," Warren said.

"Yes, he is," Anderson said. "But he can be a handful."

Warren's eyes were furtive, full of fright. He watched Anderson step from the stage and said, "Mister, I'll bring you something to eat. Just stay in the coach."

Sutter frowned. "You've never done that afore, Jay."

The man's lips tightened under his beard. "I got trouble inside."

"What kind of trouble?" Sutter said.

"The Harper brothers."

"I thought them two had been hung long since," Sutter said.

"No, they're alive and kicking. They've been drinking and they got Bessie."

"We'll see about that," Sutter said. "Bill, bring your scattergun."

"No, Ezra, you'll just get yourself killed," Warren said. "They'll let Bessie go once they've done with her."

Anderson said, "Warren, what kind of vittles are you serving?"

"I got beef and beans and buttered sourdough bread," Warren said. You go on down to the corral with Ezra and I'll bring it to you."

From inside the cabin, a woman's voice shrieked, "No! Please! No!" And a man said something coarse and laughed.

Anderson smiled. "I wouldn't dream of eating such a rate feast at a corral. I'll go inside and sit where I can enjoy it in comfort."

Warren shook his head. "The Harper brothers are pure poison, bullies and braggarts, and they'll kill you, mister."

"No, they won't," Anderson said. He smiled again at Warren, winked, and stepped into the cabin.

Dave Anderson closed the door behind him and stood there for a few moments allowing his sun-dazzled eyes to become accustomed to the gloomy interior, lit only by a smoking oil lamp, the cabin's single window shuttered.

The cabin was small, cramped, consisting of a rough-sawn table and bench, a stove to his right where a pot of beans simmered, and to his left a curtained alcove that served as a bedroom. The curtain was pulled back and two men sat on the bed, the woman called Bessie between them in a considerable state of undress.

It should be noted that some historians claim Bessie was Jay Warren's wife. She was not. Her full name was Bessie Ann Tyler, and she and Jay had lived together for several years but had never jumped the broom. A year after the incidents chronicled here, she died of cholera at the age of just thirty-six.

One of the men on the bed let go of his tugging at the woman and said, "What are you looking at?"

Both brothers were large, bearded, with ice blue eyes and wide, cruel mouths. They wore canvas dusters, pants tucked into spurred boots, wide-brimmed hats, and buckskin shirts. Even at a distance of ten feet, Anderson could smell their rank, unwashed stench.

"What I'm looking at is a pair of lousy no-good tramps abusing a lady," Anderson said.

"Is that a fact?" one of the brothers said.

"Fact. Now get up off of that bed you're fouling and be on your way," Anderson said.

The woman stared at the man with scared, pleading eyes, seeing in this slender stranger in his gambler's broadcloth and spotless linen finery a possible savior.

One of the brothers pulled Bessie closer to him, nuzzled her neck and then, his lips against her throat said, "Kill him, Luther. I aim to finish here."

"Sure thing, Floyd," Luther said. "I'll shut the pretty boy's trap permanent like."

Displaying unexpected agility, the man hopped from the bed onto his feet, grinning.

"I'll give it to you in the belly," Luther said. "You'll have something to think about for a couple of days. How does that set with you?"

"You shouldn't have abused the woman," Anderson said. "To redress the situation, maybe she'll accept your horses as compensation."

Harper's mouth hung open. "What did you say?"

"I figure even idiots like you and your brother are smart enough to steal good horses," Anderson said. "Give them to the woman you're abusing."

Luther looked like he'd seen a ghost. He stared at Anderson in disbelief, his head slowly moving from side to side. "Mister," he said, his voice taut. "I'm gonna shoot you so dead you'll be in hell before you know it."

But Luther decided to draw things out before making

the kill. Brother Floyd was enjoying the woman, so he might as well enjoy baiting the pretty boy.

Behind him, Bessie Ann Tyler was pleading with Floyd to let her go.

"Luther! Ain't you ever gonna shoot that damned rube?" Floyd said.

"I'm getting around to it," Luther said. "I'm in no hurry. I like to see the fear in the eyes of folks I'm about to shoot, Floyd. Know what I mean?"

"Let the woman go, you sorry piece of lowlife trash," Anderson said.

"We haven't finished with her yet," Floyd said. "But, mister, I'm finished with you and your yap."

It's more than likely that Luther Harper figured Dave Anderson was not armed that day. The frockcoat the gambler wore had been expertly tailored to disguise the bulge caused by a large, waist-carried revolver and he did indeed look like a man who did not go heeled.

If Luther did make that assumption, and many historians say he did, it was the last mistake of his vile and violent life.

He went for his gun . . . slow . . . making his victim wait for the gut shot . . . perhaps hoping the man would drop to his knees and plead for his life.

Anderson drew and fired. Very fast. High-ranked Texas drawfighter fast.

One shot. Roaring loud in the close confines of the cabin. The .45 bullet crashed into Luther's face and hit him right between the eyes. Luther had a split second to register a look of horrified astonishment before his body collapsed and he thudded onto the dirt floor.

Floyd, busy with the struggling woman, didn't even turn, assuming that the gambler, not his brother, was on the floor.

Anderson's voice was as sharp and thin as a razor edge.

"Git off of her, you damned animal."

Floyd jumped like he'd been jabbed with a cattle prod. He rolled off the woman, got to his feet, and stared in horror at his brother's body. After a moment his eyes lifted to Anderson's face and then to the Colt in his hand. His own holstered gun lay on the floor by the bed, out of reach.

"Mister . . . I . . . I didn't mean anything by it," he said. "The woman, I mean. I was just having a little fun and there's no harm done."

"There's harm done to me, you pig," Bessie said, holding up the torn remains of her dress to cover her nakedness.

From outside, Bob Fisk yelled, "Mr. Anderson, are you all right? I'm coming in."

"Stay where you are," Anderson said. "This isn't over yet."

"Don't kill me," Harper said.

Anderson said, "Do you really think I'd leave a piece of vermin like you alive on my back trail?"

"I'm sorry," Harper said, almost sobbing. "Sorry, sorry, sorry." He reached into his pants pocket, came up with a gold coin and offered it to the woman. "Here's ten dollars. Take it."

Bessie slapped the coin out of the man's hand. "I don't want your filthy money," she said. "I want you dead."

"Mister, I don't like you," Anderson said. "And when

I don't like a feller, bad things tend to happen. But I'll give you more of a chance than you gave me. Lady, give him his gunbelt."

Harper shrank back. "I don't want it."

"Take it," Anderson said. "Die like a man."

Harper's lips peeled back from his rotten teeth in a savage snarl. "You dried up old hag, you weren't worth it," he said.

He pulled his gun from the holster and Anderson shot him dead where he stood. He watched the man fall beside his brother and felt no regret. There are men who deserve killing.

The door burst open and Ezra Sutter burst inside, gun in hand. He looked from Anderson to the bodies and back again, a question on his face.

"Trash mistreating a woman. I won't stand for that," Anderson said.

"And you sure have a mighty sudden way of making your displeasure known, gambling man," Sutter said.

"They could've walked away from it," Anderson said. "They were advised."

Sutter nodded, then his voice tight, "Team's changed. We're ready to roll."

Anderson stepped to the stove where a loaf of bread sat on a platter along with a crock of butter and large knife. He cut a thick slice of bread, spread it with butter, and said to Sutter, "Let's go." But he hesitated at the door, touched the brim of his hat, and then said to the woman, "Sorry for what happened, ma'am."

"I'll get over it," Bessie said. "Thank you for . . . everything."

Anderson nodded and stepped from the cabin into

the sunshine. Jay Warren stood beside the stage door.

"You should've protected your woman," Anderson said.

"They would've killed me," Warren said.

"Then you should have died for your woman," Anderson said. "Like a gentleman should."

He didn't deign to look at Warren again as he climbed into the stage and shut the door.

Chapter Twenty-six

"White men ahead," Ezra Sutter said.

"I see 'em," Bill Fisk said.

"Road agents?"

"Maybe," Fisk said. He lifted his Greener from beside the seat and laid the scattergun across his knees. "We'll find out."

"White men out here, they got to be road agents," Sutter said.

"Yup," Fisk said.

"Twelve men, four of them Mexicans by their look, and only five hosses," Sutter said.

"See that," Fisk said.

"Strange, ain't it?" Sutter said.

"Yup," Fisk said.

Sutter leaned from the seat and called down to Dave Anderson.

"Hey, Mr. Anderson, there could be road agents ahead," he said.

"Except for my gun, my gold watch and two hundred dollars in my wallet, there isn't anything on this stage worth stealing," the gambler said.

"They don't know that," Sutter said. "I'm gonna pass them at a gallop, so hold on."

Anderson stuck his head out the window, stared at the twelve men, did a double take and then stared even harder. As the stage rolled closer, he yelled to Sutter, "Slow down. I know one of those men."

"Who?" Sutter yelled back.

"Frank James."

"Who?"

"Jesse's brother."

A pause, then, "Oh my God! We're all dead."

"Slow down! As a general rule, Frank robbed banks and trains, not stagecoaches," Anderson said, his words bumpy from the jolting ride.

Sutter's bald head disappeared from view and he and Fisk had a quick discussion. He slowed the team and called down to Anderson again. "I hope you two are real good friends."

"He saved my life," Anderson said. "A few years ago, he shot a loser with a knife off my back in a saloon in Sedalia."

"Then that almost makes you kissin' kin, don't it?" Sutter said.

He halted the team and when Dan Caine stepped toward him, he said, "If'n you're fixin' to rob this stage, my messenger has a Greener scattergun that's both wife and child to him and he ain't afraid to use it."

Dan said, "My name is Dan Caine and I'm the Deputy Sheriff of Broken Back town, in pursuit of bank robbers. Or at least, I was."

"Name's Ezra Sutter. Folks I don't like call me Baldy Sutter. This here feller is my messenger, Bill Fisk. He don't talk much. We're bound for El Paso with one passenger and some mail."

Frank James strolled to the stage, and from inside Dave Anderson said, "Howdy, Frank. It's been a spell."

It took Frank a moment, but then his face brightened and he said, "The Silver Slipper saloon in Sedalia."

"Going back a few," Anderson said. He extended his hand and Frank took it.

"I recollect that a railroader tried to stick a knife in your back," Frank said.

"He was a teamster. Went by the name of Watson or Wilson. I never got the right of it. You saved my hide that day, Frank."

"I won't stand idle and watch a man stab another in the back," Frank said. "You heard what happened to Jesse?"

"I heard, and I was right sorry to hear it," Anderson said.

"He deserved better," Frank said.

"Amen to that," Anderson said.

Speaking from his seat, Sutter said, "I got bad news for you boys. A couple of miles south of here, we drove past a passel of Apaches, all of them painted for war."

"At least a hundred, no women or children," Fisk said. "Bad news for somebody."

"Bad news for everybody," Dan said.

Sutter looked beyond Dan's shoulder. "Ain't much of a posse, Deputy."

"Half of them quit already," Dan said.

"Too bad," Sutter said. He gathered up the lines. "Now we got to be going. Have a schedule to keep."

"Wait just a minute," Anderson said. "Frank, I owe you."

"We're all even, Dave. You'd have done the same for me."

"You're mighty thin on the ground here," Anderson said. "I'm offering my help. It's payback time and I may never get another."

"Gambling man, the Gem saloon in El Paso is calling you," Frank said. "Your future with us could be mighty short."

"Maybe, but just once in my life I'd like to do something decent, something fine," Anderson said. "The gaming tables can wait. Frank, you need my gun."

Dan Caine, not one to look a gift horse in the mouth, said, "Yes, we do. You're welcome to join us."

"Then it's done," Anderson said. "Sutter, throw down my bag."

He stepped out of the stage, and walked to the back to untie his horse. The driver tossed a carpetbag and a saddle and Frank said, "Dave, none of us are going to get out of this alive, and even if we do, we'll make a run for Broken Back with our tails between our legs."

"We'll recover the money," Dan said. "Don't ask me how, but we'll get it."

"There's nobody asking you how, Deputy," Ephraim Traynor said. "But I wish to hell somebody would."

Dan was only half-listening. "You three bone hunters and the Mexicans can take the stage to El Paso," he said. "There's no point in you hanging around any longer."

"Mr. Anderson doesn't get a refund," Sutter said. "But I can apply it to your fares."

Professor Claringbold said, "We came out here to find dinosaurs and as far as I know, there's none in El Paso town. The Institute of Natural History would think little of me if I gave up the hunt now. I think I speak for my colleagues when I say that those wild horsewomen are bound to know where the bones are buried."

"Human bones, if'n you ask me, Perfesser," Ephraim said.

"If the lassies can identify dinosaur bones as such, and just not assume they're a pile of rocks," Angus McPhee said.

Goncharov, the Russian, said, "I can't go back to Moscow a failure. Indeed, I will do no such thing. The bones are out there, and we will find them."

Sutter said, "Make up your minds, gentlemen. Time's a-wasting."

"Well," Professor Claringbold said, "do we remain in the field?"

His colleagues readily agreed that staying on the plains was the best course of action for scientific studies.

Dan Caine was horrified.

He said to Claringbold, "Professor, there's a hundred Apaches camped right on our doorstep and there's an unknown number of She Wolves ahead of us. Both want our scalps, so you and your friends could end up very dead, dead, and dead."

"They wouldn't dare," Claringbold said.

"Perfesser, they'd dare all right," Ephraim said.

Ezra Sutter grinned. "Changed your mind, Mr. Anderson?"

The gambler shook his head. "I always pay my debts, and I'm doing the right thing here. Leave me to it."

"Then I'm outta here," Sutter said.

"Wait," Claringbold said. "Take these four Mexicans

with you. There's no need for them to risk their lives further."

"Two hundred to El Paso for all four," Sutter said. "That's half the going rate."

"I'll pay you a hundred," Claringbold said. "That's all I can afford."

"All right, a hundred, but they ride on top," Sutter said. "The inside is reserved for white folks."

Claringbold paid Sutter and gave each of the Mexicans a sum of money from his wallet that seemed to please them. Dan never found out how much it was.

After the Mexicans had clambered aboard, Sutter said, "Mr. Anderson, should I tell the law in El Paso about them two rannies you gunned at Warren's station?"

"Sure," Anderson said. "If you can find anybody who gives a damn."

That night Dave Anderson told the story of the Sutter station shooting scrape, and Dan Caine filled him in on the bank robbery, the dead men they'd encountered, and their troubles with the She Wolves. He didn't mention that Luca Moretti was a priest hunting a wolfman and the ranny was as loco as a loon. Dan figured that was more information than Anderson would care to handle at one sitting.

After Dan was done talking, the gambler said, "After hearing all that, I'd say you don't have your troubles to seek."

"No, I don't. They're right here in my lap," Dan said, looking up from the cigarette he was building.

"You have a plan, Deputy?" Anderson said.

"Well, I could ride up to the She Wolves and ask nicely, 'Would you please give me my money back.' You know what the answer would be? An arrow in the throat. Right now, that's all I have."

"Too bad," Anderson said.

Chapter Twenty-seven

First light brought more bad news and coffee was abandoned as Dan Caine and his posse stood to arms, their eyes on the five Apaches who sat their horses just out of rifle range and studied the camp.

Ephraim Traynor said, "Deputy, forget that plan you ain't got . . . but come up with another right quick. There's a hundred more where them five came from."

"Well, we got three men without horses, so we can't outrun them," Dan said.

"Then we stay right where we're at and hope those young bucks are easily discouraged," Frank James said.

"Sly, stay close with the pack mule," Dan said. "I don't want Indians running off with our supplies."

Frank shook his head. "Dan, right now I'd say that's the least of our problems."

The five Apaches rode closer and one of them used a telescope to get a better look. After a while he consulted with the other four and their vigil resumed.

"Just setting there staring at us," Dave Anderson said. "What in tarnation are they up to? Damn, that chaps my butt."

"Out of my sight! Thou dost infect my eyes!" Frank said.

"Shakespeare?" Dan said.

"Of course," Frank said.

"I guessed as much," Dan said. "But he had the right of that one."

"Hello, what's this?" Anderson said.

One of the Apaches rode forward on a black pony with a white blaze, his hands raised, showing that he carried no weapon.

"I sure hope that feller speaks American," Ephraim said. "I ain't much of a hand with Apache."

"Lower your rifles, boys," Dan said. "Let's hear what he has to say."

The Apache came on at an unhurried walk. He wore the white pants and tunic the tribe had adopted from the Mexicans and knee-high moccasins. A black white-man's vest and a blue headband completed his outfit. He was under medium height, thin and wiry, possessed of the speed, strength, and endurance of a cougar.

Dan didn't trust the Indian and though he'd lowered the muzzle of his Winchester, it was still handy. The Apache kept coming. His pony was up on its toes, tossing its head with every step.

When the warrior was ten yards away, he drew rein and said loudly, "Vengo en son de paz." The Spanish brought no reaction from the white men, and he said in English, "I come in peace."

Dan said. "State your intentions. And be warned, we're well-armed and determined men here."

"The Apache does not wish to make war on the white

men," the warrior said. "We do not wish to make an enemy of you this day."

"Peace between us and the Apache is welcome," Dan said. "We are not your enemy."

"Yes, you are the Apache's enemy, but not today and not tomorrow and not the next day," the warrior said. "My name is Delshay. I am a war chief of the Mescalero, and I speak the truth."

"And I'm right glad to hear it," Dan said. "You'll have no trouble from us."

Then the Russian surprised everybody when he took a step forward and said in English directly to the Apache, "My friend, you wish to make peace with us because you fear the power of the *volchiza,* the She Wolf."

The Apache stared blankly at the big man, understanding neither the Russian nor English term for She Wolf, but when Ephraim said, "Lobo," he got the meaning loud and clear.

For a moment, the Indian was stunned into silence, then a strange, confused expression fleeted across his face as though he experienced an emotion foreign to him, but Dan and the others recognized it for what it was . . . fear.

But only for a moment. An Apache could be as brave as he needed to be as the occasion demanded. Delshay spat and said, "Pah. Lobo. They are only women."

He turned his pony. "Will it be peace or war?"

"Peace," Dan said.

The Apache nodded.

"Been right nice to meet you, Chief," Ephraim said.

That the Indian ignored, returning to his companions at a canter.

When the Apaches were out of sight, Dan retrieved his coffee, then said to the others, "Well, what do we think?"

"For a minute there we scared the living daylights out of that Indian," Frank said. "I reckon the She Wolves are raiding into Apache territory and killing young bucks wherever they find them."

"Like the seven we found dead and scalped," Dan said.

"Yeah, just like them," Frank said.

"I just can't figure that woman, what's her name?"

Luca Moretti said, "Her name is Maria von Erbach."

"Apart from guarding her pa from you, what does she want?" Dan said.

"Deputy, for one thing, she wants your thirty thousand dollars," Ephraim said.

Moretti smiled. "She wants more than that. Yes, she knows her father is a lycanthrope and that I plan to rid this earth of his dark shadow, but she has formed an order of what she calls warrior nuns to establish a kingdom in the mesa country up on the Cimarron River in the Oklahoma Territory. Maria von Erbach didn't have to actively recruit. Just word of what she planned attracted unhappy, disenfranchised women from all over the West and even further east. One report I read claims that several suffragettes from New York have joined her order."

"How many women folk does she have?" Frank said.

"I've heard as low as fifty to a high of twice that number," Moretti said. "It's said she aims for five hundred amazon warriors."

"Who says?" Dan said.

"According to reports, those numbers are from women who didn't join up or left the order for one reason or another," Moretti said. "That's recently been changed.

Now the only way to leave the She Wolves is through death."

Ephraim handed Frank James a slice of fried bacon and a chunk of pan bread. "Breakfast," he said.

"Thank you kindly," Frank said. And then to Moretti, "Reports and more reports. How do you know they're all true?"

"Because I spoke with a woman who'd fled the She Wolves," Moretti said. "And I've no reason to believe she lied to me."

Dan Caine, like Frank chewing on bacon, said, "What was her story?"

"Her name was Della and she was married to a railroad porter by the name Jed Stone, a drunken brute of a man who beat her so badly he once made her miscarry a baby," Moretti said. "In those early days Maria von Erbach used the railroads a great deal on her recruiting drives, and she happened to be in San Antonio hoping to convince unhappy wives, servant girls, and prostitutes to join the She Wolves. Della was working as a maid in the Menger Hotel when she met Maria von Erbach and became her newest recruit. They left the same afternoon, and that evening Jed Stone was found with a bullet in his head and his brains scattered all over the inside of the Cavern saloon's outhouse. What the true nature of the relationship between Della Stone and Maria von Erbach was I do not know. When she returned to San Antonio after seven months away, that was a secret between Della and her confessor."

"How did you meet her?" Dan said.

"Through her priest," Moretti said. "He knew I was sent by the Vatican to destroy a possible lycanthrope being protected by the She Wolves and he wrote me a letter of introduction to Della. We met in the Menger where she was back working as a maid, and she confirmed all the reports I'd read about the She Wolves and Maria von Erbach's grand ambition to rule an independent amazon kingdom."

Ephraim Traynor said, "Who done fer ol' Jed, yer worship?"

"Maria, without a doubt," Moretti said.

"What did Della say about the wolf man?" Dan said.

"Nothing," Moretti said. "She told me there was a story going around among the women that a crazy old man was being kept hidden away. But that's all she knew. The old man is the lycanthrope."

"Well, I've listened to you, Moretti," Dan said. "But I've learned nothing that will help me get the money back."

"Maria von Erbach may be certifiably insane," the Italian said. "She's ruthless, hungry for power, and as deadly as a cobra. Money is power, Deputy Caine, and she won't willingly let go of it. If you want the thirty thousand dollars, you'll have to take it by force."

"So we're right back where we started," Frank James said.

Sly Barnes offered an opinion. "We could ask the army for help," he said.

"If a cavalry regiment looking for work passes this way, I'll sure do that," Dan said.

"Catching bank robbers is a civilian law enforcement matter. The army couldn't care less," Frank said. "The only problem Jesse and me ever had with bluecoat soldiers was during the war."

Moretti said, "Deputy Caine, I've spoken of Maria von Erbach, and now you know your enemy."

"And the rest is up to me," Dan said.

He looked to the east, across a vast expanse of rolling plain.

What was Maria von Erbach thinking? What was she planning?

He had questions without answers, but he would need to reply to them soon or return to Broken Back with no money and no future.

It was a grim prospect.

Chapter Twenty-eight

The old man squatted inside a gloomy, shadowed, candlelit tent, the iron collar around his neck attached to a hefty chain that was nailed to a wooden stake sledge-hammered into the ground. His white hair was long, as was his beard, and in the flickering half-light his blue eyes glittered. He wore a ragged shirt and cotton pants, and his fingernails and toenails were horny and overgrown. Withal, he looked more animal than human.

Drifting into the tent from outside, the constant shouting and laughter of young women playing baseball irritated him, and deep in his throat he growled his displeasure.

"Damn you, stop that," Maria von Erbach said. "You've lived long enough. Why don't you just die, old man? You're fast becoming a burden to me."

Baron Dieter von Erbach grinned, showing long teeth the color of ancient ivory piano keys. "I won't give you that satisfaction, my dearest daughter," he said. "I'll linger on for as long as I can."

"I should surrender you to the priest Luca Moretti," Maria said. "He'll kill you with silver bullets."

"It was Cardinal Ahren von Recke, the lowborn churl, who sent the demon hunter Luca Moretti here to kill me."

"Von Recke's blood is almost as noble as our own," Maria said.

The old man angrily pulled on his chain, but the stake didn't budge.

"Set me free," von Erbach said. "I'll tear Moretti's throat out."

"As you did the monks?" Maria said.

"Yes, as I killed the monks."

"The monks were already dead, old man. You didn't kill them."

"One by one, I tore out their throats."

"You bit at their throats, but they were already dead," Maria said. "The monk who survived told Moretti you were a lycanthrope. You're not, you're just an insane old man who needs to die."

A shout went up from outside as somebody made a hit.

"I am a werewolf," the old man said. "When I was seventeen, I was bitten during a hunt in Bavaria. The wolf made me his brother." His fingers strayed to his cheek. "That is why you bear my mark."

"Old man, the bite inflamed your madness," Maria said. "You became so insane that your own mistreated peasants revolted and threw you off your estate."

"I should have gone back with a regiment of hussars and whipped the serfs into submission, the dogs."

Maria said, "Kaiser Wilhelm knew you were mad and he ordered your arrest and execution. It was I who smuggled you out of Germany and brought you here. I saved your life, but now you refuse to die. Why won't you die?"

"Tell me why you hate me so much," the old man said.

"You know why, adulterer."

"Your mother died because her heart failed."

"And only because her heart was broken by your unfaithfulness. Thrice damned fornicator! You even threw your peasant sluts onto the marital bed."

"Maria, you're an unnatural creature," von Erbach said. "Against my wishes, you became a nun, a grotesque calling, and then the church banished you for the mortal sin of sapphism. Now you lord it over strange women who listened to your talk of freedom and forsook their husbands and children to be with you. Perhaps you are the one who should die and remove your black shadow from the earth."

"You talk nonsense, old man," Maria said.

"I live," von Erbach said. "And sometimes I howl at the full moon. You are ashamed of me, and that's why you keep me hidden. Why don't you use that knife at your waist and cut my throat? Yes, do that. Add patricide to all the other mortal sins that have already damned you to hell."

Maria von Erbach moved quickly, long, shapely legs under her short tunic covering the few paces between she and her father. She stood behind the old man, dug her fingers into his matted hair, and jerked his head back, the edge of her bowie drawing a thin ruby ribbon of blood.

"How easy it would be to destroy you, *mein liebster Vater*," the woman whispered in von Erbach's hairy ear, a soft feline purr.

"Then do it now, this instant. Free me of this miserable existence," the old man said. "Me, Baron Dieter von Erbach, descended from Teutonic Knights, a nobleman who broke bread with the Kaiser and is now chained to a post in the wilderness."

Maria withdrew the blade and violently shoved her father's head forward.

"No, not yet," she said. "You are the bait that will draw in the murderer Luca Moretti, the slaughterer of innocents."

Von Erbach smiled, a grotesque grimace. "You hate the Italian priest, but not because he burned witches and shot a few Lithuanian peasants. You hate him because he exposed your great mortal sin to Cardinal Ahren von Recke, who banished you from the Vatican."

"Yes, he did, and me of nobler blood than his own, the upstart dog."

The old man said, "Keep Moretti alive for a while after you capture him. I want him to kill me with silver bullets."

"I'm sure that can be arranged," Maria said.

Maria von Erbach ducked under the tent flap and stepped outside into the sunlight, and the mane of blond hair that cascaded over her shoulders gleamed like molten gold.

The women still played noisy baseball, and a couple more bathed naked in a shallow creek that flowed through the tree line to the north and had its origins in the Oklahoma Territory. Two dozen Sibley tents, based on the Indian teepee, dotted the landscape. These were large tents, eighteen feet in diameter and twelve feet high. Like the teepee, the tent could be raised to provide ventilation in warm weather. A few had cooking stoves inside with iron chimneys that poked through the open top.

Maria von Erbach stood and looked around her. She saw a camp of canvas but dreamed of something more permanent built of stone and brick across the border in Oklahoma. The horse lines were to the east of the camp and behind those the pack animals and several parked freight wagons.

Maria prided herself on founding an order of warrior nuns, but nowhere in sight was there anything that suggested a church.

A baseball rolled at the woman's feet and a black girl with her hair done up in yellow ribbons waved her arms and yelled, "Throw it back to me, Mother Superior!"

Maria smiled and threw the ball, but it went way wide of the girl, and the women cheered and laughed and Maria von Erbach laughed with them.

It was unfortunate that two men rode out of the pines and wild oaks to the north and happened on this idyllic scene. As they rode closer, first cousins Andy Brown and Curtis Holder, on the scout after a botched stage robbery in the Indian Territory that involved a passenger cutting, saw half-naked women playing ball, three fully naked women jumping out of a creek and reaching for towels . . . and at once reckoned that they'd died and gone to heaven.

But as one historian put it, "A more accurate assessment was that they'd died and gone to hell."

Chapter Twenty-nine

The pair rode closer, grinning. Andy, like his cousin, possessed a slack-mouthed, small-eyed face dominated by an ugly flat nose and big ears, the product of generations of inbreeding. He reached into his saddlebags and came up with a bottle of rotgut that he shook at the silent women.

"Look what I got, little ladies," he grinned, revealing a grotesque, snaggle-toothed overbite.

"An' we got something else for ye," the leering Holder said, a violent, vicious man and casual murderer. "If'n you have a mind for it."

"And if'n you don't have a mind for it," Brown grinned.

The women left their game and stepped toward the men. Several carried heavy wooden bats they'd whittled from hickory or ash axe handles. Two dozen women surrounded the horsemen and stared intently at them, heads tilted, faces expressionless. Studying. Not a word was said. The quiet was profound and smarter men than Holder and Brown would have found it both threatening and sinister.

Curtis Holder grinned and leaned from the saddle,

his hairy face turned to a pretty brunette with a silver wolf head on a chain around her neck. "Give us a kiss, l'il darlin'," he said.

The girl shrank away and a ripple of movement went through the She Wolf pack.

"Who's gonna give me a kiss?" Curtis said. "Or do I have to come down and steal it?" He drank deeply from the bottle and passed it to Brown. "We're gonna have ourselves some fun today, cousin," he said.

But Andy didn't answer. He stared at the women silently surrounding his horse and said, his voice cratered by his growing unease, "Curtis, I reckon we should be riding on."

Curtis guffawed. "Are you crazy? We got enough womenfolk here to keep us busy for a six-month. Take a drink and relax. They're shy is all, and I'll soon fix that."

Then urgently, Andy said, "Why are they here?"

"I don't know, and I don't care," Curtis said.

Maria von Erbach, the alpha She Wolf, moved at an unhurried pace toward the horsemen. As was her pack-given right, the other females dare not attack without her.

Curtis Holder's and Andy Brown's lives were now measured in minutes.

Curtis saw a tall, statuesque woman with a red stain on her cheek step toward him. He leaned back in the saddle, smiled, and said, "Well, well, well, what do we have here? Couldn't stay away, huh, girly? Tell Uncle Curtis what you want."

Maria could've answered, "Your death," but she was as silent as the rest.

She walked to Holder's horse and finally the silence was broken. "What do you want here?"

Curtis grinned and waved a hand. "I'm Curtis Holder and this is my cousin Andy Brown. Now, look around you, girlie. Ain't it obvious what we want here?" He leaned from the saddle. "Give us a kiss, sweet thing."

Showing considerable strength, Maria grabbed Curtis by the front of his shirt and dragged him out of the saddle. The man hit the ground hard and his gun flew out of the holster. He didn't get a chance to retrieve it. Maria's knife flashed as she stabbed downward . . . not a serious wound, just a jab to the man's belly that didn't go too deep. Some of her cubs needed to learn how to kill, and she left the rest to the women. They descended on him like a starving wolf pack on an injured deer. Knives plunged and bloodily plunged again and the blows from the baseball bats thud . . . thud . . . thudded . . . breaking bones.

It must have hurt because Curtis shrieked. He shrieked a lot.

Andy Brown saw what happened to his cousin and set spurs to his mount. But one of the yelling women waved a white towel in front of the horse and made it rear. Brown slammed onto the ground on his back. He managed to draw his gun and fired but several women had grabbed his arm and the shot went wild. As far as Andy Brown's fate was concerned, a year after these events a reporter for the *Prescott Morning Courier* wrote:

> Regarding the she-wolf affair, Andy Brown was the second cousin to die and it would be a most melancholy task to describe his demise in detail. Let me just state that one of the ladies then present later said that after she and the others were done, his body looked

like a side of beef on a butcher's slab. She
added as an afterthought that the unfortunate
gent did not scream "too very much."

When the killing was done, Maria von Erbach stood
over the bloodied bodies and told her women that intrud-
ers of any kind would not be tolerated. "Sisters, these men
broke our law and they have paid for it. They have been
executed." She smiled and said, "Tonight we will dance
to the flute and the tambourine and celebrate our victory."

But not all of the She Wolves had carried out the
killings. The older women were bloodstained, their hands
glistening crimson. Six of the new, younger girls, including Cora and Elsie Curry, had held back and took no part
in the executions. They stood pale and wide-eyed, seem-
ingly haunted by what they'd seen.

Maria was angry.

Calling on the deer hunter's ancient tradition of honor-
ing a first kill, she ordered the girls bloodied. A couple of
the older women with bloody hands drew a finger down
each girl's cheek, leaving a red streak.

"Warpaint," Maria said. "You will not wash off the
blood until sundown."

Suitably chastened, the girls slunk away, and Maria von
Erbach returned to her tent and lay on her cot. She'd
something to think about . . . a plan that would change
her life forever. But she could not think clearly, not then.

She'd felt it coming on for hours and now the migraine
hit with savage ferocity, like a thunderstorm in her skull.
Pain spiked at her head and she felt nauseous as dazzling
lights flashed around her and her vision blurred.

The woman wanted to scream. She didn't need this

agony, not now when her reinforcements were due at any time. Her soul-destroying headaches usually lasted three days, and she didn't have that kind of time. As they always did, when she'd been away from them too long, the women from the She Wolves permanent camp at Black Mesa would ride in boisterous and unruly and would require strict discipline.

Maria had been trying to break her morphine habit, but now she needed it like a baby needs its mother's teat. She rose from the cot, immediately sank to all fours, dizzy, in pain, as though a sledgehammer was driving railroad spikes into her head. She crawled to her small campaign desk, taken on a raid into Mexico, and reached up to one of the drawers. It was stuck. The woman almost screamed in pain and frustration. She got up on her knees and this time managed to yank the drawer open. Maria grabbed a small wooden box bound with red leather, sat down, and opened the lid. For a few moments she shut her eyes against a sudden, tidal wave of pain, and then filled the syringe from the morphine bottle. She plunged the needle into the crease of her left arm and depressed the plunger.

Morphine doesn't act instantly, and Maria von Erbach dragged herself across the floor and crawled into her cot. Someone pounded drums in her head.

Ten minutes passed . . . fifteen . . . the pain began to subside.

The woman closed her eyes and fell into uneasy sleep.

Outside her tent, the baseball game resumed . . . as though the death of two men had never been.

Chapter Thirty

Dan Caine shook his head. "Thanks for volunteering, Frank, but I'll take Ephraim Traynor with me. He knows how to scout."

"If it comes to a gunfight, you'll need me," Frank said.

"It won't come to shooting," Dan said. "I only want to scout the She Wolf camp, maybe see where the money is being held."

"Now there's a needle in a haystack," the gambler Dave Anderson said, smiling. "I'd call that mighty long odds."

"I know, but I feel it's my duty to do something," Dan said. "I can't stay any longer, just sitting around drinking coffee." He saw doubt on Frank James's face and said, "If it looks hopeless, and I think it might, I'll give it up and we'll return to Broken Back." Dan frowned. "Damn, that would be a bitter pill to swallow."

"Swallowing a pill is better than being dead," Frank said. "You and Dan'l Boone over there be careful."

Ephraim scowled and said, "I'm a better scout than Dan'l ever was, sonny. So put that in your pipe and smoke it."

Frank smiled. "No offense."

"None taken," Ephraim said. "I mean, now I've set you straight about Dan'l Boone." Then to Dan, "Ready to saddle up and ride, Deputy?"

"Yeah, I'm ready," Dan said. "Now, remember what I just told you."

"What do I keep in mind?" Ephraim said. "Tell me again."

"That we're looking for the money sacks," Dan said. "Nothing else."

"Then you do the lookin', an' I'll do the shootin'," Ephraim said.

"Sounds like a deal to me," Frank said.

"Deputy, look for the lycanthrope," Luca Moretti said. "It's of vital importance."

"It's only of importance to you, Moretti," Dan said. "Not to anyone else. But if I see a ranny running around on all fours howling at the moon, I'll be sure to let you know."

"What is this lycanthrope?" Professor Claringbold said. "Professor McPhee, do you know?"

"I've never heard of the beastie," the Scotsman said.

"A sort of werewolf," Moretti said. The professor was of little use to him, and he answered the man's question without interest.

"Ah, now I remember," Doctor Ivan Goncharov said. "There was said to be a werewolf infestation in a dozen villages near Volgograd in 1860 while I was still a student at the Moscow Institute of Paleontology."

His interest sparked, Moretti said, "Did the Vatican intervene?"

"No, Czar Alexander did," Goncharov said. "He sent in Cossacks." He saw that the word drew blank stares from the others and said, "Cavalry who sabered every adult male in the villages. The infestation soon stopped."

"Huzzah for the man from Russia," Ephraim said. He was already mounted, his Henry rifle under his left knee.

Dan Caine swung into the saddle and said to Moretti, "The Vatican should hire some Russian Cossacks. Get rid of those lycanthrope critters right quick."

"The edge of a saber kills, but does nothing else," Moretti said. "The Holy Father sent me, a priest, in the hope that I could destroy the lycanthrope but save its immortal soul."

A silence fell after that statement, and Frank James promptly filled it. "Be careful, Dan," he said. "Just remember that saving the money isn't worth your life."

Dan nodded. "I'll keep that in mind." Then to Ephraim. "You got your telescope?"

"Sure do," the old man said.

"Got the jerky?"

"Sure do."

"Then let's get this thing over with," Dan said.

Suddenly it dawned on him like a fist to the gut. The She Wolf camp was a dangerous place and he had little hope of coming back . . . with or without the money.

Chapter Thirty-one

Campfires were visible in the distance when Dan Caine and Ephraim Traynor stopped for the night. There were no stars and little moon as the sky clouded and a strong wind picked up that stirred the long grass into slow-moving waves. The evening was as dark as pitch, and the-far off fires looked like small orange cinders fallen to earth off the tail of a shooting star.

Dan and Ephraim made a cold camp and chewed on beef jerky for supper. Oppressed by the night, neither man felt like talking until Ephraim said, "You reckon that there is the camp of them wolf women?"

"It's got to be," Dan said. "The gal that spoke to us under a white flag hadn't ridden far and she went back in this direction."

"And you taking pots at her the whole time," Ephraim said, smiling.

"Not one of my finest moments, I agree," Dan said.

"So how do you want to play this, Deputy?" Ephraim said.

"I've been studying on it, and I reckon we should take advantage of this moonless night," Dan said.

"How so?"

"We ride closer and then dismount and injun our way to the camp," Dan said. He glanced at a sky that didn't tell him anything and then consulted his pocket watch, holding it close to his face. "It's nine o'clock, so I surmise we got about ten hours of darkness left. That's all the time we need to take a looksee at the camp and make it back to the horses before first light."

"And we're looking for the money," Ephraim said.

"Yeah, white money sacks or a place where they might be hidden," Dan said. He smiled. "Don't worry old man, I'll do the looking."

Ephraim chewed, then swallowed the last of his jerky and said, "Then let's go. We got a sight of belly crawling to do before first light."

The She Wolves' campfires still burned red in the distance when Dan Caine and Ephraim Traynor ground tied their horses and went forward on foot. The darkness enclosed them like a black cloak and the only points of light in any direction were the fires.

"Feel that?" Ephraim said after ten minutes of walking.

"Yup, rain," Dan said. "Of course, it's raining. It was bound to happen."

"It might put them fires out," Ephraim said.

"Doesn't matter," Dan said. "We keep walking in a straight line and we'll get there."

"Wet," Ephraim said. "We'll get wet. I hate getting wet. I feel like a rooster under a drainpipe when I get wet."

"Then don't keep crowing about it," Dan said.

"Very funny," Ephraim grumped. "Yeah, like a wet rooster. That's how I feel."

The rain was not heavy, but it fell steadily enough to gutter the campfires. Distant thunder rumbled and lightning orked from a black sky, but the storm remained far to the north.

Dan and Ephraim inched forward on their bellies, a laborious, wet business.

Now they were close to the camp, and the place seemed deserted, nothing moving but the flames of the dying fires. A strong north wind flapped and tugged at the canvas tents and made a sound like battle banners snapping. Over at the horse lines, the animals were restless and one of them whinnied . . . and froze Dan and Ephraim in place.

After a while, Ephraim whispered, "Do you see anything?"

"Tents and rain," Dan said. "We have to get closer."

"No money sacks?"

"No money sacks," Dan said. "They wouldn't leave them out in the rain."

Ephraim fell silent, and Dan knew exactly what the old man was thinking . . . this is nothing but a wild goose chase that could get us both killed.

Dan agreed with that assessment, but there was something in his gut driving him, as though he felt that the theft of the thirty thousand dollars was his fault. His first posse had brought back nothing but dead men, and that disaster had stayed with him. Now his second group of vigilantes were doing no better.

Rain dripping from his hat brim, he crawled forward, silent old Ephraim beside him.

The only thing that could save Dan Caine's honor, his very soul, was to bring back the bank's money . . . the people of Broken Back's money.

The question was . . . where in this rainswept hellscape was it?

Now he was closer, Dan Caine studied the camp layout and what immediately struck him was that one tent, larger than the rest, was set a good distance apart from the others. The treasury? Or just a place to store supplies? The first was unlikely, the latter was probable . . . unless there was a whole passel of women asleep in there. But why was the big Sibley at least thirty yards from the other tents? Did it contain something valuable? That was a mystery Dan intended to solve.

He rolled closer to Ephraim and whispered in his ear, "I'm going in there to take a looksee at a big tent. If I'm not back in half an hour get out of here. Tell the others I've been captured or worse."

"But . . . but what do I ask them fellers to do?" Ephraim was flustered.

"Come rescue me or head at a gallop for Broken Back. If it was up to me, I'd advise the skedaddle."

Ephraim, his hairy face concerned, opened his mouth to speak, but Dan said, "Remember, thirty minutes. No longer. Wish me luck."

Dan rolled away and then got to his feet. He was confident that nothing was stirring in the She Wolf camp, and he crouched low and headed directly for the big tent.

Steel needles of rain fell around him, and the ground was already muddy.

* * *

Dan Caine reached the large tent. He stopped at the entrance and looked around him at the canvas cones of the other silent tents and the steady fall of the rain.

Then a woman cried out and he froze, an alarm bell clanging in his head.

Almost immediately one of the closer tents filled with the orange glow of an oil lamp and the tent canvas bulged as women hurried around inside. A few slow minutes passed and then the lamp was extinguished.

Relief flooded through Dan. A woman had cried out in her sleep and now the camp was silent again. There was no sound from the tent beside him.

It was now or never. Dan swallowed hard and drew his Colt. He opened the tent flap and ducked inside into darkness. After a while his eyes adjusted to the gloom but he could see only a few feet in front of him. The tent seemed to be empty and Dan shuffled forward, his eyes searching the murk. He felt a surge of concern . . . if the money sacks were stashed in there, it would take time to find them.

He stopped in his tracks, his gun coming up to waist level, staring blindly into a wall of blackness. Someone . . . someone close . . . was breathing. No, not breathing . . . panting. Panting like a hound dog.

"Who's there?" Dan whispered.

In the answering quiet, the four clicks of his Colt's cocking hammer sounded loud enough to wake the dead.

"Who's there?" he said again in a husky whisper.

No answer. But the panting seemed closer.

And then worse, much worse.

Dan heard a low growl, savage, menacing, coming from directly in front of him.

"Stay back," he said. "I can drill you from here."

A chain clanked and Dan thought he was faced with some kind of large dog, a mastiff maybe. But then a man's voice dispelled that notion. The words were accented, mantled with a brutal veneer of hate.

"Swine, I will kill you. I will tear your throat out."

Then three things happened very quickly.

The first was that something large and strong and hairy jumped on Dan Caine. The second was that he had time to thumb off a wild shot. The third was the baseball bat that thudded into the back of his head and laid him out cold.

Chapter Thirty-two

Ephraim Traynor heard the shot, then the commotion that followed as armed women in night attire ran toward the source of the shooting.

It seemed to the old man that every tent was now lit with a diffused orange glow, including the large one that Deputy Caine had planned to investigate.

No one looked in his direction, and he rose to his feet. Who had fired the shot? Was it the deputy or had someone, a guard maybe, plugged him? His straining eyes saw a crowd of women, but there was no sign of Dan Caine.

What to do?

Frantic with worry, Ephraim ran in the direction of his horse, turned, and ran back to the camp. As before, shouting, excited women crowded around the big tent. He ran toward his horse again, stopped, and wondered if he should run back.

Finally, he forced himself to calm down. Running around like a chicken with its head cut off wouldn't help Dan Caine . . . if he was still alive.

Ephraim made up his mind. He'd return to the posse and raise the alarm. Yeah, that's what he'd do.

* * *

Ephraim Traynor rode up to the camp leading Dan's mount.

"Halt! Who goes there? Friend or foe?"

A voice from the darkness.

"It's me, Ephraim. Sly, is that you?"

"Yeah, it's me. Advance, friend, and be recognized."

Ephraim rode into camp where a small fire burned, sizzling in the rain, thanks to Sly Barnes who'd loaded up his mule with firewood from the live oaks and pines to the north of their position.

"Damn it all, who taught you how to challenge folks like a soldier boy?" Ephraim said.

"Mr. James. He said I have to holler out, 'Halt! Who goes there, friend or foe?' every time somebody comes near the camp."

"Then don't let Mr. James teach you anything else, or I'll shoot you down like a mad dog," Ephraim said.

Frank James stepped out of the gloom. "Do I hear somebody taking my name in vain?" He saw Ephraim's stricken face and said, "What happened?"

"Bad news," the old man said. "Deputy Sheriff Caine is either dead or taken. I don't know which."

Dave Anderson stepped beside Frank, and now everyone stared at Ephraim. Finally, Frank said, "Tell us what happened, Ephraim."

"We'd only been on the edge of the camp for about fifteen minutes when the deputy left me to take a look at a big tent. It was a lot bigger than the other tents and set a long ways from them," the old man said. "A few minutes later, I don't rightly know how long it was, I heard a shot and then all them She Wolf women made straight for the big tent. What a commotion, like there was a snake in the chicken coop."

"What did you do, Mr. Traynor?" Professor Claringbold said.

"What did I do? I hightailed it out of there, Perfesser," Ephraim said.

"Bad news, gentlemen," Claringbold said. "Bad news indeed."

The news had come as a shock, and Frank James took time to sort out his thoughts. Finally, he looked around at the others and said, "Well, as Dan liked to say, I'm open to suggestions. But the one I don't want to hear is that we charge into the She Wolf camp with guns blazing."

"No indeed, Mr. James, such an action will achieve nothing but your death. Will you give me one minute to confer with my colleagues?" Claringbold said.

"Go right ahead," Frank said. "Take all the time you want."

The professor took his two companions aside and after a few minutes of earnest talk and some arguing he stepped back to Frank and said, "I have a suggestion."

"Speak your mind, Professor," Frank said. "I'm all ears."

"I suggest, and my colleagues agree, that this present crisis needs determined action and a strong, steady hand," Claringbold said.

"Uh-huh," Frank said. "Go on."

"Therefore, my course of action is that we three learned professors borrow your horses and ride into the, uh, female camp," the professor said. "We will present stern countenances to the ladies, always bearing in mind that we have the full power of the New York Institute of

Natural History behind us. Once the women are suitably cowed, we will demand that they surrender Deputy Sheriff Dan Caine or hand over his body for suitable interment."

"Those hussies won't tangle with us, or give us back talk," Professor McPhee said. "The Edinburgh Explorer Society is not to be trifled with."

Dr. Goncharov growled something in Russian that no one could understand, but he seemed most determined and stood in the faint firelight, fists clenched, looking like a great bear.

"There you have it," Claringbold said. "A suggestion . . . nay . . . a solution . . . to this perplexing problem. Boldness, Mr. James. First and foremost, let boldness drive us forward to victory."

Luca Moretti said, "Professor Claringbold, do what you suggest and Maria von Erbach will skin you alive and hang your hide on her wall."

"Professor, I have to agree with Moretti," Frank said. "This is Texas. You're a long way from the New York Institute of Natural History."

Ephraim let out a hee-hee-hee giggle and then said, "Them She Wolves will never trust a perfesser until he's skun."

"And that's why I'll be the one who finds out what happened to Dan Caine," Moretti said. "I've done this kind of thing a few times before. I will go with or without your blessing."

"And I'm not going to argue with you," Frank said. "It seems you're the expert."

"You're volunteering, your worship?" Ephraim said, surprised. "You're a shining example of the clergy."

"Indeed, he is," Frank said. "How far that little candle throws his beams! So shines a good deed in a weary world."

"Is that the Shakespeare feller again?" Ephraim said.

"Yes, it is," Frank said.

"He has a sayin' for everything, don't he?"

"Just about," Frank said. Then to Moretti, "How are you going to handle this?"

"I'll leave now, head north then east and get into position among the trees before dawn," Moretti said. "If I see a chance of freeing Dan Caine during the hours of daylight, I'll take it. Otherwise, I'll again wait for dark."

"Mighty thin, ain't it?" Frank said.

"As a fiddle string," Moretti said. "But as they say in my native Italy, *A chi bene crede Dio provvede* . . . Have faith and God shall provide."

"You still haven't told me why you're doing this," Frank said.

"Dan Caine refused to sell me out to Maria von Erbach," Moretti said. "I owe him." He looked at Dave Anderson and said, "You know all about that."

Anderson nodded. "A man should pay his debts."

"Now see here," Professor Claringbold said, "I insist that I make peace with the women and perhaps arrange for the return of the bank's money. I can be both strict and persuasive when the need arises. Remember, I was once their captive, and at the time I was most firm with them and took no sass. That's why they let us all live."

"Professor, they let you live because they wanted you to die a slow death from thirst, starvation, or hungry wolves," Frank said. "Either that, or they wanted to slow up Dan Caine's posse."

Ephraim cackled and said, "Perfesser, you're all-fired determined to get your head on a pike. But maybe you'll change your mind when I tell you what I saw when I was crawling across the grass in the dark."

"Saw what?" Claringbold said, irritated. "Speak up, man."

"Well, I didn't exactly see it, I bumped into the dang thing," Ephraim said. "It liked to take some skin of my knee I can tell you."

"You bumped into what?" Claringbold said.

"A rock."

"What kind of rock?"

"A hard rock."

"Describe it," the professor said. Despite himself, he was interested.

"I didn't linger, you savvy that, huh?" Ephraim said.

"Yes, yes, go on, go on."

"The rock was kind of rounded, but it had a passel of what you might call deep grooves on the top of it," Ephraim said.

"How many grooves?" Claringbold said.

"I don't know. A lot. Some long, some a tad shorter."

Claringbold's eyes sought Angus McPhee in the darkness and he said, "Are you thinking what I am thinking?"

"A rib cage, by God," the Scotsman said. "Ivan, what do you think?"

"Yes, yes, it could be a dinosaur," Dr. Goncharov said. "We must investigate at once."

"Yes indeed, and it must be done instanter! Mr. Traynor, could you lead me to the place where you saw the rock?" Claringbold said.

"Where I bumped into the rock, you mean? Yeah, Perfesser, I believe I could take you there. It's about half-way between us and the She Wolf camp."

"Then we must set out at once," Claringbold said. "There's not a moment to be lost."

"In the dark?" Frank said. "And in the rain?"

"Mr. Traynor, our stalwart frontiersman, will lead the way."

Frank couldn't resist a dig. "What about taming the She Wolves?"

"Ah, that business will have to wait," Claringbold said. "Science must come first." He shook his head in apparent distress. "Oh dear, all our tools are gone, stolen. Not even a trowel between us."

"Then we'll dig with our bare hands," McPhee said. "It's what the Edinburgh Explorer Society would expect of us."

"Quite so," Claringbold said. "Yes, indeed. And so would the New York Institute of Natural History and the Moscow Institute of Paleontology."

Frank James drew a large, broad-bladed bowie knife from the sheath on his belt and said, "Here, Professor. You can dig a hole to China with that."

Claringbold was profuse in his thanks as he accepted the knife. Then Frank and the others looked on, fascinated, as he buttoned up his tan jacket and straightened the pith helmet on his head. His two colleagues stood at a form of attention as the professor inspected them, buttoned one of McPhee's breast pockets, and set Goncharov's helmet straight.

"Never at a jaunty angle, my dear doctor," he said. "Remember, we're scientists."

Professor Claringbold stood back, studied the other

two for a moment, and then nodded. "Splendid. Now, Mr. Traynor, will you lead the way?"

Ephraim swung into the saddle, and said, "Follow me, your honors. And don't wander away because you could get lost in the dark."

After the professors walked into the gloom, Dave Anderson said, "I saw it, but I don't believe it. Do they know there's Apaches out there?"

"Believe it," Frank said. "And yes, they know there are Apaches out there, but they don't care. Jesse and me ran into bone hunters a time or two in Kansas and Missouri, and they're a strange breed."

"Anybody know what them . . . things the professor talks about are?" Sly Barnes said.

"Dinosaurs?" Frank said.

"Yeah, that's it. Dinosaurs. What did they look like?"

"I don't know," Frank said. "Like gigantic chickens, I guess."

"Well, I'll be," Sly said. "Glad I never tried to steal one of them."

Frank smiled and turned his attention to Luca Moretti. The man was mounted, wearing his gun, a rifle booted under his right knee. He had field glasses hanging on his chest, and he wore black leather gloves, the first time Frank had seen them.

"I'm riding out," he said.

"The rain is lessened, but it seems the night has gotten darker," Frank said.

"I'll use my compass," Moretti said. "Head north until I reach the tree line and then swing east and probe the camp from its northern edge."

"We'll wait until the day after tomorrow and then come

looking for Dan Caine," Frank said. "It's likely all we'll do is pick up the pieces."

"If there's a way, and he isn't already dead, I'll save him," Moretti said.

"Then good luck," Frank said. He looked slightly puzzled. "Moretti, tell me this. Are you really a priest?"

The man smiled. "Hard to believe, isn't it? Yes, I'm an ordained Catholic priest."

"You don't look like a holy man," Frank said.

"Crusaders seldom do," Moretti said.

He kneed his horse forward and was soon swallowed by the night.

"That man sees more devils than vast hell can hold," Frank said. He smiled. "I'm misquoting the Bard again."

"I catch your drift," Anderson said. "Dan Caine told me about him. A gambler spends a sight of time reading people, and I can tell you this . . . Luca Moretti is a mighty dangerous man."

Chapter Thirty-three

Dan Caine woke to pain.

His head throbbed and when he opened his eyes the harsh morning light spiked at his brain.

Where was he? More to the point, was he dead or alive? Alive, he reckoned. The dead don't feel pain. *Think, Dan, think.* Slowly, inexorably, the events of the night came back to him, random pieces fitting together like a child's jigsaw puzzle.

He remembered leaving Ephraim . . . the big tent . . . no sign of money sacks . . . then some . . . thing . . . sprang on him . . . he fired a shot . . . recollected the blow to his head . . . and then . . . oblivion.

He opened his eyes again and immediately realized two things. The first was that he was sitting at the edge of the She Wolf camp, and the second, and more alarming, his raised arms were roped to the wheel of a parked freight wagon. His boots had been removed, and his ankles were also bound. Last night's rain was gone, but the ground under him was still wet and muddy.

As his blurred vision focused, Dan saw excited, yelling

women run toward some sort of commotion. He turned his head, paid for the move with a jolt of pain, and saw the cause of the celebration. A troop of mounted women, about twenty in number, had just ridden into camp, and a joyous reunion was taking place. Half the women were horse archers, arrow quivers on their backs, short, Apache bows in their hands. The remainder carried Winchesters, and a few had Henrys. All rode bareback. Rightly, Dan figured the She Wolves had just received reinforcements. Bad news for somebody . . . probably Frank James and the others.

Dan fought against his bonds, but he was tied fast by the wrists, cruelly tight, and couldn't move. His hat was gone, and he feared the noon sun would burn him to a crisp. As it was, he needed water, and soon that need would grow into a raging thirst. He shook his head and voiced his thoughts. "If someone is coming to rescue me, now would be a real good time."

By Dan's reckoning, an hour passed, and the sun climbed higher in a blue sky. Women came and went, some of them gossiping, laughing, but none looked in his direction, as though he was invisible. All the She Wolves wore the same short tunic and knee-high moccasins, and most had their long hair tied back. A few were beautiful, some were pretty, and others quite plain, but they were all young and seemed self-confident and walked around with an air of purpose. White women, black women, Hispanics, and a few Indians, they had one thing in common, they were all running from something and had found a home and a purpose with Maria von Erbach, the founder of a future Amazon nation. That they were living a madwoman's dream didn't seem to enter their thinking.

Dan Caine wondered what fate the She Wolves had in store for him. His thoughts went around and around about the question, but always came back to the same conclusion . . . they were going to kill him. Probably painfully.

Well, there was not a damned thing he could do about it.

He closed his eyes and dozed in the growing heat of the day.

Somebody was kicking his feet, telling him to wake up.

Dan Caine opened his eyes and saw a towering female figure looming over him. Backlit by the sun, she was a dark silhouette, surrounded by an aura of brilliant opalescent light. Dan turned his head and averted his eyes from the dazzle . . . and was rewarded with a hard backhand across the face that sounded like the crack of a pistol shot.

"Look at me, you pig," the woman said. "Look at me."

The left side of his face numb, Dan opened his eyes again and said, "Lady, if I'm a pig, then you're a hog."

His lame attempt at a joke was not worth another slap across the face, this time so vicious and powerful that it made his head spin.

The woman moved closer, blocking out the sun and her aura vanished. Dan saw shapely thighs and as his gaze moved higher, the swell of large, unconfined breasts and higher still, the face of a Renaissance courtesan, its beauty marred by the scarlet birthmark on her cheek in the shape of a wolf's head.

"I am Mother Superior Maria von Erbach," the woman said. "Why are you here?"

"Water first," Dan said, his voice croaky.

The woman turned to the girl at her side and said, "Give him water."

A trim little blonde, the girl dipped water from a pail with a clay cup and held it to Dan's mouth. She was surprisingly gentle, let him drink what he needed and rubbed the excess moisture from his lips with the palm of her hand.

Maria scowled at the girl and kicked her away from the prisoner and said, "Now, tell me why you are here."

"My name is Dan Caine, I'm the deputy sheriff of the town of Broken Back, and I'm here to recover the bank's stolen money."

"Liar! You came here to assassinate my father, the Baron Dieter von Erbach," Maria said. "Was the criminal Padre Luca Moretti with you?"

"Lady, I've got no quarrel with you or your pa," Dan said. "Give me the money, and I'll be on my way."

"You shot at my father," the woman said.

"I was attacked by something in the dark," Dan said. "That's what I shot at. I didn't know who or what it was. I sure as hell didn't think it was somebody's pa."

"You lie through your teeth," Maria said. "There is no truth in your eyes."

"Lady, you wouldn't know the truth if it came up and kicked you up the butt," Dan said.

That impertinence was rewarded by another spiteful slap across the face.

"Tomorrow is the feast of Saints Pontian and Hippolytus

and we will celebrate with your execution," Maria said. "I warn you, it will not be a pleasant one." She glanced at the sky. "Enjoy the sun."

The woman stepped away. She had a hip-swaying walk that Dan had seen only in whores.

Chapter Thirty-four

It was not yet first light when Luca Moretti tethered his horse in a grove of mixed pine and wild oak where there was a sufficient amount of grass. He loosened the girth and patted the bay's neck. "This is the best I can do for you, boy," he said in English. "I'll be back as soon as I can."

Moretti doubted that the animal understood a word he'd said, but he hoped his tone was reassuring. The horse stood with its head down and seemed stoical enough.

Carrying only a half-full canteen, field glasses hanging from his neck, he made his way through the trees, sparser here than they were farther east. But the darkness hid his movement until he was in position close to the northern edge of the She Wolf camp. As the night turned into a steely dawn, Moretti found a brush-covered area that was mostly juniper, mesquite, and lotebush, and from there he could overlook just about all of the camp. He settled into the thick cover and studied the area through the binoculars, tents, horse lines, and a wagon park. What he saw gave him pause. He focused on one of the bigger freight wagons and saw a man lashed to one of its iron-rimmed wheels. And that man was Dan Caine.

"*Cavalo!*" Moretti muttered aloud in Italian, a very unpriestly, "Holy crap!" in English.

He'd expected Caine to be dead or captive, but somehow seeing him roped to a wheel shook Moretti to the core. Perhaps Maria von Erbach planned to expose him to sun and thirst until he died. She was a malevolent witch and capable of any such atrocity.

Dan was out in the open for all to see, and Moretti's options were limited. The obvious solution that sprang to mind was a merciful bullet to end the man's suffering. But Moretti's rifle was back with his horse, and he could not make the shot with his revolver. There was only one other solution and that was to use the cover of darkness tonight and cut the deputy free. But by then Dan might already be dead . . . or dying.

Risking a flash of sunlight on his glasses, he scanned the entire compound. Women walked constantly to and fro among the tents, and he smelled frying bacon and coffee as breakfast was prepared. Chores were being done, caring for the horses, drawing water from a nearby creek, clearing litter from the ground, and washed linen hung on rope clothes lines strung between the branches of nearby live oaks. Moretti estimated that there were at least forty women in camp, and as he'd expected, Maria von Erbach ran the place with Teutonic efficiency.

He had only one question in mind—where was the lycanthrope?

His guess was that the large tent set apart from the rest housed the man-beast. When it came time to destroying the monstrosity, that tent was where he would find it. The more he thought about it, the more he was sure that his guess was the right one. The lycanthrope was there . . . he felt its evil presence, and he could almost smell its foul, feral stench.

The iron discipline of the experienced hunter exerting itself, Luca Moretti lay still as a living corpse bracing himself for the torment of the long, scorching day. Twice he'd seen women give Dan Caine water, but he was offered no shade. They were obviously keeping him alive for a reason, probably for torture of some kind and then a slow death.

Maria von Erbach was in league with the devil, and her dark master would suggest a hundred different ways to kill a man so he felt every agonizing moment of his long dying. Moretti blinked the sun glare grit out of his eyes and glanced at the sky. Still blue. Dear God in his heaven, would the night never come?

A group of women practiced archery at makeshift butts, canvas targets spread across mounds of earth. They were both skilled and noisy, cheering every hit, jeering every miss. But what attracted Moretti's attention were the actions of an Indian girl, probably Apache, who wandered away from the others and strolled closer to the tree line. She stood and curiously gazed into the trees, her bow with a nocked arrow in her hands. The girl had a broad, attractive face framed in thick braids twined with green ribbons, and her black eyes were fixed on a point close to where Moretti lay.

Did she sense his presence? Some women, no matter

their race, at birth received the devil's gift of second sight. Was this Indian girl one of them?

Slowly, making no sound and little movement, Moretti's hand moved to the knife on his belt, a stiletto with a long, slender blade and needle-sharp point. He drew the blade from its sheath and kept it by his side. A quick thrust to the throat would kill the girl and silence her instantly. He hoped that it wouldn't come to that. Knifings were always a messy business.

The She Wolf took a step to her left and her eyes tracked across Moretti's position. He tensed. Had she seen him? His hand tightened on the knife's ivory handle.

Then behind him a rustle in the brush and slowly, tentatively, soft footfalls passed his position. A slight breeze blew from the east and he was downwind of the young whitetail buck that sensed him at the last moment and exploded into a frantic, bounding run. Moretti saw the Indian girl react. She instantly swung to her left, drew her bow, and let the arrow fly. A splintering crash in the brush as the deer fell. But the animal rose to its feet again, and the girl loosed another arrow. Hit twice, the whitetail tried to rise, but it was done. The buck collapsed, and the girl let out a whoop of triumph, bringing other women to the scene at a run.

Panic spiked at Luca Moretti and he flattened himself and tried to burrow into the soft earth. But his fear of being discovered was unfounded. The She Wolves' attention was entirely on the dead buck . . . and the presence of Maria von Erbach, by ancient right first at the kill.

Women chattered in excitement as the Indian girl kneeled by the deer and gutted the animal with her bowie. She reached a hand into the steaming, bloody cavity and came out with the animal's quivering liver that she passed to Maria. The mother superior bit into the meat, tore off a chunk and chewed, then swallowed. Her mouth and chin were bloody. In unison, the women tilted back their heads and howled . . . the triumphant cry of the wolf pack.

Maria wiped off her mouth with the back of her hand, gave an order, and the deer carcass was dragged away to be butchered.

Luca Moretti had watched Maria von Erbach's actions, mesmerized. As he'd often asked himself before, how could a creature so divinely beautiful be so savage? Truly, she was the work of the devil.

Chapter Thirty-five

"Boy, when we meet these women keep your mouth shut and your eyes in your head," Singer Tyler said, slapping his two-mule team into a shambling trot, jolting the wagon forward. "We're there to sell guns, nothing else. Understand?"

The youth beside him, sixteen-year-old Adam Tyler, nodded. "Sure, Pa."

"I mean it, now," Singer said, a stocky, hard-faced man with a weakness for whiskey. "Up Black Mesa way in the Oklahoma Territory, I've done business with Maria von Erbach before, and each time after I left, I touched my head to make sure it was still on my shoulders. But she pays well."

For the past year, after his ma died, young Adam had traveled with his father. They'd peddled their stock of rifles, revolvers, and ammunition in towns all over the frontier, braving poorly maintained dirt roads with axle deep mud, terrifying drop-offs overlooking deep, mountainous ravines, washed-out chasms, flooded river crossings, and a whole array of other problems. Gun trading was not an occupation for the weak at heart or the indecisive. It took strong men with even stronger resolve to survive in the business, and Singer Tyler was one of those.

But Adam Tyler thought his pa was tense, uneasy, as though his coming visit to Maria von Erbach's camp worried him. The boy said, "Pa, maybe we should just head to Fort Concho like we planned. There's always Indians there who'll buy a rifle. Besides, we don't even know if the woman is where the peddler said she'd be."

Singer Tyler shook his head. "I've known Leb Kagan for years, and he's never steered me wrong when it comes to finding business. The peddler said he sold two hundred dollars' worth of merchandise to Maria von Erbach and that she's three days due north of Ned Baxter's stage station. Well, that's where she'll be." Tyler turned and looked at his son, a skinny towhead whose broad shoulders hinted at the strong man to come. "At Fort Concho, an Indian will try to trade some mangy pelts for a new Winchester, and soldiers never have any money, but Maria von Erbach pays in gold. It's worth the detour."

The boy smiled. "And worth the risk?"

"There's no risk if you mind your manners," his father said. "What did I just tell you?"

"Keep my mouth shut and my eyes in my head."

"Then remember it, because I can see tents in the distance," Singer Tyler said.

Dan Caine saw the wagon drawn by two big mules drive into the camp and then stop. The driver sat rigidly upright in his seat, the youth beside more curious, looking around at everything before his gaze stopped at Dan. The boy's face registered shock as he turned to the man and whispered urgently into his ear. The driver said something short and angry, just a few words and one of them a cuss. The towheaded youngster then sat as straight and erect as his parent, his eyes to the front, staring fixedly at the butts of the harness mules.

Dan was suffering from the heat, the sun burning even his tanned skin, but he was interested in the wagon, and for a moment forgot his misery. The wagon was of medium size with a wood cover and attached to the top of that a carved wooden rifle about four-feet-long proclaimed the owner's trade.

For the most part, the She Wolves ignored Singer Tyler's wagon. A visit from a peddler with his stock of female dainties would have generated much more excitement.

Dan saw Maria von Erbach step out of a tent, the young blond girl at her side. She said something to the gun dealer and he climbed down from his seat and he and the two women walked to the rear of the wagon where Tyler rolled up and tied the canvas curtain. Tyler reached inside and, smiling, showed Maria a rifle, an 1866 model Yellow Boy. The woman sighted along the barrel, tried the action, and then nodded. More rifles followed, Winchesters and Henrys mostly, and Dan reckoned that Maria von Erbach bought at least twenty firearms and ammunition as Tyler, notebook in hand, kept the tally.

The woman distributed the rifles among the She Wolves and then entered her tent again. When she came out, she had a bag of coins in her hand. She passed the bag to Tyler who counted them out into his hand and nodded his satisfaction.

As Dan watched the gun trader leave, he felt a pang of regret. He'd been all wrong about where the money was kept. It was obviously in Maria von Erbach's tent, not the large one. But what if he'd known? Sneaking into a woman's tent in the dead of night, especially a woman like Maria von Erbach, could get a man's head blown off. He might have tried it . . . but his chances of success would've been small and his chances of getting shot mighty high.

Dan closed his eyes to the sunlight. Well, it didn't matter now. Nothing mattered now.

One of the girls who'd brought him water was Cora Curry and she whispered that he must make peace with his maker because Maria planned to burn him alive.

It was a terrible death and Dan, not a church-going man, said a fervent prayer that God would help him stand up to the flames like a deputy sheriff should.

Chapter Thirty-six

Ephraim Traynor heaped a plate with pan bread and fried salt pork, and Frank James, aware that their supply of meat, flour, and baking powder was dwindling, said, "You going to eat all that yourself?"

"It's for the perfessers," the old man said. "Them boys will starve to death if'n I don't make them eat. They're digging away at that big skeleton I found, and food and drink never enters their minds."

Frank smiled. "Then carry the plate careful, Ephraim. If I was you, I'd keep my horse to a walk."

"Sound advice as ever was," Ephraim said. He gave the plate to Frank. "Here, hold that." He mounted his horse, took the plate back, and said, "Thank'ee."

"Be careful, Ephraim," Frank said. "We got She Wolves and Apaches on our doorstep."

"I'll be careful," the old man said. "After I feed the perfessers, I aim to go find the deputy."

Frank was taken aback. "Moretti . . ."

"I don't trust him," Ephraim said. "You don't send a priest to do a mountain man's job. If Dan Caine is still alive, Moretti ain't the feller to save him, but I am. I may be old, but I can still move like a puff of smoke when I have to. Sneaking around dangerous folks is what I'm good at."

"If anyone goes it should be me," Frank said.

"No, this is a job for an old man who's got nothing to lose," Ephraim said. "Frank, you got a lot of life and the living of it in front of you. All my living is behind me." Frank opened his mouth to speak, but Ephraim held up a silencing hand. "I'm going, and that's an end to it."

Dave Anderson said, "Wait up, Ephraim." He took the plate from the old man's hand and in its place gave him a pearl-handled, .41 caliber Remington derringer. "If you run into trouble, this stinger will be your ace in the hole," he said. "It's saved my life a time or two."

"Thank'ee, thank'ee kindly," Ephraim said. He tucked the derringer into the pocket of his buckskin shirt. "I sure hope I don't need it. A belly gun is for close work, and I don't want to get that near to any of them She Wolf ladies." He smiled. "Now give me my plate back, sonny. I got starving perfessers to feed."

Using just Frank James's knife and their bare hands, the three professors had uncovered much of the dinosaur's rib cage and neck.

"We believe it could be a Ceratosaurus, Mr. Traynor," Samuel Claringbold said. "It's a carnivore, and I'm sure you'll agree with my colleagues and I that it's late Cretaceous."

"Yeah," Ephraim said. "Sure as shootin' it's . . . what you said all right."

"Crackerjack!" Claringbold said, clapping his hands. "We are in agreement."

"And now it's time to eat," Ephraim said. He handed the three men bread and salt pork. "It will give you strength to dig up the big bird."

"It's a dinosaur, Mr. Traynor," Professor McPhee said. "It's got nothing at all to do with birds."

The professors ate as they dug and talked about bones and dinosaurs and other stuff Ephraim couldn't understand. They devoured their food, but he was sure they didn't taste it.

Ephraim glanced at the sky and stepped into the saddle. "I'll be goin' now, your worships," he said.

Claringbold looked up from the hole he'd dug and said, "What did you say, Mr. Traynor?"

"I'm ridin'," Ephraim said.

"Oh, yes, yes, of course," Claringbold said. "Thank you for the food." He turned to Dr. Goncharov and snapped, "No, Ivan! Don't dig there."

An argument followed between all three of the professors, and as Ephraim rode away, he was glad he wasn't with them.

As he'd done with Dan Caine, Ephraim Traynor rode close to the She Wolves' camp and then dismounted and went the rest of the way on foot. This time he'd the advantage of the growing darkness, and he walked to the perimeter of the camp before dropping to the ground. He was prepared to stay there all night and into the next day as long as he saw any hope of freeing the deputy.

Lying on his belly, Ephraim looked around. All the tents were lit from within and only a few women walked here and there in the compound. Where was Dan Caine? Ephraim's old eyes scanned the camp, searching for a clue, anything that would indicate where Dan was being held. That is, if he was still alive.

Then Ephraim saw something in the fading light that at first puzzled him and later horrified him.

To his left, at the rim of the encampment, a stake in the shape of a bare tree trunk had been dug into the dirt so that about eight feet of it still showed above ground. Brush was piled around the bottom of the stake to a height of three feet and another pile stood ready for use. Ephraim had seen its like before. The Plains Indians burned their bitterest enemies at the stake, especially the Comanche, and it was a terrifying death.

With awful certainty, Ephraim knew burning was the death planned for Dan Caine, and he would not let it happen.

But what the old man didn't know was that events were already set in motion that would drive the She Wolves into an all-out war with the vigilantes from Broken Back and soon much blood would be spilled.

Chapter Thirty-seven

Darkness was Luca Moretti's friend. He'd done some of his best work for Cardinal von Recke in the murk . . . when witches cast demonic spells and werewolves come out to hunt and kill.

The Italian rose to his feet, the stiletto in his hand, his Enfield revolver holstered. This night called for silent, close work . . . work for the blade. The rising moon was lost behind cloud and the whole compound lay in darkness, only the oil lamps burning in the tents providing scattered cones of orange light.

Moretti gave the horse lines a wide berth. The last thing he wanted was to scare the animals and raise an alarm. He stepped into the grassland and walked in a wide arc around the remuda and the pack mules and then turned and headed for the parked wagons. So far, he'd not been seen, and Moretti prayed that his luck would hold for a while longer.

He froze in his tracks and then immediately hit the ground. A sentry was walking the camp perimeter! A woman carrying a Winchester across her chest emerged from the gloom. She stopped, looked along the horse line, seemed satisfied, and walked on.

Moretti took a tighter grip on his knife.

For some reason the woman, slim and dark haired, tarried at the place where the mules were tethered and her eyes probed the darkness. She unlimbered the rifle, thumbed back the hammer, and stood ready to fire. Long moments passed that the anxious Moretti counted as hours, and through a fringe of grass he saw the woman tense, the forefinger of her gun hand on the trigger. She didn't call out or say a word, the She Wolf just stood there in silence. Waiting. Ready. Unafraid.

But in the end, the cottontail that hopped out of the darkness was considerably less than ferocious. The woman smiled and eased down the rifle's hammer. She shooed the rabbit and it bounced away into the night.

And Luca Moretti breathed a sigh of relief.

The woman strolled toward the wagons and passed just six feet away from the Italian hidden in the darkness. She stopped and then walked to the big freight wagon where Dan Caine was tied to one of its wheels. The She Wolf said something that Moretti couldn't hear well enough to understand, and Dan made an inaudible reply. The woman laughed, walked along the side of the wagon, turned and took up her position on the perimeter again. A few moments later she was swallowed by the gloom.

Moretti rose to his feet. Cautiously he stepped to the freight wagon and stubbed his toe on a pair of spurred boots. They must have been taken off the deputy's feet and carelessly tossed aside. Moretti carried the boots with him and then dropped to a knee beside Dan. "We don't have much time," he whispered. "That sentinel woman will be back." His knife was busy sawing on the ropes. "What did she say to you?"

"First of all, thank you for scaring the living daylights out of me, coming from the dark like that," Dan said. "And the woman made me a proposition she knew I couldn't accept."

"Too bad," Moretti said. "Maybe you'll meet again under better circumstances."

"Maybe, but I doubt it," Dan said. "Shh . . . what's that?"

Moretti listened into the night.

After long moments he whispered, "It was a She Wolf moving between the tents. She stopped and talked to another woman, but now they've both moved on."

Dan said, "I'm scared. Moretti, are you scared?"

"Scared of being caught, yes," the man said. "Now be quiet. I've got work to do."

After freeing the deputy's hands, a job that seemed to take forever, Moretti worked on Dan's ankles. The stiletto is not a cutting knife, and it made hard work of the tough hemp rope, but after a couple of minutes he was free.

Dan pulled on his boots and said, "Did you find my gun?"

"No," Moretti said. "Just the boots. Now come with me."

Dan followed the Italian into the long grass and the covering darkness and then the man turned north and Dan followed.

Moretti said, "In case we're separated, I have a horse tethered in the trees. Just keep in this direction until you reach the tree line and then walk west. You'll find it."

Then disaster struck.

Looking back, Dan believed the whole thing could

have been avoided and in later years he blamed himself for what happened.

It started when they were walking in the gloom near the horse lines. Moretti, who could see like a cat in the dark, said, "Deputy, where did you get those scratches on your face?"

Dan could have said, "I got them when I struggled with the She Wolves after they caught me." Or he could have said, "I got them running through the trees trying to escape."

In other words, he could have lied. But he didn't.

"When I went into the large tent looking for the bank money, something big and hairy attacked me," he said.

Moretti stood and stared into Dan's face. The man's eyes glittered.

"How big was it?" he said.

"It was dark, and I couldn't really see the thing," Dan said. "I shot at it and missed." Then, realizing what harm he'd done, he tried to undo it. "Maybe it was a big hound dog," he said.

Luca Moretti said, "It was not a dog, it was a monstrous creature that I must destroy. Now do what I told you, Deputy. Get into the trees and find the horse."

He hesitated a moment to say, "God help me," and then he was off and running, gun in hand, sprinting toward the large, isolated tent.

For a moment Dan Caine was gripped by uncertainty, but then he quickly told himself that his loyalty lay with his posse and the good citizens of Broken Back. Let Moretti chase his wolf man. It was none of his concern. He ran into the darkness . . . and didn't stop until he reached the pines of the tree line.

* * *

Gun in hand, Luca Moretti stopped outside the tent and looked around him. Nothing stirred and the lone sentry was nowhere in sight. He opened the flap and ducked inside, into the vile stench of a man living in his own filth. An oil lamp was lit, illuminating the creature chained to a stake in the middle of the trampled, brown grass floor. The man was overgrown with hair, naked from the waist up, and his large feet were bare, the toenails long, curved, and horny. He looked old, he was old, but his arms and hunched shoulders were still muscular, still powerful, strong enough for grasping and holding. The eyes above the white beard were sky blue, empty of fear, showing no malice toward his unexpected visitor.

"Good evening," Moretti said, speaking English.

"I am Baron Dieter von Erbach. What do you want with me?"

"Do you know who I am?" Moretti said.

"No. Why should I know the name of every peasant I meet?"

"My name is Padre Luca Moretti. And I'm here to destroy you."

"An Italian priest, the worst kind," von Erbach said. "The Vatican sent you, ha?"

"You killed the holy monks who came to convert the heathen," Moretti said.

"No, you fool, my daughter killed them. I merely finished them off, bit their throats."

"Ha! So you admit you're a lycanthrope, Herr Baron," Moretti said in triumph.

"No, I am a man like any other. I bit their throats to

prove to my daughter that although I am old, I could be as savage as her and any of the She Wolves. At that time, I wanted to live, and Maria didn't kill me then, but she will when the time is right. She used me as bait, to draw you to her, because she hates you, Moretti."

"You lied to me," Moretti said. "You'd heard my name before tonight."

"Yes, I had. Why does she hate you so much?" von Erbach said.

"Mostly because I had her banished from the Vatican, but she also blames me for the suicide of her lover who threw herself into the Tiber in Rome," Moretti said.

"All you said is known to me," von Erbach said. He smiled, a grotesque grimace. "You have destroyed lycanthropes before. Now kill this one." He tapped the middle of his forehead with an index finger and said, "Put the silver bullet right there."

Moretti holstered his Enfield. "No, I won't kill you. I can see that you're not a lycanthrope. You're a sad old man and there's nothing of the wolf about you. I believe you didn't murder the four monks and thus my long trip from Rome has been in vain."

"Then kill my daughter," von Erbach said. "She is the true evil, the nun from the deepest chasms of hell."

"I have no orders to destroy Maria von Erbach, but I believe she'll be the architect of her own destruction. I can't talk to you longer, old man. I need to breathe fresh air."

"Wait, your blessing, Padre, before you go," von Erbach said. "Perhaps it will help me feel clean again."

Moretti said, "You are a poor demented creature, but even an animal shouldn't be chained as you are." He raised a hand, and making the sign of the cross, said, *"In Nomine Patris, et Filii et Spiritus Sancti*, Amen." And then, "May God help you, my son."

Moretti bowed out of the tent . . . into the waiting rifles of Maria von Erbach and a dozen She Wolves.

Chapter Thirty-eight

Ephraim Traynor was well aware of the sentry walking the perimeter of the camp and he crawled back into the gloom until she passed. From his position he couldn't see the freight wagons and had no idea that Dan Caine was now on the run.

As the long night dragged on and brightened into morning, he realized an old scout with bad eyesight and the rheumatisms wasn't going to free the deputy . . . if he was still alive. Ephraim was about to give up all hope and make his way back to his horse when he saw something that chilled his blood and got his full attention.

The shouting, laughing, She Wolves, and there were a lot of them, were dragging a man by a rope around his neck. Some of the women had clubs they used to beat on him, and every time he stumbled and fell, he was viciously pounded until he staggered to his feet again. As the rowdy crowd came closer, chanting, "Luca . . . Luca . . . Luca . . ." Ephraim faded back into the grassland and watched. He was near enough to see that the priest Luca Moretti had taken a terrible beating. Both his eyes were swollen shut, his lips were split and bleeding, and more blood fell across his face from a head wound. He'd been dragged through the compound's only campfire and could no longer walk. Now he was hauled along the ground by his neck, and when that stopped, the beatings continued again.

Ephraim was appalled. He'd liked his worship Luca Moretti and enjoyed having a priest around to say a word for him to St. Peter if he stopped a fatal bullet and was headed for the pearly gates. Now the holy man was being beaten to death, and Ephraim had no way of stopping it. The old man's immediate thought was, "Moretti, what did you do wrong?" But the obvious answer was that like himself, he'd come to rescue Deputy Caine and was now getting punished for succeeding. Ephraim felt a jolt of sudden fear.

He knew it was high time to skedaddle out of there, but he forced himself to watch the martyrdom of Padre Luca Moretti to the very end. Mercifully, it was not long in coming.

"Oh my God, ain't this something," Ephraim whispered to himself.

Now the rope around Moretti's neck was removed and used to lash him to the stake at the edge of the camp. The She Wolves fell silent as Maria took a burning brand from the fire and walked to the condemned man.

Ephraim wiped a tear from his eye with the back of a gnarled hand.

Maria raised the burning torch over her head and said, "This is the murderer of the innocents and the sworn enemy of free women like us." This brought boos and hisses, and Maria said, "Padre Luca Moretti also caused the death of someone very dear to me. For that I want him to burn." Then, her voice rising to a strident yell, "I want this man to suffer as I suffered."

Moretti's bloody head hung, dripping gore, and Ephraim did something he'd never done before and would never do again . . . a thing he kept secret until his dying day. He pushed his face into the grass and sobbed.

Maria von Erbach's last statement was not as well received as she'd expected. There were few cheers now that burning a man at the stake had become a harsh reality.

Maria shoved the flaming brand into the dry brush that was piled around Moretti's feet, and it burst into flame immediately. Maria piled on more brush and then more as the man burned. Some apologists for Maria von Erbach say Padre Moretti was dead ere the flames reached him. But Ephraim Traynor who witnessed the execution had a different story to tell. He said the man writhed and cried out on the stake for God's mercy and it took him "quite a spell" to die.

There are those who say Luca Moretti died a martyr's death and urge his sainthood. But that is unlikely to happen since the Church disowned him once his actions in Lithuania and elsewhere were investigated and fully understood.

Ephraim Traynor had seen enough. He walked into the remaining darkness and found his horse close to where he'd left it. He rode back to the vigilantes and told them that Luca Moretti was dead. He didn't tell what he'd seen nor did he ever, for the rest of his life, mention it again.

Chapter Thirty-nine

Dan Caine rode in just after daybreak on Luca Moretti's horse and got the word that the Italian was dead.

"He saved my life," Dan said. The coffee Frank James shoved into his hand was welcome. The makings in his pocket had survived his ordeal and now he built a cigarette and told of his capture and being roped to a wagon wheel.

"Moretti cut me loose, told me where he'd left his horse, and then he went after his wolf man or whatever it was," Dan said. "They must've caught and killed him."

"Yeah, I guess that's what happened," Ephraim Traynor said.

Frank said, "Did you see anything, Ephraim?"

"Not a thing," the old man lied.

"I saw something," Dan said. "I saw where the money is stashed. It's in the tent of Maria von Erbach, and it's right in the middle of her camp."

"How do we get at it?" Frank said.

"We don't," Dan said. "We'd all be killed trying."

The statement was followed by a silence until Dave Anderson, less emotionally involved than the others, said, "So we know where the money is, but we can't get at it, huh?"

"That about sums it up," Dan said.

"Then it's over," the gambler said.

"Yes, it's over," Dan said. "Over and done." His shoulders slumped in defeat. "All we can do now is go back to Broken Back and tell the town that we failed . . . again."

"You tried your best, Dan," Frank said.

"But my best wasn't good enough," Dan said.

"I'll stand by you," Frank said.

"So will I," Ephraim said.

"And that goes for me too," Sly Barnes said. Then, "For what it's worth."

Dan managed a smile. "I appreciate it, Sly," he said.

Frank said, "Listen to us. What a sorry bunch we are, crying into our coffee. Damn it all, there has to be a way to get the money back."

"If there is, we haven't found it yet," Dan said.

"It's like robbing a bank," Frank said. "We go in fast, grab the cash, and run."

Old Ephraim Traynor frowned and said, "Who's gonna do the grabbin' and who's gonna do the runnin'?"

"Give me time, Ephraim," Frank said. "I haven't worked out all the details yet."

Dan shook his head. "We'd all wind up dead, Frank," he said. "We'd have to do it under cover of darkness, and all the odds are against us. One mistake, one yell from Maria von Erbach, and the She Wolves would swarm over us like ants from a kicked-over nest."

Frank looked around. "Well, does anybody like my idea?" He got no response and said, "Anybody?"

Ephraim, a man who called a spade a spade, said, "No. It stinks."

"Frank, I have to agree with Ephraim," Dave Anderson said. "I wouldn't play the odds on that one."

"Then we're left with only one alternative," Frank said.

"Go home," Dan said.

"You said it."

"I'll hand in my resignation, tell Broken Back to pin their star on somebody else," Dan said. "A man more worthy than me."

"Deputy, defeat doesn't destroy a man, but quitting does," Frank said. "Wear your star with pride. No man could've done more than you."

"Thank you kindly," Dan said. "But the defeat is all mine, and I'll need to find a way to live with it." Then to Ephraim, "Call in the professors, tell them we're leaving."

"They ain't gonna like this, Deputy," the old scout said. "They still got a dinosaur to dig out of the ground."

"Bring them in, Ephraim," Dan said.

Professor Samuel Claringbold was outraged.

"Deputy Caine, we can't leave now when we're so close to uncovering the tail," he said. "I think once I've done that, I can establish without doubt that we have a complete skeleton of a Ceratosaurus, a discovery that will be hailed from New York to Moscow."

"And to Edinburgh," Angus McPhee said, shaggy eyebrows lowered.

"Yes, of course," Claringbold said. "How remiss of me, Professor McPhee; the excitement of the moment made the Edinburgh Explorer Society slip my mind."

"No offense taken, Professor Claringbold," McPhee said. "Please carry on."

"Don't you realize what this means, Deputy?" Claringbold said. "It all but guarantees further financing from our institutes. We can mount another expedition just as soon as I can arrange for a large wagon, tools, tents, and hardy diggers."

Frank James smiled. "How are you going to find the skeleton again, Professor?"

"Ah, Mr. Traynor has very kindly agreed to be our scout," Claringbold said.

"I'll find it for you, your worship," Ephraim said. "Don't you fret none over that."

"I'm sorry, Professor, but we're pulling out today," Dan said.

"I beg of you, Deputy Caine, just give me two more days, that's all I ask," Claringbold pleaded, his face a mask of anxiety. He turned to Frank. "Mr. James, you're a man of some learning, talk to the deputy on my behalf."

"Dan, are you in a big hurry to get going?" Frank said.

"I don't think Maria von Erbach has forgotten me," Dan said. "She thinks I tried to kill her father, but I escaped her clutches and the bonfire she'd made ready for me. I reckon it's a lead pipe cinch that she'll come after me, probably with forty or fifty She Wolves."

"Maybe better to meet them here than the open prairie with horses carrying two riders," Frank said. "We sure as hell can't outrun them."

Dave Anderson smiled. "Five of us men against fifty fighting women." He shook his head. "We're all going to end up dead anyway."

Dan stood lost in thought. Finally, he said, "All right

Professor, you've got your two days. Depending on the She Wolves, you might have a lot less than that."

"Thank you, Deputy Caine," Claringbold said. "And be assured that I will mention your excellent cooperation the next time I'm in the Institute of Natural History. As for the She Wolves, as you call them, a severe countenance and a stern word will send them on their way."

Dan said, "I sure wish it was that easy."

Frank James stood gazing at the prairie to the east. They'd come from that direction, probably in a line abreast. They'd advance at a walk and when they came within rifle range the She Wolves would charge at the gallop. There would be no stopping them, not with five men, one of them an old timer who couldn't see and another a chicken thief who'd never handled a gun before.

Frank looked up the cobalt blue arch of the beautiful morning sky, smelled grass and sage on the breeze.

"Enjoy it while you can, Frank," he told himself. "Enjoy it while you can."

Chapter Forty

Maria von Erbach made up her mind about solving two problems. The first was to wipe out Dan Caine and his bunch for assisting the vile priest Luca Moretti, the second was to kill her father, the murderer of her sainted mother. The old scoundrel had lived too long.

But first the safety of the money she'd taken from the bank robbers had to be assured. There was a chance Caine had seen where it was kept, a slim chance certainly, but one that could not be ignored. The man was now desperate and might make an attempt to take the money back by force. And there was another consideration in Maria's mind. All of the She Wolves had prying eyes because she'd trained them to be aware, and most knew that there was thirty thousand dollars in her tent. That much money could keep a woman in comparative luxury for the rest of her life and temptation was a dangerous thing.

She'd move the money that night and stash it somewhere in the tree line for a couple of days and recover it on her way to . . . not Black Mesa, but somewhere with lights and music and life. Jane Hall, the pretty blond girl who shared her tent, would help. She was an ignorant little slut but knew how to keep her mouth shut.

"Mother Superior."

The voice of Martha Nichols, an older, masculine-looking woman who was Maria's unofficial second in command.

"Hold on, I'll come out," Maria said.

She stepped outside into morning sunlight. The camp was a hive of activity as the women prepared for the anticipated move to their permanent settlement at Black Mesa. The timing of the move was what Martha Nichols wished to discuss.

"My plan is to attack the Dan Caine rabble with the She Wolves just after dawn tomorrow," Maria said. "Once they are all dead, we'll return and break camp."

"We may have dead and wounded," Martha said.

She was a tall woman, about forty years of age, wide shouldered and bony, and her face was saved from mediocrity by piercing blue eyes. She claimed she'd fled the Kansas plains, leaving her constantly ailing common law husband to plow his hundred and sixty acres alone.

"We'll strike with overwhelming force, and I think our casualties will be small as they were in our battle with the bank robbers," Maria said. "But we'll deal with that when the time comes."

"Attack with our whole strength?" Martha said.

"Yes. How many in camp?"

"Forty-eight, but five were wounded in the previous battle and will not fight. Say forty-three."

"Forty-four," Maria said. "I'll lead the charge."

"Arms?"

"Rifles. Bows for those that are competent with them," Maria said. "Any more questions?"

"None for the moment," Martha said.

"Are you looking forward to our return to Black Mesa?" Maria said.

Martha smiled. "Yes, and I very much look forward to the day when we have a city of brick, its streets paved with black lava, and my house will sit nearly five thousand feet above the flat."

"And so you shall have all those things," Maria said. "We'll call our city state Amazonia and keep out men except traders and those we summon by invitation or keep as slaves. Trespassers will be hanged without trial."

Martha Nichols had just glimpsed the tormented mind of a mad woman she thought of as a living saint, and yet her loyalty to the memory of Maria von Erbach never wavered until her death in 1903.

The camp slumbered in the night, the tents dark, as Maria von Erbach and Jane Hall carried four small sacks of paper money and coin into the trees close to the trail that headed north to the Oklahoma border and Black Mesa.

Maria found a natural hollow at the base of a post oak that accommodated the sacks. She covered them over with leaves and pine needles and then used her knife to cut a V-shape into the bark of the tree to mark the spot.

"Nobody will find it there," she said.

Irritated at being out at such a late hour, Jane Hall was sulky. "Nobody was going to steal it from our tent between now and when we leave for the Territory tomorrow."

"I didn't want to take a chance that the hick deputy might try a raid tonight," Maria said. "I won't rest easy until he's dead tomorrow." She stared out into the darkness.

"I think he could attempt it. I feel something threatening out there . . . watching . . . waiting. Can't you feel it?"

"I feel cold and I feel tired," Jane said, pouting. "That's all I feel."

Maria's mouth hardened. "I should slap your face for doubting me, you little whore."

The girl felt a sudden stab of alarm. The wolf's head on the woman's cheek stood out blood red and Jane was immediately contrite. "I'm sorry, Mother Superior," she said. "I spoke out of turn."

"Don't let it happen again," Maria said. "Now, go back to our tent and wait for me there."

Jane nodded. "Yes, Mother Superior."

The girl ran into the night and Maria von Erbach watched her go with harsh eyes. That one needed disciplining.

Maria von Erbach made her way into the feral, acrid stench of the large tent. The lamp wasn't lit, and the inside was pitch dark. She stood for a moment until she heard the chink-chink of a chain. "It is me, *mein geliebter Vater,*" she said. "I bring you wonderful news. I will kill you tomorrow."

Baron Dieter von Erbach growled and rattled his shackles.

"No? It's not good news?" Maria said. "I'm so disappointed. I thought it would make you happy to be on the eve of your death."

"No matter what they told you in the Vatican, you were never a nun, daughter," the old man said. "You were always a demon. Why do you torment me so?"

"Torment you? There is no torment. It's a time for

rejoicing," Maria said. "I'll cut your throat tomorrow and set you free."

"And you? What of you?" the old man said. "You will build your female utopia in the middle of a wilderness? Pah, an impossible dream."

"Perhaps," Maria said. "I already grow weary of it. My archenemy, the priest Luca Moretti, is dead. I buried all that was left of him, and my hatred went with him to the grave. Tomorrow I will destroy those who aided and abetted him, and then, who knows? Paris, Vienna, the world."

"What about your She Wolves?" von Erbach said. "What about the women who were willing to follow you into a wasteland to share your dream?"

"They were nothing when I found them, and they'll be nothing when I'm gone," Maria said. "God has seen fit to send me a large sum of money and I intend to spend it, spend it on myself, old man, every last penny."

"God didn't send you money, you hellhound, the devil did," the old man said. His usually harsh voice was very weak, a whisper. "I curse you, and I curse your ill-gotten money. May it be your death."

Maria frowned. "I had intended tomorrow to be a celebration," she said. "And now you've spoiled it for me."

She turned and stormed out of the tent into the darkness.

Chapter Forty-one

Dan Caine stared into the night and worried about the three professors. If there was an attack from the She Wolves in the next couple of days they'd be first in the line of fire and the first to die.

Frank James stood beside him. "You can't sleep either, huh?"

"Not with Sly Barnes standing sentry," Dan said. "He's never used a gun before."

"But he takes his job very seriously, and he stays awake," Frank says. "Back in the old days, I could've used a man like him. He's a human owl."

Ephraim Traynor and Dave Anderson were asleep by the fire, both with guns close at hand. The moon was hidden behind a cloud, and beyond the small circle of firelight the camp was surrounded by absolute blackness that hugged it close.

"I worry about the professors," Dan said. "They're way out there on point."

"And they're unarmed save for my knife," Frank said.

He reached into Dan's shirt pocket and took out the makings.

"I didn't know you smoked," Dan said.

Frank looked down at the tobacco and paper in his fingers. "I don't usually, but I want one tonight." He licked the cigarette closed and Dan thumbed a lucifer into flame and lit it. Frank inhaled deeply and small clouds of smoke puffed out of his mouth with every word as he said, "Do you feel something in the air?"

"Do you mean am I uneasy?" Dan said. "If you do, the answer is hell, yes."

"The She Wolves?" Frank said.

"What else can it be?" Dan said.

"I think they'll attack tomorrow, probably at first light," Frank said.

"You're guessing?" Dan said.

"Yes, I'm guessing," Frank said.

"Well, my guess is they'll attack tomorrow at first light," Dan said.

"Suppose they don't come?" Frank said. "Could be they'll figure we're not worth the trouble."

"Do you really believe that?" Dan said.

"No."

"Neither do I."

"Maybe we should bring the professors back," Frank said.

"Die where you're at or die here," Dan said. "That's the choice I'd give them."

"You don't give us any chance at all," Frank said.

"There's too many of them, Frank," Dan said. "They'll

charge and ride right over us. We might drop a few of them, but the rest will keep on a-coming."

"I always figured I'd meet my end from a lawman's bullet or a railroad bull's shotgun," Frank said. "I never expected to get my ticket punched by a bunch of sage hens."

"Me neither," Dan said.

As was his habit, Ephraim Traynor groaned as he rose from his blankets and then stood and stretched the frost out of his old bones.

"What are you boys talking about?" he said. "Don't answer that. Is there coffee in the pot?"

"Yes, and it's hot," Dan said. "Help yourself."

Ephraim poured himself a cup and said, "Now, what were you boys talking about?"

"Our chances of survival," Frank said. "They're mighty slim."

"Well, the way I see it, we can't run, we can't hide, and we can't surrender," Ephraim said. "So what does that leave us? Not a damn thing but to die well and me, I've got my place all picked out for when I go over the river."

"And where's that, Ephraim?" Dan said.

"Well, listen up," the old scout said. "I've lived most of my almost eighty years among rough and profane men, unschooled frontiersmen with wild ways. But now the good Lord has seen fit to allow me to die among educated gentlemen."

Frank smiled and said, "Well, Dan, it sure ain't us."

"No, it ain't. It's the three perfessers," Ephraim said. He drained his coffee, then, with great dignity, "Now, if you will excuse me, I got to get going."

Ephraim saddled his horse and mounted. He leaned

from the saddle and then stuck out his hand. "So long, Deputy Caine."

"So long, Ephraim," Dan said. Then, uttering the words that popped into his head, "Die well."

"You too, Deputy," the old man said. He put out his hand again. "Frank, so long."

Frank James took the proffered hand and said, "So long, Ephraim, and good luck."

"You too, Frank. Good luck."

The curtain of the night parted and then closed behind horse and rider.

Dave Anderson and Sly Barnes slept through Ephraim Traynor's departure, and Dan Caine didn't waken them. They would have to face soon enough the grim reality of what the morning would bring.

"When we see the She Wolves coming, we'll bring the horses forward and shoot them," Frank James said. "They'll provide cover."

"And make the battle last a little longer," Dan said.

"Yeah, just a little," Frank said. "I'm looking for miracles here."

"Maybe at dawn a regiment of cavalry will happen by," Dan said.

"That's a miracle we could sure use," Frank said. He added some mesquite branches to the fire and then said, "During the war, Jesse and me, we were always scared the night before a battle. But when the fighting started most of the fear would go away."

"You scared now, Frank?" Dan said.

"I don't know. I feel something, but I don't know what it is."

"You feel what I'm feeling," Dan said.

"What's that?"

"Fear," Dan said.

Frank smiled and said, "Yeah, that's it. I'm just plumb scared."

Dan Caine woke Dave Anderson an hour before sunup.

The gambler complained that he'd been dreaming about Lillie Langtry and that when Dan shook him awake, he'd just asked her to marry him. "Now I'll never know her answer," he said.

Anderson's humor was a little forced, and Dan recognized that he was feeling the strain like everyone else. Sly Barnes, now free of guard duty, said that he wanted it over, that the waiting was taking a toll on him.

"But if I survive this, I'll never steal a cooling pie or a chicken again," he said.

"If we survive this, I'll buy you a pie," Frank James said. "What kind do you like?"

"I'm right partial to peach," Barnes said. "But I reckon I like blueberry the best."

"You got it," Frank said.

"Mr. Traynor, I will not allow anyone to die on this expedition, and that includes you," Professor Samuel Claringbold said. He glared at Ephraim. "Do I make myself clear?"

"Your worship, come daylight the She Wolves will attack, and we'll be the first to go," Ephraim said.

"Who says that?" Claringbold demanded.

"Why, everybody," Ephraim said.

"Who is everybody?"

"Well, me for a starter and then Deputy Dan Caine and Frank James."

"Apart from you, my dear sir, they're hardly people I'd put my faith in," Claringbold said.

"Why would those lassies kill us?" Professor Angus McPhee said. "We've done them no harm."

"Perfesser, just being with Dan Caine's posse is harm enough," Ephraim said. "Them wolf women want your hide and everybody else's."

"No, I will not allow it," Claringbold said, looking pompous. "As I told Deputy Caine, I'll turn those harridans aside with a stern look and harsh word."

"But Perfesser . . ."

"Listen to me, Mr. Traynor," Claringbold said. "When they charge, if they charge, I will stand right there on the edge of this trench, beat my chest and say, 'I'm a member of the New York Institute of Natural History.' That will work wonders."

"Them gals will come a-shooting, Perfesser," Ephraim said. "A bullet doesn't listen to speechifying."

"Then we'll wait and see, won't we?" Claringbold said. "Now come look at this, Mr. Traynor. Doctor Goncharov pointed it out and it's most interesting. Step down into the trench, if you please, I want your opinion on this matter."

Ephraim spoke to his restive horse and then slid his Henry from the boot.

"You won't need that," Claringbold said.

"I just might," the old scout said. He stepped down into

the trench, looked around him and said, "This hole is a right good defensive position, Perfesser."

"This trench is a scientific excavation," Claringbold said. "Not a hole in the ground. Now look here." He used Frank James's knife as a pointer. "See how six vertebrae at the back of this creature's neck are severely crushed."

"Crrrushed," Goncharov said, closing his fingers into a fist.

"Quite," Claringbold said. "It's the doctor's view, and I agree with him, that this meat-eater met its demise in the jaws of a bigger carnivore. What is your opinion, Mr. Traynor?"

Ephraim peered at the fossil and said, "Something mighty big took a chomp, right enough."

Claringbold clapped his hands and said, "Huzzah! Once again your succinct judgment has set us all to rights." He shook his head. "Indeed, Mr. Traynor, in the Cretaceous it was the law of the jungle, the strong devour the weak."

"And that's what I've been trying to tell you, your worship," Ephraim said. "We're the weak, and the She Wolves are the strong."

"Then take heart, my friend, I will make you stronger," Claringbold said.

"The professor has a way with the fair sex," Professor McPhee said.

And Dr. Goncharov nodded his agreement.

Chapter Forty-two

The night had not yet grayed into day, but the She Wolves camp was already stirring as women tended to their horses and armed themselves for the attack on the hated Caine posse.

For Maria von Erbach the death of Dan Caine would be sweet revenge on the man who'd harbored the priest of blood, Padre Luca Moretti. But Maria would not lead the attack. She had other plans on what she considered the first day of her new life.

Maria sought out Martha Nichols who was bridling her mount at the horse lines. She saw Maria and smiled. "I've already saddled your sorrel, Mother Superior. And the Yellow Boy is in the boot."

Most of the She Wolves rode bareback, but some of the older women used saddles, and Maria was one of them.

"Thank you, but I will not lead the attack today," Maria said.

"Are you having one of your headaches?" Martha said.

"Yes. It's just starting."

Martha laid her hand on Maria's arm and said, "You poor thing. Lie down and try to rest."

She did not question Maria von Erbach's courage. The woman had proven her bravery too many times in the past to be considered a coward.

"I will take your place," Martha said. "It is a great honor you do me."

Maria laid her hand on the other woman's shoulder and said, "Bring me back Caine's scalp."

"Consider it done, Reverend Mother," Martha said. Then, "Can I bring you coffee and some breakfast?"

"No, thank you," Maria said. "I'll lie down for a while, but first I want to see for myself how the preparations for the attack are coming."

There was still an hour before sunup and women were standing around eating breakfast, horses tethered outside the tents. Some wore the pelts of the gray wolf and others had tied up their hair for the coming battle. Most of the She Wolves were young, under thirty, but there were a few older women in their ranks who helped steady the youngsters during their frequent raids into the Oklahoma and New Mexico territories.

It is claimed by some historians that Martha Nichols, one of the older women, was in fact Martha Jane Cannary, later known as Calamity Jane, and that in her cups she sometimes talked of her adventures with the She Wolves and her lasting admiration for their founder . . . but was not believed.

Busy as they were with their battle preparations, the women paid little heed to Maria von Erbach as she led her sorrel from the horse line and walked to the large tent. She left her mount, reins trailing, at the entrance to the tent and ducked inside.

Feeling her way into the gloom, she took a match from the box that lay on the table, scraped it into flame and lit the oil lamp. Instantly a pale light flooded the tent and banished the darkness.

"Finally, you have come to kill me," Baron Dieter von Erbach said. "I can sense death surrounding you. You wear it like a cloak."

"Yes, I have come to kill you," Maria said. "You have lived too long, old man."

The woman carried Luca Moretti's Enfield revolver in the holster of the dead man's gunbelt.

"This is a happy day," Maria said. "For both of us. You will get a silver bullet in your brain and I'll finally be free of you."

"Shoot me and your women will come running," von Erbach said. "They will see what you've been hiding from their sight, this monstrous thing that was once a man."

"All they will see is the body of an insane old man who took his own life," Maria said. "They'll talk about it among themselves for an hour perhaps, and then it will be gone, forgotten. And you will be forgotten, Herr Baron, as though you never existed."

"Let me live," von Erbach said. "For God's sake don't take my life."

"I thought you wished to die."

"No, as death draws nearer, I've come to realize that every moment of life is precious. I want to leave here and feel the sun warm on my face and hear the birds sing."

"You old fool, I'm here to kill you, not save you," Maria said. "Vile adulterer. Murderer. Wife killer."

"I was all of those things, and I wish to atone for them,"

von Erbach said. "To atone, I need life. It's not too late. Have mercy on me, daughter."

"There will be no mercy for you, not from me," Maria said. She smiled. "You know, I believe I'll go to Rome. Yes, I can pose as a rich European tourist and would such a person be suspected of the murder of Cardinal Ahren von Recke? I think not. I can kill him. It can be done. I will destroy the man who was instrumental in the death of my beloved Adriana."

"And your soul will be damned for all eternity," von Erbach said.

"A small price to pay for the death of a man I hate with every fiber of my being," Maria said. "I damn him with every breath I take, every beat of my heart. I once knew a love so intense, so wonderful, a loathsome creature like you could never understand it. Von Recke took it from me."

"Sapphist. Even at this late date have you no shame?"

"Have you?"

"Yes, I have. I discovered it in the darkness that surrounds me," the old man said. "Spare me to repent and save my immortal soul from the fires of hell."

"Now that death is near, you fear the torment that lies ahead," Maria said. "What a coward you are."

She drew the Enfield.

"Silver bullets, *mein Vater*. You never lived like a man, now try to die like one."

Von Erbach lowered his head. "I will not beg for mercy any longer. Do what you have to do."

"For my mother," Maria said. She thumbed back the hammer. "For all the dreadful harm you did to her."

"Shoot. Damn you, shoot."

Maria placed the muzzle in the middle of Baron Dieter von Erbach's forehead and squeezed the trigger. As the racketing roar of the shot reached every corner of the camp, Maria placed the revolver in her father's hand, curling his still warm fingers around the grip.

She smiled, her eyes alight, and then as outside women's voices were raised in alarm, she composed her face into an expression of grief and left the tent.

To the assembled women and their frantic questions, she raised a silencing hand and said, "It breaks my heart to say this, but my beloved father just took his own life." To cries of sympathy, Maria added, "He was sick and old and couldn't leave his tent. I think his life became too much of a burden and he chose to end it."

Martha Nichols, tears running down the cheeks of her homely face, grabbed Maria and hugged her close. "I'm so sorry, Mother Superior," she said. "I feel your pain."

Maria pushed the woman away and said, "Thank you. I appreciate your concern. It will be light soon, Sister Martha, time to get your people ready for the attack."

Martha Nichols opened her mouth to say something, but the words never came . . . because at that moment vengeful Apaches tore into the She Wolf encampment like a hundred slashing bullwhips.

The deaths of eight young Apache warriors was a blow to the Mescalero and one that had to be avenged. That the women called the She Wolves, who'd raided isolated villages in the recent past, were the killers the Apaches had no doubt. The women were known to be numerous and well-armed and a call went out to the

Chiricahua and the Jicarilla to come help until a hundred warriors gathered and willingly placed themselves under the command of Delshay, the young Mescalero war chief. A mighty warrior thirsting for revenge, he led the crashing attack on the unsuspecting She Wolves.

Chapter Forty-three

In the half-light of the somber dawn, the She Wolves were taken by complete surprise. Over the past several years Maria von Erbach had trained them to be horse warriors, but when the Apaches attacked only a few were mounted and played no major role in the battle.

Delshay, carrying a war lance, planned to trap the She Wolves between the hammer of his attack and the anvil of the tree line. In that, he was successful. Most of the women bunched in the middle of the encampment and attempted to make a stand. Maria von Erbach, with a better grasp of strategy, would have opened up the ranks and ordered a fighting retreat to the cover of the trees. Whether or not this maneuver would have been effective against the Apaches will never be known. What is certain is that shocked, leaderless, the women were packed so closely together the archers could not properly deploy their bows, and the rifle fire was not concentrated. Delshay, seeing this confusion, urged his warriors to charge into them. He lost several men in the initial assault, but then he and his Apaches were among the She Wolves, using their short bows and lances to great effect. The women

lost all cohesion and broke and fled, and now the camp
became a killing ground. No longer formidable fighting
She Wolves but a disorganized mob of frightened women,
some fled, screaming, into the open prairie and were
hunted down and killed by mounted Apache warriors. A
few tried to surrender and were shot where they stood by
angry and revengeful Mescaleros.

A couple of minutes before the Apache charge,
Martha Nichols had managed to disengage from the tan-
gled mob of She Wolves and led four women toward the
trees. Skilled with a revolver, she shot a couple of
Indians who'd come too close and managed to reach
the tree line undetected. She and the others hid in the
brush until dark . . . and, apart from Maria von Erbach,
were the only survivors. The Curry girls were nowhere
to be seen, unfortunately—odds were they never would
be again. The Apache were capable of anything.

It should be noted here that Martha Nichol's handi-
ness with a gun strengthens the hypothesis that she was
Calamity Jane Cannary, renowned, even in the male-
dominated West, for her shooting skills.

When the Apaches charged the camp and the shooting
began, Maria von Erbach didn't waste a moment to flee
the coming massacre. She drew the Enfield revolver and
mounted her horse. The money was hidden close, giving
her time to retrieve it and ride deep into the cover of the
trees.

"Mother Superior, wait for me!"

Maria turned her head and saw Jane Hall. She swore
under her breath. The little slut would only slow her down.

Above the racketing of gunfire, Maria yelled, "Go away. Fight with the others."

"No, I want to come with you," the girl said.

She clutched at the mane of Maria's sorrel and, frantic now as screams of the dying clawed across the fair face of the morning, pleaded, "Take me with you!"

Maria tried to kick the hysterical girl away and when that failed, she lowered the Enfield and fired. A silver bullet crashed into the top of the girl's skull and she fell, dead when she hit the ground.

Maria took a second to glance at the once lithe, now crumpled body, and said, "Slut."

She kicked her horse into motion and galloped into the trees.

As his warriors rounded up the She Wolves' horses and gathered their rifles, pistols, and food supplies, Delshay rode his black pony around the compound. He had made a great victory. For the cost of four dead and five wounded he'd killed many of the hated She Wolves. Even the sick had been dragged from their beds and knifed to death, so terrible was the revenge of the Apache. The hated tents had been pulled down and dragged into the grassland where they were ripped apart, never to be used again. Warriors called out to Delshay praising him for his triumph and the number of horses he'd captured, and even a normally reserved Jicarilla, himself a war chief, said in camp that night he'd sing of Delshay's courage and leadership.

Delshay rode past the place where the largest tent had stood, where the strangely contorted body of an old man had been found by his warriors. The man had been chained to a stake and had long white hair and a beard to his waist. His finger- and toenails had grown to the length of bear claws. Someone had shot him in the head before the battle, and the warriors said this was a strange thing. They agreed that by the look of him the old man had not been human at all, but some kind of white man's demon.

The Apaches then gathered up their spoils of war and did not again come near the strange devil.

Chapter Forty-four

The expected attack on the posse's camp never came and the sound of a distant battle at dawn explained the reason why.

"Frank, what do you reckon?" Dan Caine said after the firing died away.

"Maybe the army caught up with the She Wolves," Frank James said.

"A surprise attack just before sunup makes sense," Dave Anderson said. "The soldier boys could've murdered the women while they were still warm in their blankets."

"Killing to the sound of bugles is not murder," Frank said. "The war taught me that."

"We'll stay where we're at until noon and if it's still quiet go take a looksee," Dan said. "Sly, do we have enough wood for a coffee fire?"

"I reckon we do," Barnes said. "I'll get it going."

The scarlet sky slowly faded into pale purple, and a west wind picked up, stirring the long grass. Gunfire no longer shattered the morning, and the prairie was silent as though waiting to see what would happen next. To the east, buzzards quartered the sky, their lazy circles slowly gliding closer to the She Wolves camp and the site of the recent gun battle.

Dan and the others were standing around drinking coffee when Ephraim Traynor rode in, his Henry rifle across his saddle horn. He nodded and said, "Good mornin' all," and then stepped out of the saddle and patted his black's neck. "Told this old feller to leave me, but he wouldn't go. Now that I ain't been massacreed, I'm kinda glad he stayed."

"What was all the shooting about, Ephraim?" Dan said.

The old scout helped himself to coffee before he answered. "Do you mind them hundred Apaches Ezra Sutter, the stagecoach driver, told us about? Well, I reckon they attacked them wolf women. Forgive and forget don't enter into a Mescalero's thinking."

"You think they were getting even for the eight young Apaches the She Wolves killed and scalped?" Dan said.

"Depend on it," Ephraim said.

"Then who won the fight?" Frank said.

"That I don't know, but I guarantee the Apaches lost at least half their warriors in a scrape that sure didn't last long," Ephraim said. "Perfesser Claringbold said no longer than five minutes from first gunshot to the last."

"If it was Apaches, I wonder if Maria von Erbach is still alive," Dan said.

"If the Apaches won and she's still alive, I reckon about now she's wishing she wasn't," Ephraim said.

"Do you think the Indians are still there?" Dan said.

"I don't know, they might all be dead," Ephraim said. "But I don't much want to go take a looksee."

Dave Anderson said, "The war chief that spoke to us . . . what's his name?"

"Delshay," Ephraim said. "It means warrior and chief in Apache."

"He made peace with us," the gambler said.

"For how long?" Ephraim said. "Time means different things to a white man and an Apache."

"We don't know for how long," Dan said. "Let's hope it's for a considerable while."

Frank said, "And now I have to ask the question . . . who has the bank's money, including my five thousand dollars?"

"Could be some Apache took it to light the fire in his wikiup," Ephraim said. He cackled and added, "And use the coin to decorate his wife's dresses."

"That ain't funny, Ephraim," Dan said.

"Then where is the money, Deputy?" Ephraim said. "It could be anywhere, north, east, south, or west. Take your pick and give this here posse a direction."

"It may still be with the She Wolves," Dan said.

"If they won the fight that is," Frank said.

Dan tossed away the dregs of his coffee and said, "Damn it, I'm not waiting around here guessing any longer. I'm taking a look at the women's camp."

"I'll come with you, Deputy," Ephraim said. "Keep you out of mischief and see you don't get tied to any more wagon wheels."

Dan said, "Frank, Dave, and Sly, if I haven't returned by sundown you know what to do."

Frank nodded. "Hightail it for Broken Back."

"You got your saddle on the right hoss, Frank," Dan said. "Keep going and don't ever look back."

Frank smiled. "I'll keep that in mind." He unbuckled his gunbelt and handed it to Dan. "Here, you might need this," he said. "By this time some She Wolf or young Apache buck is wearing yours."

"I appreciate this, Frank," Dan said as he strapped the ivory-handled revolver around his waist. "I'll take good care of it."

"Think nothing of it," Frank said. He stuck out his hand. "Seems that I'm forever saying this, but good luck, Deputy Caine."

Chapter Forty-five

On their way east toward the She Wolf encampment, Dan Caine and Ephraim Traynor stopped to speak to the three scientists and told them to rejoin the others.

"What was all the shooting about?" Professor Claringbold said. He and his colleagues stood in the trench they'd dug, dwarfed by the huge dinosaur skeleton they'd uncovered.

"I don't know for sure, but we think the She Wolves and the Apaches got into a fight," Dan said. "Ephraim and me are going to find out what happened."

"It was a short fight, no more than five minutes," Claringbold said. "I'm not a soldier, but if I remember my history correctly that usually means someone scored a one-sided victory."

"The question is who?" Dan said.

"My money is on the Apaches," Ephraim said. "There surely was a whole passel of them."

Claringbold shook a sorrowful head. "This is most distressing," he said. "There may be wounded."

"If Apaches were involved, that ain't likely, your worship," Ephraim said.

Claringbold said, "Before I became a paleontologist, I was a qualified surgeon. Perhaps I should accompany you, Deputy Caine, though without my bag there's little I can do."

"Professor, Ephraim and I might well get into a fight ourselves," Dan said. "The best thing you can do is go join the others."

Claringbold nodded. "Yes, perhaps you're right. Professor McPhee, Dr. Goncharov, do you agree?"

Both men agreed, but McPhee said, "Ach, I fear that when all this is over, our skeleton will be lost."

"Don't you perfessorships worry none," Ephraim said. "I've got a map in my head, and X marks the spot. I'll find the big bird for you."

"It's not a bird, it's a dinosaur, Mr. Traynor," Claringbold said. "We must try to remember that and make sure we don't repeat it among other paleontologists."

"Now I got that warning stuck in my brain, Perfesser," Ephraim said. "I won't say big bird again."

"See that you don't," Claringbold said. "Now good luck to both of you."

Under a deep blue sky where sharp-eyed buzzards flew in lazy circles, Dan Caine and Ephraim Traynor rode into a charnel house made terrible by death and destruction.

Dan looked around at the sprawled, bloody bodies of the dead She Wolves, most of them clustered in one spot where they fell. Shocked beyond measure, he said, his voice strangely flat, "Tell me about it, Ephraim."

The old mountain man dismounted and scouted the ground. He picked up an arrow, studied it and said, "It's

Jicarilla. It was Apaches all right. I reckon they hit the women by surprise about sunup and overran them. Over there where all the bodies are is where the She Wolves tried to make a stand and were wiped out. The Apaches hit them gals hard and fast and then it was all over."

Dan looked around him. All the tents had been pulled down and dragged away and the ground was littered with the debris of the looting after the battle, female clothing, small bottles, hairbrushes, shoes, and bits and pieces of dropped food supplies. He kneed his horse forward and rode at a walk among the dead, searching each gray face for the scarlet mark of the wolf. He did not find Maria von Erbach.

Dan rode to where the large tent had stood and into more horror.

The bent body of a man was still staked to the ground by a chain. He was on his hands and knees, ragged, over-grown with white hair and his fingers and toes looked like claws. Dan realized that this poor creature had to be Luca Moretti's lycanthrope. He swung out of the saddle and approached the dead man then almost jumped three feet in the air when the body moved. But it only toppled onto its side, perhaps from the vibration of Dan's booted steps. It was then he saw the man's face. His blue eyes were wide open, his mouth under the beard fixed in a snarl, and there was a neat bullet hole in the middle of his forehead.

"Some Apache done for him," Ephraim said. He stood beside Dan and looked down at the contorted face of the dead man. "Look at the burned black powder around the wound. He was shot at close range, the muzzle of the gun touching his skin."

"Strange that," Dan said.

"Strange for an Apache," Ephraim said. "They usually ain't that pernickety about where they place the bullet."

"Another body over there by the trees," Dan said, indicating with his chin. "She must've been making a run for it."

"On a horse, looks like," Ephraim said. "There's only one set of tracks over there."

Dan looked closer at the dead girl. She'd been short and slender and had been terrified, running for her life. Too bad. She'd almost made it.

Then Ephraim called him over and everything changed.

"Two sets of tracks here, Deputy," the old scout said. "And I can't figure them. And the girl was shot in the top of her head and I can't figure that either." He held up a slender chain with a silver wolf head pendant. "This was around her neck, something the Indians missed. I'll hold on to it."

"She was running from an Apache and he caught up with her and shot her," Dan said. "That's one way of reading it."

"Is there another?" Ephraim said. "That's the story the tracks tell."

"Maria von Erbach's body is not here, and apparently the Apaches took no prisoners," Dan said. "I think the woman had it all planned out to abscond with the money, but the Apaches spoiled it for her. You savvy so far, Ephraim?"

"Yeah, go ahead," the old scout said. "I get your drift."

"The She Wolves plan was to attack us at first light, but suppose Maria held back, maybe pleading sickness, leaving her free to take the money. I reckon she hung the money sacks on her horse and then led it to the big tent. Then the Apaches attacked and she had to hurry. She shot her father and mounted her horse and headed for the trees. The girl saw Maria and begged to go with her and the woman shot her."

"It's mighty thin, but I can comprende. What I don't understand is why would she shoot her own pa?" Ephraim said.

"Look at him," Dan said. "I think he was chained up and abused for years, here and at Black Mesa, because for some reason his daughter hated him."

"So you think she took the money and fogged it for . . . where? Black Mesa? The Indian Territory? Fort Worth?" Ephraim smiled. "Here we go again."

"I don't know where she's headed, and Ephraim, that's why you're going to scout the trees like you never scouted before," Dan said.

"Then I'll make a start," Ephraim said. "I've got to get away from this place. One time I seen a Crow village that had been attacked by Cheyenne, bodies everywhere, men, women, and children, but even that wasn't a patch on this."

It was Dan Caine, not Ephraim Traynor, who found the evidence that directly linked Maria von Erbach to the killing of the young She Wolf.

He'd leaned over in the saddle, searching for tracks, when the sun filtering through pines glinted on something that looked like metal. Dan swung out of the saddle and parted the grass, uncovering a broken necklace identical to the one the dead girl wore. He examined the wolf head pendant, about the size of a silver dollar, turned it over and read *Love Jane* engraved on the back.

Dan called Ephraim over and asked to see the necklace he'd taken off the body of the dead girl. On the rear of the pendant the words *Love Maria* were crudely engraved, probably the work of an itinerant tinker.

"The girl must've broken the chain when she reached out to Maria von Erbach for help," Dan said.

"And all she got was a bullet," Ephraim said. The old man sighed. "Ah well, the woman left tracks aplenty, all headed due north."

"Then she's making for the Oklahoma Territory border," Dan said. "Ephraim, Maria von Erbach isn't far ahead of us and we can catch her."

"Then what are we waiting for? Let's go," Ephraim said.

Chapter Forty-six

As she had half-a-dozen times before, Maria von Erbach turned in the saddle to scan her back trail. It was unlikely she was being followed, but this was not a time to take chances. And as had happened before, she saw no one.

Maria had no intention of crossing the Red River into the high country of the Oklahoma Territory and heading for Black Mesa. That part of her life was over, the thirty thousand dollars convincing her that there was a better way. She'd very quickly abandoned her dream of an all-female city . . . anyway, its future leading citizens had been killed by Apaches, and it would take years to recruit more.

Booming Fort Worth was a three-or-four-day ride to the southeast across the rolling plains country, a good place to plan her future travels. Nobody knew her there, and she could lose herself in the crowds. But not the way she was dressed. She still wore the She Wolf short tunic, scarlet battle corset, and knee-high moccasins, and a change of clothing was a must. She studied the terrain in front of her. This region of the plains was said to be good plow country, and there must be a farmhouse somewhere. All she had to do was find it.

As it happened, after two hours of riding, Maria didn't find a farm, but a sod cabin with a timber addition, built on top of a flat, limestone shelf near an extensive stand of post oak and mesquite. The Stainless Banner of the Confederacy hung listlessly from a pole attached to a gable end of the building and there was a small corral near the trees. Smoke rose straight as a string from a brick chimney that, like the cabin, was covered in white stucco. There was a well out front, but no plowed land and Maria figured the bleak, rundown place must cater to occasional travelers and outlaws on the scout. Did a woman live there? It didn't look like it.

She rode up a section of the rock shelf that seemed to have been broken down by a sledgehammer and drew rein in front of the cabin.

A moment later the roughly sawn timber door opened and a man stepped out, a scattergun in his hands. He was tall and stringy, about forty years old, dressed in black pants and vest and a collarless gray shirt that had once been white. The man's name was Tag Dobbs and before he spoke, he summed up Maria von Erbach. Beautiful woman, naked thighs, corset, mark on her cheek. He wanted her. Big sorrel gelding he could never afford. He wanted the horse. A revolver and what looked to be a Yellow Boy rifle. He wanted them both. And he wanted to see what was in the white sacks that hung from the woman's saddle horn.

"What can I do fer ye?" Dobbs said, lowering his gun. "Are ye sharp set?"

"Does a woman live in this cabin?" Maria said. She instantly despised the man, an ill-bred and dirty peasant.

"Sure there's a woman," Dobbs said. "My wife Dora." He smiled, showing few teeth and those black. "I rent her out by the half-hour, but you wouldn't be interested in that."

"I'm hungry," Maria said.

Dobbs smiled again. "Then come on in. We got salt pork in the pan and sourdough bread to go along with it. Whiskey too, lady, if ye'd care for a taste."

"I'll water my horse first," Maria said.

"Let me help," Dobbs said. "The well's deep and it can be tricky." He leaned his shotgun against the cabin wall as Maria dismounted and the man's greedy eyes nearly popped out of his head. He wanted this woman, more than he'd ever wanted anything in his life.

Dobbs untied a rope from an iron ring hammered into the well's waist-high brick wall and dropped the metal bucket down the shaft. It was a long time before Maria heard a faint splash.

After a while the man hauled up the full bucket, laid it on the wall, and tied the rope to the ring again. "I haven't lost a rope yet," he said.

"Good for you," Maria said.

"Come on into the house," Dobbs said. "My wife will put food on the table."

Maria followed the man inside, bringing the money sacks with her. She stepped into a cramped, smoky cabin, the slightly slanted limestone shelf its only flooring. Two chairs stood in front of the stone fireplace that took up most of the room consisting of a table and two more chairs, an oil lamp, a chest, and a shelf to hold dishes. Another shelf over the fireplace was piled end to end with pots and pans. A single window with four greased paper panes filled the room with a strange, pasty glow. There were no photos of dead or distant kinfolk, no books, not even a Bible, nothing to cast light on the lives of the people who lived there. A half-open door led to the timber extension where a pole bed covered with a patchwork quilt was just visible.

Maria took this in at a single glance, noting that no firearm was visible. Unless Dobbs kept a rifle or pistol in his bedroom, the scattergun was his only weapon. It was something to know.

"Sit ye down at the table . . . I didn't get your name," Dobbs said.

"That's because I didn't give it. It's Maria."

"Then sit, Maria," Dobbs said. "Let me take your gun. You'll be more comfortable."

The woman unbuckled her cartridge belt and removed it from her waist. She hung the ungainly Enfield on the back of the chair, the handle toward her, and sat, the white sacks at her feet.

"You can trust me and my wife, lady," the man said. "We'll do you no harm."

"We'll see," Maria said.

"I'll bring you food and drink," Dora Dobbs said, after leaving a knife, fork, and tin cup on the table. She was a tall, joyless woman, thin. Her bloodshot eyes looked like rusty iron, and she had a little, steel trap of a mouth that years before had lost the habit of smiling.

Maria von Erbach's only interest in the woman was the size of her dresses. They would be tight around the bust and hips but were close enough.

Dora brought a plate filled with fried salt pork and

slices of bread. She poured coffee from a sooty pot into the tin cup.

"Eat hearty," Tag Dobbs said, smiling.

As he watched the woman eat, Dobbs's mind was working. If she'd been homely, he probably would've strangled her and took her horse and whatever she had. But, despite the scarlet stain on her cheek this woman was exquisite, and he wanted to keep her to himself until he tired of her, and that might be a long time. If he could disable her long enough to tie her up, she might come around to his way of thinking pretty damn quick.

Dora, who over the years had indulged her husband's fantasies when it came to women, could hit her over the head with a heavy pan and put her down and out long enough to truss her up real good.

Tag Dobbs smiled. It might take time, but he'd break this woman like he'd done others . . . break her with patience and a dog whip.

Maria von Erbach, her instinct for danger honed to a fine edge, saw it. She saw the glance exchanged by Dobbs and his woman and then the barely perceptible nod of the man's head.

As Dora stepped to the fireplace, took a heavy cast iron frypan from the shelf, and then edged her way behind Maria, Tag thought to distract her. "The meal was to your liking?" he said.

Those were the last words Dobbs ever said, going out like a third-rate head waiter.

Maria planted her feet on the limestone floor and then pushed back with all the strength of her legs, a move that was fast and violent. The chair crashed into Dora who staggered back and slammed into the section of wall to the left of the fireplace.

His face registering his alarm, Tag Dobbs sprang to his feet, his eyes frantically searching for his shotgun. He needn't have bothered. Maria pulled the Enfield from its holster and pumped two silver bullets into the man's chest. As he sank to the ground, Dobbs's eyes were unbelieving. This was not how it was supposed to end. He'd wanted a beautiful and helpless woman in his bed . . . not his death. The man died with his face on the limestone, his life blood seeping out from under him, scarlet, like the stain on Maria von Erbach's cheek.

Maria didn't wait to see Dobbs fall. She spun around and saw Dora come at her, the woman's face made ugly by hate, the heavy pan raised.

She fired, one shot into Dora's head, sparing the dress. She could hardly wear a garment with a bullet hole. Quickly, before it got blood stained, Maria stripped off the dead woman's clothes, a task she found distasteful. Dora's black dress was sweat stained and smelled and her undergarments were gray, not white.

She couldn't wear those dirty rags.

Disappointed, Maria tried the bedroom. Maybe there was something better in there. A bed and a mirrored dresser, that was all. But then she noticed the small steamer trunk under the bed. She pulled it out, dumped it on the patchwork quilt, and opened the lid . . . and found treasure. In it was a folded buttercup yellow dress, cotton, that looked as though it had never been worn. Maria took it from the trunk and held it against her. The dress combined femininity and functionality and had a fitted bodice with a square neckline at front and back, a three gored, floor length skirt with a half skirt at the back that suggested a bustle. There were also bloomers and petticoats that were as white as the day they were made. She quickly stripped off her tunic, reluctantly abandoning her comfortable cotton underpants, swapping them for roomy bloomers and a cascade of petticoats, one on top of the other. To Maria's surprise the dress fit fairly well, presentable, or so the mirror told her, but a pair of ankle boots in the trunk were too small and she was stuck with her moccasins for a while longer. There was a hat in the trunk, a straw confection with paper flowers on the brim, that she ignored. She'd wear the poke bonnet that hung on a nail inside the cabin door. It would protect her from the sun and cover the telltale birthmark on her cheek. Not that she expected to be followed. It would take an expert Indian scout to pick up her trail.

Maria von Erbach looked at herself in the mirror. She would do. Dora Dobbs must have kept the dress for a special occasion that never came. Well, too bad for her.

Her holstered, unhandy Enfield, with just one cartridge in the chamber, she left on the bed. If she needed protection, the .44 Yellow Boy with its fifteen-round magazine was more than enough.

It was a three-day ride to Fort Worth and she'd need some food. She found a large, clean bandana on a shelf and used it to wrap the rest of the sourdough bread, a few slices of cooked salt pork, and four sugar cookies. It wasn't much but it would suffice until she reached her destination.

Two bodies on the floor took up a lot of space in a small cabin, but they might as well have been dead cockroaches for all the attention Maria paid to them. She stepped over the sprawled corpses as she collected the money sacks and walked outside into bright sunlight.

Maria von Erbach filled her canteen at the well, draped the canvas bags over the saddle horn, and then hiked up her dress and mounted the sorrel. She kneed the horse forward in the direction of Fort Worth and didn't look back.

Chapter Forty-seven

Ephraim Traynor stepped into the sod cabin's attached bedroom and picked up the Enfield revolver from the bed. "She left this, Deputy," he said.

"That was Moretti's gun," Dan said. "I guess she'd no more cartridges for it. She's probably got a rifle."

They stepped back into the cabin.

"Why did she shoot them?" Ephraim said. "That doesn't make any sense to me."

Dan Caine picked up Maria's discarded tunic. "Well, she needed to change clothes and was shy," he said.

"Now you're joshing me," Ephraim said.

Dan smiled. "Yes I am. I don't know why she shot them."

"Maybe they knew she was carrying a heap of money and tried to rob her," Ephraim said.

"That's the likeliest reason for gunning them," Dan said.

Ephraim kneeled and placed his hand on the wood ashes in the fireplace. "Still warm," he said.

"Be dark soon," Dan said. Then, after a pause, "What are we going to do, Ephraim?"

"About what?"

"Do we just leave them lying there?"

"Or bury them?"

"Yes. Do we take the time to bury them and let Maria von Erbach open up even more git between us and her?"

"Deputy, you're the boss of this here outfit. It's your decision to make," Ephraim said.

"The decent thing is to bury them," Dan said.

"The Christian thing is to bury them," Ephraim said. "Be dark soon anyway. The wolf lady will need to stop for the night."

"All right, let's find a shovel," Dan said.

Dan Caine and Ephraim laid both bodies in one hole, fairly shallow because of bedrock, but it made Dora and Tag Dobbs closer than they'd ever been in life.

Both men stood in silence, lit by the oil lamp as darkness surrounded them, staring at the grave. And then Ephraim's uncertain singing voice wavered out . . .

Shall we gather at the river?
Where bright angel feet have trod

Dan's deep baritone joined in the singing...

With its crystal tide forever
Flowing by the throne of God.

Together he and Ephraim struggled through as much of the hymn as they could remember and when they were finished, the old scout said, "I don't know who they were or what they were, but we done them two proud."

"Seems like," Dan said. He picked up the lamp. "Let's go inside and see if there's any grub."

That night, Dan Caine and Ephraim Traynor dined on fried bacon, and thanks to the old scout finding flour, lard, and buttermilk, a very tasty pan bread. They shunned the blood-stained cabin and slept outside in their blankets and were awake at first light.

"I've sacked up some supplies," Ephraim said. "And I filled the canteens at the well."

"Do you think we can catch her before she reaches Fort Worth?" Dan said.

"If she slows up some," Ephraim said. "If she don't, we'll lose her."

"Maybe we can get close enough to run her," Dan said. "Tire her out."

"It could happen," Ephraim said. "But it ain't likely. Her horse is carrying a lot less weight than ours. In a pinch, she could outrun us all the way to the city."

"We'll never find her in Fort Worth," Dan said. "I hear it's a boom town and crowded with people, especially a district by the name of Hell's Half Acre where the saloons, dance halls, and brothels are located."

"The wolf lady will stay out of there," Ephraim said. "She'll look for something a little more genteel."

"Ephraim, Maria von Erbach ain't genteel," Dan said. "She's the woman who shot her own father, burned Luca

Moretti to death, shot that Jane girl and promised me I was destined for the stake and that she'd make sure I died slowly. And yesterday she shot two more people for a reason we don't know."

"And she stole our money," Ephraim said.

"Yeah, in addition to all that, she stole our money," Dan said. "That makes her a wanted outlaw in my book, and wanted outlaws go to ground in Hell's Half Acre."

"Deputy, I can track her there, just like I tracked her to here," Ephraim said. "I was a mountain man, I'm at my best in wild places and Fort Worth is a wild place."

"I hope you're right, Ephraim," Dan said. "But maybe it won't come to that. If we catch her, the game's over."

"For who?" Ephraim said. "The lady knows how to use a gun."

"I know. And that's why I don't plan on taking any chances with her," Dan said.

"You ever shot a woman?" Ephraim said, looking straight ahead at an endless prairie.

"Yes," Dan said. "I'll tell you the story someday. You?"

"Only once, by mistake."

"For God's sake, how do you shoot a woman by mistake?"

"It was up on the Platte in the summer of '59. I put lead shot from a fowling piece into the butt of a three-hundred-pound Arapaho woman who was stirring a cooking pot outside her tepee."

"Did you hurt her bad?" Dan said.

"Nah, a medicine man picked out the lead and she was fine. But I wasn't. That was one angry Arapaho and she hit me over the head with her ladle, laid me out cold for an hour."

"How did you manage to shoot the woman in the first place?" Dan said.

"I took a pot at a landing duck, missed, and hit the woman by mistake." Ephraim shrugged. "It happens."

"What happens? Missing a duck or shooting an Arapaho woman?" Dan Caine said.

Ephraim shook his head. "Deputy, it's a wonder to me that you've lived this long," he said. And Dan laughed.

Three long days in the saddle and Dan Caine and Ephraim Traynor never got so much as a glimpse of Maria von Erbach. By the time they rode through ranching country and Fort Worth came in sight they knew that the woman had by now lost herself in the city and may be impossible to find.

Chapter Forty-eight

At that time in the West, Fort Worth was the brawling, bawdy, and dangerous Gomorrah of Tarrant County, Texas. It was the city where the frontier began, a place where many a lively young blade had met his sudden demise by the gun, knife, garotte, sap, billy club, or bad whiskey and badder women. As Dan Caine and Ephraim Traynor would soon learn the hard way, the trouble was confined to the Third Ward, known as Hell's Half Acre, a crime-ridden, suppurating pit of perdition that infected the whole city like a cancer. It was the first stop for drovers coming up from the south on the old Chisholm Trail, attracted to its brothels, dance halls, opium dens, and a scattering of honest businesses that supplied the cowboy with all that was not sinful. The Acre's north-south thoroughfares were Main, Rusk, Calhoun, and Jones and its lower boundary ended at 15th Street. In between, gunmen, highway robbers, card sharps, whores, and goldbrick artists prospered mightily.

One local newspaper summed up Hell's Half Acre thusly, "It's a slow night which does not pan out a cutting or shooting scrape among the Acre's male denizens or a fatal morphine experiment by one of its frisky females."

And somewhere in this seething morass of violence and depravity was Maria von Erbach with thirty thousand dollars of stolen money.

As he and Ephraim Traynor rode down Main Street, Dan Caine had never seen the like, not in all his born days.

The street neatly bisected Hell's Half Acre, a bustling, noisy, smelly bedlam of rickety timber buildings, some of them three stories high, the upper reaches propped in place by slanted logs. Painted fronts advertised saloons, dance halls, and bawdy houses, but to his surprise Dan passed several thriving churches, grocery, clothing, jewelry, saddle, and candy stores and a couple of bakeries. The throngs of people he saw in the street seemed respectable enough, prim matrons with their broadcloth-clad spouses and young belles in giggling gaggles of two, three, or four wearing the latest Eastern fashions, tiny hats, bright red, yellow, and blue day dresses with enormous bustles and high-heeled ankle boots. Vendors shouted their wares from the boardwalks, and horse-drawn drays with massive, steel-rimmed wheels made their way through the throngs, their drivers cursing one another for rogues. Bakers with tin trays of bread and pastries on their heads rubbed shoulders with butchers wearing bloodstained aprons, and the din was constant and unbelievable. Dan heard a dozen different tongues—men, women, and children babbling in languages he didn't understand.

Ephraim leaned from the saddle and yelled in Dan's ear, "Livery stable up ahead. We can put up the horses."

Dan shouted back, "Do you have any money?"

"Two dollars," Ephraim yelled.

"That's not gonna go very far in this town," Dan shouted back.

"No siree," the old scout said.

The livery fronted Main Street but was just north of the Acre in a quieter part of town. The silence and coolness of the stable was a welcome relief from heat and noise.

The man in charge watched Dan and Ephraim lead in their horses and said, "Two bits a day for a stall. Two bits a day for hay. Two bits a day for oats. Take it or leave it."

"You're expensive, mister," Dan said. "Maybe I should take my business elsewhere."

"I don't own the place and I don't set the prices," the man said. "I was a drover once, went up the trail for the first time when I was fourteen and now after twenty years of punching, I'm about as stove-up, used-up, and stiffened-up as a man can be, and what I don't need right now is backtalk or sass. Do you want the stalls or don't you?"

Dan bowed to the inevitable and said, "Yeah, we want the stalls." He looked around. It seemed that almost all the stalls were in use. "Any horses come in real recent?" Dan said.

"How recent?" the livery man said.

"Maybe as recent as last night," Dan said.

"Not that I know of," the man said. He thought about it for a moment and then added, "No, I don't reckon so."

"How many liveries in Fort Worth?" Dan said.

"How many fingers you got?"

"Ten."

"Then there's your answer."

As Dan's heart sank to his boots, Ephraim said to the stableman, "What's your name, sonny?"

"I ain't afraid to put it out," the man said, immediately defensive.

"Of course, you ain't," Ephraim said. "Mine is Ephraim Traynor. I've had that name man and boy."

"Bill Lowery," the livery man said. "I'm from the Cow Bell Creek country in the Arizona Territory."

"Right pleased to meet you, Bill," Ephraim said.

The two shook hands and Lowery said, "When I first laid an eye on you, I saw the buckskin shirt and took you for an Indian. But then I saw that you're a white man."

"A white man through and through," Ephraim said. "I was a mountain man with Kit Carson and Joel Estes an' them, and then an army scout, and now I'm retired."

The two men shook hands again and Lowery, obviously impressed, said, "*Como esta,* Ephraim?"

"I'm doin' just fine and thank'ee for asking," Ephraim said. "Now, Bill, can you recommend a cheap hotel?"

"Real cheap," Dan said.

"Sorry, boys," Lowery said, friendlier now. "There ain't no such thing as a cheap hotel in Fort Worth, not even in the Acre."

"What's the Acre?" Dan said.

"Hell's Half Acre, the bad side of town," Lowery said. "You rode through the middle of it to get here. Some say it's the wickedest place on earth, but I don't know about that. Wait a minute, you could try Ma Tandy's boarding house up on Twelfth Street. I hear she's cheaper than most and keeps a clean place."

"How do we get there?" Dan said.

Lowery said, "Keep going north on Main and then make a right onto Twelfth. You'll pass the Golden Garter saloon, then a vacant lot, and the next two-story building is Ma's. You can't miss it."

"Much obliged, Bill," Ephraim said, and shook hands for a third time.

"Right nice feller," he said when he and Dan walked onto Main Street.

Chapter Forty-nine

Ma Tandy, a tall, broad shouldered woman still wearing black widow's weeds for a husband who died twenty years before, didn't like the look of Dan Caine and Ephraim Traynor, so she kept them on the front doorstep.

Dan was completely unaware that to civilized people he and Ephraim looked like tough, dangerous men, lean as cougars, uncurried, all the fat burned out of them by long riding and desperate encounters, watchful eyes and faces browned by sun and prairie winds.

"Fifty cents a day and that includes breakfast," Ma said. "Seventy-five cents if dinner is included. Pay for rooms in advance. No whores in the rooms. No spurs in bed. I do not accept drifters, saddle tramps, bunco artists, vagabonds, rogues, or scum. No gambling is allowed, and sleeping in the parlor is strictly prohibited. Dinner tonight is chicken and dumplings and will be served promptly at eight. Do you have any questions?"

"We'll take two rooms with breakfast," Ephraim said.

"Ephraim . . ." Dan sounded alarmed.

"Your friend looks as though you can't afford the rooms," Ma Tandy said.

"We can't," Dan said.

"Yes, we can," Ephraim said. He swept off his hat and made a low bow. "May I crave your indulgence, ma'am?" Without waiting for an answer, and showing considerable spryness, he sat on the doorstep, pulled off a boot, displaying a sock with a hole at the toe, and fished inside the scuffed footwear. He broke into a grin and his hand reappeared, a ten-dollar gold coin between his thumb and forefinger.

"I've been standing on this for nigh on three years," Ephraim said. "Been saving it for a rainy day. Well, this is a rainy day."

Ma's attitude changed immediately. "Well, do come in out of the heat," she said. "And I believe the coffee is on the boil, and I do have a suspicion that there are sugar cookies left from last night's dinner." She looked at Ephraim. "Put on your boot first."

Inside, the house was shadowed and gloomy with heavy mahogany furniture, dark drapes, and darker rugs. The top of the staircase opposite the door leading to the upper story vanished from sight, as though it had been swallowed by a dark fog. The place smelled of boiled cabbage, reminding Dan that every boarding house he'd ever been in smelled the same way.

"I'll show you your rooms first," Ma said.

She led the way to an upstairs corridor and opened adjoining doors, revealing rooms with a brass bed, a dresser and a table with a blue, ceramic pitcher and bowl, and a folded white towel. A worn rug covered part of the floor, and an oil lamp with a short wick that would smoke like a factory chimney stood on a bedside table.

Ma served coffee and cookies in the parlor, having first grabbed Ephraim's ten dollars, promising change when he left.

Dan took the opportunity to ask the woman where he could find the local lawman.

"We have an acting city marshal until the job is filled," Ma said. "His name, so he says, is Bully Boyd. I hear he's one for the ladies and fond of the bottle."

"Where is his office?" Dan said.

"He doesn't use an office. Most days you can find him holding court in the White Elephant saloon. He's a friend of Luke Short, the gambler who runs the place. I will say this"—Ma poured more coffee into Dan's cup—"Short is just a little man but he keeps good order and they say the White Elephant is the best and most respectable saloon in town. It only caters to men, and I'm told it's also the most expensive."

"And where is it?" Dan said.

"It's on the three hundred block of Main, just north of here. You can't miss it." A pause, then, "You have business with the marshal, Mr. Caine?"

"Indeed, I do, ma'am," Dan said. "I'm a deputy sheriff of a town west of here, and I'm in pursuit of a criminal with thirty thousand dollars of our bank's money."

"Well land's sake!" Ma said, her hands fluttering like a pair of white doves. "And here all the time I took you and your friend for a couple of outlaws on the scout. Now I'll sleep easier tonight."

"Fear not, you're safe with us, dear lady," Ephraim said.

"Another cookie, Mr. Traynor?" Ma Tandy said, smiling.

"Perhaps some other time, ma'am," Dan said, rising to

his feet. "I believe we'll go talk with the marshal and see if he can offer us any help."

"I'm sure he can," Ma said. "Well, I'm not sure, but you being a law officer and all . . ."

Dan smiled. "I'm sure he'll help."

Chapter Fifty

The Excelsior was the best hotel in Fort Worth, and Maria von Erbach took full advantage of it. As she reclined in a luxurious brass bathtub in her suite drinking champagne, salesladies from the city's finest female clothing businesses came to her. A pretty model strutted her stuff in a succession of dresses, hats, and underwear while the eager saleslady stood to one side and beamed.

After an hour, Maria rose from the tub and the hotel maid immediately wrapped her in an oversized towel. As other maids carried the tub away, she sat in an easy chair beside the fireplace and gestured toward the pile of clothing. "Then it's the dark green traveling dress and matching cloak and the red and the blue gowns. Underwear we've already discussed and the hats."

"Does madame wish both pairs of ankle boots and the parasol?" the saleslady said.

"Yes, both pairs and the parasol," Maria said. "Oh yes, and the bath robe with the red roses"—she turned to the maid—"that I need right now. And the silk dressing gown." She slipped into the robe. "The rest you can take back."

Maria paid for the clothing with money she removed from a drawer in the large vanity and when the saleslady and her model were gone, she said to the maid she considered doltish and unpretty, "Carry these old clothes away and burn them."

The maid gathered up the Dora Dobbs dress and underwear, gave the moccasins and poke bonnet a puzzled look, and then curtsied and left.

There was a scratch at the door and Maria bade the visitor enter. He was a short, plump man with slicked down black hair, a perfumier who called himself Francois and flounced. At a time when most American women wore lavender oil, complex French perfumes were not cheap in the West, but Maria bought several tiny bottles and paid Francois from her cash drawer.

Hairbrushes, combs and pins, face powder, lip color and rouge, at that time considered very daring, and eye makeup had all been bought earlier as had a large clothes trunk and roomy carpetbag.

Maria now pressed the button of the new-fangled annunciator electric bell call system that buzzed the front desk. She still had an important purchase to make.

The hotel manager knocked on the door, and the woman let him in. The man was young and Maria's spectacular beauty obviously made him nervous. Even the strange birthmark on her cheek did not detract from her raw, latent sexuality. "What can I do for madame?" the manager said. He tried his best to keep his eyes averted from the woman's breasts swelling under the thin silk of her dressing gown.

And Maria told him what she needed.

"That is very unusual, madame," the manager said.

"I know it's a most singular request," the woman said. "But it is a matter of the greatest moment that I do not continue on my Western travels unarmed. I'm but a frail and fearful woman and may fall prey to unscrupulous men who may think to do me harm."

Maria had sold her horse and the Yellow Boy at a bargain price to an army officer who'd happened to be in the livery stable when she rode in the day before. Now she badly needed a gun, something small and handy that would fit in her purse.

"I need a small revolver that will fit in my purse," Maria said. "Surely there's a gun store that could supply such a weapon."

"Ebner Braunstein has a gun and rod shop just a block away," the manager said. "I can send a boy to fetch him, but whether or not he'll come, I do not know. Ebner can be testy."

"Do try," Maria said. "I do not wish to frequent such a store myself. It would not be ladylike."

"Of course, I understand," the manager said. "If not Ebner, I can probably find someone else anxious to show his wares."

To Maria von Erbach's surprise the manager returned very quickly with a small, gray haired man in tow. "This is Mr. Ebner Braunstein, the gunsmith," the manager said pompously, as though he was introducing royalty. "He will take care of all your firearm needs."

Maria smiled. "Thank you, now you may go. Mr. Braunstein, please be seated."

After the manager left, the woman said, disappointed, "Is that all you've got, one pistol?"

"Dear lady, I've brought all you'll need," Braunstein said. He opened the wooden box on his lap and produced a small, nickel plated revolver. "This is a J.H. Marlin five shot, eighteen-seventy-two model pocket or purse pistol in thirty caliber with a custom two-inch barrel and an ivory handle. It's a tip-up revolver and I worked on the trigger myself. It's as smooth as silk and breaks like a glass rod." He reached into his pocket and brought out a small, rectangular carboard box. "And I have cartridges for the weapon."

"It's small," Maria said. "But it seems to be just what I need."

"Indeed, it is, ma'am," Braunstein said. "If someone gets on his high horse with you, this will knock him off it."

"Tip-up? I'm not familiar with that. Show me how it works," the woman said.

The little gunsmith showed Maria how to load the revolver and had her try the trigger.

"Excellent, Mr. Braunstein," she said. "I'm sure this will serve me well. How much do I owe you?"

"Because of the custom barrel and ivory, the revolver is eight dollars," the man said. "The box of twenty cartridges will be another dollar."

Maria went to her money drawer. "There's ten dollars, Mr. Braunstein. A little extra for your trouble."

The man bowed and said his thanks, and said, "I can't quite place your accent, ma'am."

Maria smiled. "I'm German, from Bavaria. And judging by your name, you must be of the Jewish faith."

"Yes, I am," Braunstein said.

"Then you must visit my beautiful Bavaria some time," Maria said. "You'll be made welcome. We're very fond of Jews in Germany."

"Perhaps I will someday," Ebner Braunstein said.

He bowed and stepped to the door.

"Wait," Maria said. "You may keep the box. I don't need it."

Maria von Erbach buzzed the hotel's front desk one last time that day and asked the manager for a train schedule. She discovered that the following afternoon there was a Fort Worth and Denver Railway Company cannonball to the New Mexico border and then a change for Denver. From there she could join the transcontinental railroad at Cheyenne, a first step on her journey to Europe.

The train would leave left the Fort Worth Union Depot at eleven o'clock sharp, and Maria planned to be on it . . . with a gun in her purse and a small fortune in her luggage.

Chapter Fifty-one

The White Elephant was a block north of Hell's Half Acre and the gentlemen-only saloon had more than its share of gunfights and shady deals. Yet, by the time Luke Short took over as manager it had already staked its claim to fame by supplying more quality gambling, top-shelf liquors, and gourmet food than any other establishment in the Southwest. The gambling lawman Bat Masterson gave it respectful mention in his 1907 recollections as did Wyatt Earp who praised the first-class food, fine whiskies, and the gaming tables that attracted big-time gamblers and the high rollers of Fort Worth society. The White Elephant employed a staff of twenty-five to thirty men to staff its around-the-clock operation and these included dealers, porters, and shoeshine boys. But the princes of the staff were the bartenders, skilled mixologists who could, in the words of the *Fort Worth Mail* prepare the recently invented cocktail on demand. "There is no drink known to modern or ancient times they cannot concoct with all the latest improvements."

Dan Caine approached one of these men, a magnificent creature in a brocaded vest, cravat with diamond stickpin, pomaded hair slicked down and neatly parted in the middle and enquired of the whereabouts of town Marshal Bully Boyd.

Not every high roller in Fort Worth wore broadcloth and snow-white linen, yet the bartender seemed willing to take Dan at face value despite his battered hat, slightly ragged shirt, scuffed boots, untrimmed mustache, and unshaven chin. And he didn't even raise an eyebrow at Ephraim Traynor's buckskin shirt and feathered hat, a man who looked more Indian than white.

"And you are?" the man asked.

"Name's Dan Caine. I'm the deputy sheriff of Broken Back, a town west of here."

The mixologist nodded. "Marshal Boyd is in the dining room where he's lunching with Mr. Short, our manager. Deputy, I'd advise you and your friend to leave your sidearms behind the bar and pick them up on your way out. If Marshal Boyd and Mr. Short see armed men approaching them . . . well, let's just say that their reactions could be quite unpredictable."

"That makes sense," Dan said. He unbuckled his gunbelt and passed it to the bartender and Ephraim did the same. To the mixologist, the old scout said, "Nice place you got here, sonny."

"Thank you, sir," the man said. "I'll pass that on to Mr. Short. The dining room is the door to your right."

Dan and Ephraim stepped into the opulent, mirrored dining room, walking on a thick carpet that absorbed all sound. It was early in the day, and the sporting crowd were still abed and would not stir until sundown. Only two tables were occupied, one by a trio of elderly men dressed in broadcloth, the other by two other men, one big-bellied and sprawling, the other small and neat with careful eyes.

When Dan and Ephraim stopped a respectable distance from the table, the small man slipped his gun hand under his well-tailored gray coat and without smiling said, "What can I do for you boys?"

"Name's Dan Caine, I'm a deputy sheriff here to speak to Marshal Boyd. This here is Ephraim Traynor, a member of my posse."

"When we had a posse," Ephraim said.

The big-bellied man, he had a heavy-featured face with a network of broken veins from alcohol and the harsh downstroke of the razor, said, "I'm Marshal Boyd. Where are you a deputy sheriff, Mr. Caine?"

"A town called Broken Back, a long way west of here," Dan said.

"Never heard of it," Boyd said. "How come you're so far off your home range, Deputy?"

"I'm here to recover thirty thousand dollars robbed from the bank in Broken Back," Dan said. "I believe the money is now in the possession of a woman named Maria von Erbach and that she's here in Fort Worth."

"And you want me to help look for her. Is that it?" Boyd said.

"Yes. She has a red birthmark shaped like a wolf's head on her right cheek and shouldn't be too hard to find," Dan said.

"So how come you haven't found her then?" the marshal said.

Luke Short smiled. "Good question, Bully."

"We just got in this morning and have had no time to look," Dan said. "My search begins here."

"At the White Elephant?" Short said. He smiled again. "I haven't seen her. Women, even a woman with thirty thousand dollars, aren't allowed in here."

"It's the marshal I came to see," Dan said.

"And you'll have my complete cooperation, Deputy," Boyd said. "I have spies everywhere in this town and if . . . what's her name again?"

"Maria von Erbach," Dan said.

"Well, if Maria von Erbach is in Fort Worth, I'll find her," the marshal said.

He called out to a passing waiter, "Bob, another gin sling."

"Coming right up, Marshal," the man said.

Boyd looked up at Dan and said, "Was there something else, Deputy?"

"No. That was all," Dan said.

"Well, keep in touch," Bully Boyd said.

Chapter Fifty-two

When Dan Caine and Ephraim Traynor walked into Main Street after picking up their guns from the White Elephant bartender, they agreed that Marshal Bully Boyd wasn't going to be much help.

"Seems to me he never leaves that chair," Ephraim said. "And what's a gin sling?"

Dan said, "I don't know, some kind of fancy drink, I suppose." He was silent, thinking, and then said, "If Maria von Erbach suspicioned that she might have been followed, she'd want a place to hide out for a spell."

"And that place is Hell's Half Acre," Ephraim said. "She'd lie low and blend into the crowds."

"Right. And that's the place we should go look for her," Dan said.

"Deputy, when we find her, are you going to arrest her or shoot her?" Ephraim said.

As they walked toward the Acre, Dan said, "I just don't see myself pulling the trigger on the woman. Damn it, Ephraim, it just ain't natural, like gunning your ma."

"Truer words was never spoke," Ephraim said. "When we find the wolf woman, we'll put the manacles on her."

"We don't have manacles," Dan said.

"Then we'll get some from Marshal Boyd," Ephraim said.

Dan smiled. "I don't reckon that Bully Boyd has seen a manacle in his life."

They stayed on Main, and when they reached Thirteenth Street, they were in the beating heart of the Acre. It was early and the saloons and dance halls were quiet, waiting for evening and the sporting fraternity. No one took any notice of Dan and Ephraim as they made their way along the boardwalk, passing punchers in big hats, sallow gamblers looking for an early game, shifty-eyed men on the make, and a few prosperous businessmen in broadcloth. The usual flotsam and jetsam of the frontier, hollow-eyed men who did not fit into any category, ignored the expensive girls in candy-cane dresses who stood on the balconies above the saloons and dance halls urging passersby to come inside for a heck of a good time. Their business was with those whores past their prime, their naked shoulders scarred from bite wounds, who did their business transactions in the street.

A dull roar of a thousand voices filled the Acre from dusk until dawn. It was a bustling, hustling annex of hades, bursting at the seams, a place where sin came easy but never cheap.

Dan's destination was the National Hotel, its huge painted sign hanging above the door visible at a distance. He and Ephraim passed a grocery store, a variety store, a vacant lot, and then a millinery shop and finally reached the hotel . . .

. . . and that's when the trouble began.

Dan and Ephraim were about to enter the hotel when

its door burst open and a half-naked woman ran out screaming, "He's going to kill me! He's going to kill me."

Such goings on were routine in the Acre and passersby hardly gave the woman a second glance, especially when she was so obviously a whore having a violent disagreement with her pimp.

A man charged through the door after the woman, grabbed her by the arm and slapped her face, back and forth, each blow sounding like the crack of a whip. The man was tall, black-bearded, well over six feet, big meaty shoulders and thick arms bulging under his beautifully tailored broadcloth suit coat.

"You try to shortchange me." SLAP! "You cheap whore." SLAP! "I'll teach you a lesson." SLAP! "You . . ."

It was more than Ephraim Traynor could stand. "Here, that won't do!" he yelled.

He stepped in front of the man, measured the distance to his bearded chin, and threw a roundhouse right. The punch would've dropped a lesser man, but it hardly made the big pimp blink. But it did make him angry, angry as hell, ready to burn some powder.

"Damn you, pops," the big man gritted through clenched teeth. "I'm gonna perforate your hide."

"No!" a woman in the gathering crowd shrieked.

But the gunfighting pimp made his play. His hand dropped to the pearl-handled Colt tucked into his waistband and he'd almost hauled out the revolver before a bullet crashed into his chest and cut his suspenders. The man fell flat on his back and then raised his head in disbelief . . . and saw Dan Caine standing there, the gun in his hand trickling smoke. "But . . . but . . ." the pimp said and then all the life in him fled, and he knew no more.

Dan stepped to the dead man. The pimp wore a ruby stick pin in his cravat, matching the blood that pooled under him, and a diamond ring on the little finger of his left hand.

"Jack! Oh, Jack, they've killed you!" the beaten woman cried out in great distress. She threw herself on top of her pimp's body, covered his face and neck with kisses. She took his left hand and pressed it to her lips. "Jack," she sobbed, "wait for me in heaven where all sorrows cease."

A man who looked like a desk clerk came out of the hotel and pulled the woman off the dead man. "Easy, Maggie," he said. "Stay here until the marshal arrives."

The woman nodded and said nothing.

When Dan looked at the dead man again, the ruby stickpin was gone, as was the diamond ring from his finger.

Dan said to the woman named Maggie, "You took your back wages, huh?"

"You guessed it, cowboy," the woman said. There were angry red welts all over her face and one eye was bruised. She opened her mouth and the ring fell out into her open hand. "Times are hard all over," she said.

"What was his name?" Dan said.

"Jack Winter." She stared hard at the young man. "You didn't give him an even chance."

"And he gave me no choice," Dan said. "He would've killed my friend."

Maggie shrugged. "What the hell does it matter? Jack was a pimp and he knew he'd come to a bad end eventually. Most pimps do."

Dan said, "I'm sorry I had to be the one that killed him."

"Save your sorrow for them as needs it, cowboy," the woman said. "Jack Winter was a woman-beating lowlife, and he doesn't deserve it."

"Deputy Caine, you wouldn't like our jailhouse," Marshal Bully Boyd said. "It's cold and damp and over-run with rats. So your story better be good, tip-top you might say. Why did you kill Jack Winter?"

Dan said, "The man was slapping around a woman . . ."

"Never get between a pimp and his whore," Boyd said. "Go on. I'm listening."

"Ephraim tried to put a stop to it, and punched Winter in the face," Dan said. "The man then proceeded to go for his gun, and I shot him."

"Why didn't you shoot him . . . Traynor, isn't it?" Boyd said.

"That's my handle all right, Marshal," Ephraim said.

"Why didn't you shoot Winter?" Boyd said.

"Because I'm mighty slow on the draw," Ephraim said. "He would've done for me for sure."

"So to save your friend, you shot him," Boyd said. "Is that right, Deputy?"

"I shot him to save a member of my posse," Dan said. "I had no alternative but to act."

A respectable looking man had been standing by, and the marshal said, "What did you see?"

"I saw Mr. Winter get socked on the chin and then he drew his revolver, or tried to," the respectable man said.

"But Winter made a play first?" Boyd said.

"Yes, but he wanted to shoot Mr. Traynor, not Mr. Caine, if that makes any difference."

"It doesn't," Boyd said. "This is a clear-cut case of self-defense. I won't even bring it to court." Then, "You can go," he said to the respectable man.

After the man left, Boyd said, "Shed no tears for Jack Winter. He was a boil on the butt of Fort Worth." Then, "Have you made any progress finding your fugitive, Deputy?"

"No. That's why we were planning to inquire in this hotel," Dan said.

"She isn't here," Boyd said. "I already asked the desk clerk."

"Apart from that, have you made any progress, Marshal?" Dan said.

"No, not so far. These investigations take time," Boyd said. "You're a lawman, you must know that. But be assured, my spies are on the job. Patience, Deputy Caine, patience."

"If I lose Maria von Erbach here, I'll never find her again," Dan said. "That would spell ruin to a lot of people in Broken Back."

"If I find out anything, where can I reach you?" Boyd said.

"We're staying at Ma Tandy's boarding house on Twelfth Street," Dan said. "I guess you could reach us there."

"Yes, I know where that is, near the Golden Garter saloon," Boyd rose to his feet. "A word of advice, Deputy Caine, don't kill another man in Fort Worth."

"I didn't want to kill Jack Winter," Dan said. "He opened the ball when he tried to draw down on Ephraim."

"Deputy Caine saved my life," Ephraim said.

"Yes, yes, I know, you've already told me all that," Boyd said. "But no more, huh?"

"I can't guarantee what will happen when we find Maria von Erbach," Dan said.

"I'll tell you what will happen," Boyd said. "You'll stand aside while I arrest her. Is that clear?"

"As a bell," Dan said. "I'll do anything you say, so long as we get my town's money back."

Chapter Fifty-three

"So the hick lawman gunned Jack Winter," Luke Short said. He shook his head. "It's hard to believe."

"Well, it's a natural fact," Bully Boyd said. "Skinned the iron faster and dropped him with one shot. A few folks seen that."

Short said, "I still can't believe it, Diamond Jack Winter dead. Killed by a rube who looks like he should still be nursing on his mama's teat. Say, do you remember that time when Jack cut Lute Benson in half with a scattergun in the Happy Dove cathouse? Some disagreement over a woman, wasn't it?"

Boyd sampled his gin sling and said, "It's always over a woman. Jack died today because he slapped around one of his whores. It seems that Deputy Caine and his sidekick took exception to that. I mind Lute Benson. He wasn't much. He threatened to kill Jack on sight."

Short said, "Winter went looking for him and tracked him down to the Happy Dove and let him have both barrels."

"In the back," Boyd said. "But since Lute had threatened Jack and was armed at the time it was a clear-cut case of self-defense. Oh, what the heck, Winter won't be missed."

"I don't know about that," Short said. "He was a lousy poker player, but he was a high roller and a big tipper. Somebody should write that on his gravestone, 'Here lies Jack Winter. He was a high roller and a big tipper.'"

"You gonna bury him, Luke?" Boyd said.

"Hell no, he didn't tip that big."

Luke Short, not a heavy drinker, ordered another gin sling for Boyd and a glass of beer for himself. "Do you think the deputy . . . what's his name?" Boyd supplied the name and Short said, "Do you think Deputy Sheriff Caine will find the gal he's looking for and get his money back?"

"In Fort Worth, following a cold trail? He ain't got a prayer," Boyd said.

"Did you tell him that?"

"No. I don't want to break his heart."

"Do you have anybody looking?"

"Only Gus Knott."

"That little ferret?" Luke Short said.

"He's a good detective," Boyd said. "He'll stay on a case like a dog with a bone."

"Do you think he'll find the woman?"

The marshal sighed. "No. But Gus is still a fine detective."

Short said, "You'll eventually have to run the rube out of Fort Worth. You know that, don't you?"

"He's living in a cheap boarding house and has no money," Boyd said. "He'll leave town soon enough, along with the old mountain man."

"Well, as long as he don't overstay his welcome," Short

said. "We got enough penniless rubes in Fort Worth as it is."

"I think Dan Caine is probably a good lawman," Boyd said. "He's handy with a gun. He proved that today. If I accepted the permanent job of marshal, I'd hire him as a deputy."

"If you don't accept the job, your free booze and food at the White Elephant ends," Short said. "Think about that, Bully."

Boyd shivered.

"Luke, my dear friend, the very thought of that makes me feel quite ill," he said.

On Main Street, south of the White Elephant Dan Caine and Ephraim Traynor stood in the doorway of an Acre general store and discussed their next move. The street was its usual chaotic state, crowded with people, wagons, and riders, including a puncher wearing a red shirt who drove three longhorn steers toward the slaughterhouse.

"We've tried every hotel, boarding house, and a brothel by mistake and nothing to show for it," Ephraim said.

"We can only keep trying," Dan said. "She's got to be in this town somewhere."

"Be dark soon," Ephraim said.

Irritable, Dan said, "I figured that out by myself."

"I was only saying," Ephraim said.

"I'm sorry," Dan said. "Seems like I got a burr under my saddle."

"You can't find the gal with the thirty thousand, and you was forced to kill a man to save my life," Ephraim said. "It ain't surprising that you're a mite testy."

Dan nodded. "You're right, it ain't surprising."

Boots sounded on the boardwalk and a youngster with a large canvas bag hanging from his shoulder handed Dan and then Ephraim a handbill. "From the mayor's office. He wants everybody in the Acre to read it."

The kid hurried away, passing out handbills to people as he walked.

Dan and Ephraim read theirs, written in fine copperplate and then printed.

WARNING

FROM THIS DAY FORWARD THIS CITY WILL NO LONGER PUT UP WITH OR TOLERATE HUCKSTERS, THREE-CARD MONTE ARTISTS, THIEVES, THUGS, FAKIRS, BUNCO STEERERS, ,AND DANCE HALL LOUNGERS.

ANY PERSON ARRESTED ON ANY OF THESE CHARGES WILL SPEND 10 DAYS IN THE TARRANT COUNTY JAIL AND WILL BE FED A DIET OF BREAD AND WATER.

REPEAT OFFENDERS CAN EXPECT TO BE TARRED, FEATHERED, AND RUN OUT OF TOWN.

And it was signed, *John Peter Smith*, Mayor.

"Well, he ain't talking about us," Ephraim said. Then after a long pause, "Is he?"

"I reckon if we're in Fort Worth for much longer he'll be talking about us right enough," Dan said.

"Deputy, when do we give up the chase?" Ephraim said. He held up his hands. "Just asking."

"Before our money runs out at Ma Tandy's boarding house," Dan said. "We'll need supplies for our return journey."

"And that means we buy what we need and leave this burg tomorrow morning," Ephraim said. "How does that set with you?"

"It doesn't set well with me, Ephraim, but I've got no other choice," Dan said.

"In Broken Back they'll know you tried," Ephraim said.

"In Broken Back they'll never forgive me," Dan said. "I'm finished there as a lawman because I couldn't get the job done."

"Me, Frank James, Sly Barnes, and John Brooks and them others who quit the posse, there's enough of us to spread the blame thin," Ephraim said.

"There's only one person to blame, Ephraim, and that's me," Dan said.

Thunderclouds had gathered over the Acre and now lightning flashed and rain fell in a torrent, soaking everything. The streets cleared as the sporting crowd and other pedestrians sought shelter and Dan and Ephraim stepped farther into the store doorway. The door opened, a bell jangled, and the proprietor, a bald, stocky man wearing a tan-colored canvas apron stepped out, glanced at the black sky, and shook his head. "This damn storm will cost me money," he said. Then, "Are you boys buying or just looking?"

"Sheltering," Dan said.

The man nodded. "It's a day for it." He walked back inside and the doorbell jangled again.

"Well, we can't stand here all day," Dan said.

"It'll pass," Ephraim said. He waited until a drumroll of thunder ended and then said, "We gonna try more hotels and boarding houses?"

Dan said, "That would take us the rest of the day and into tomorrow and maybe the next day and by that time we'll be sleeping rough. Ephraim, we've set ourselves an impossible task. We don't even know if Maria von Erbach is in a hotel. Who knows? She might have kin or friends in Fort Worth. We can't go door to door asking if she's to home."

"A good way to get ourselves shot," Ephraim said. "I reckon folks are mighty suspicious in these parts." The old scout raised his chin and scratched his hairy neck. "Well, Deputy, what do we do?"

"We go back to Ma Tandy's and have chicken and dumplings for supper," Dan said. "And tomorrow after breakfast you get your change from the ten dollars you gave her and then we saddle up and head for Broken Back."

"Well, it's been a ride I'll never forget," Ephraim said. "Wolf women, Apaches, perfessers, the bones of a giant chicken . . . I'd never seen the like afore."

Dan's smile was slight. "Me neither. I reckoned I'd lead a posse of vigilantes, catch up with the outlaws who robbed the bank, and get the money back. And that's where the story would end. But it sure didn't work out that way."

Thunder rumbled and a competing tinpanny piano played in one of the saloons.

"And I shot a man today," Dan said.

"Nobody's holding that agin' you, Deputy," Ephraim said. "You did what you had to do."

"Call me Dan, Ephraim. I don't reckon I'm a deputy any longer."

"You're a deputy sheriff until we reach Broken Back," Ephraim said.

"And then?" Dan said.

"And then they're gonna hang you."

Despite his black mood Dan Caine laughed.

Dan Caine and Ephraim Traynor ate chicken and dumplings in Ma Tandy's guest house, a meal that Ephraim declared to Ma was, "Tolerable, but made a feast by the sweet distraction of you, dear lady, at the head of the table." The old scout hoped his flattery would lead to a reduction in his bill. It didn't.

That night Dan lay sleepless in his bed, going over and over in his mind about all the mistakes he'd made, trying to figure what he could've done differently. He found no answers. He was still awake when dawn chased the shadows from his room.

Come morning, he and Ephraim were eating a breakfast of scrambled eggs and skillet potatoes when there was loud and frantic pounding at the front door.

"Oh dear, what can that be at this early hour," Ma Tandy said. She dabbed her mouth with a blue and white checkered napkin and rose to her feet as the thumping at the door continued. "Hold your horses," she yelled. "I'm coming."

The time was ten twenty.

Chapter Fifty-four

"You're so kind."

The smiling words of Maria von Erbach as a porter carried her luggage from the Excelsior Hotel's private carriage to the Union Depot's ticket office.

"This train, ma'am?" the uniformed man behind the brass grill said.

"Yes, this train to the end of the line and a connection to Cheyenne," Maria said.

Union Depot was built near the stockyards and the recent rain had turned the ground to mud and the stench from the cattle pens and a nearby pond that received runoff from the yards was a palpable thing.

"I trust once I'm on the train I won't smell that disgusting odor," Maria said, a small white handkerchief against her nose.

"Not as bad, ma'am, not nearly as bad," the ticket agent said. "Keep your window closed." He passed the woman her ticket and glanced at the clock. "Ten twenty-five, we're on time and the cannonball will leave at eleven on schedule." The man smiled. "Do you need help with your luggage?"

"Yes, but only the trunk goes in the baggage car," Maria said. "I'll carry the carpetbag into the carriage."

The woman looked out the window to the deserted platform. "Am I the only passenger?" she said.

"No, ma'am," the ticket clerk said. "There's a family of seven already on board, a couple of businessmen, and a soldier returning to his regiment. The return trip will be much busier. People love to visit Fort Worth."

"I can't imagine why," Maria said.

She carried her carpetbag onto the platform where the locomotive hissed and steamed like a sleeping dragon. She boarded an empty Pullman fitted out with uphol-stered seats and carpet on the floor and took a place at the window overlooking the platform.

She smiled. She'd made the first step on her journey to a different and better life, and nothing could stop her . . .

And then the crashing migraine hit with the sudden-ness of a thunderclap.

Though she clearly showed her annoyance, Ma Tandy said nothing when Marshal Bully Boyd used the back of his right hand to shove her aside as he hurried into the dining room. There were half a dozen boarders at the table including Dan Caine and Ephraim Traynor.

"We've found her!" Boyd yelled.

Dan whooped and jumped to his feet, and the other breakfasters, alarmed, looked as though they were about to dive under the table.

"Where is she?" Dan said.

"Right now she's at the Union Depot, on board a train that leaves at eleven o'clock," Boyd said. "It's now ten thirty-five, and we got some walking to do."

Dan and Ephraim got their guns and hats and Dan said to Boyd, "Where was she?"

"I'll tell you on the way," Boyd said.

Outside the sun was climbing in the sky and the morning was coming in clean, washed by the rain. A stray black dog kept pace with them as they hurried toward the rail depot, its tail wagging.

"Where is the Union Depot?" Dan said.

"East of the stockyards on Front Street, only there is no street there," Boyd said. "But I can tell you what is there, a swampy bog of open ground between us and the depot, so deep in places horses founder in it. So watch your step."

Boyd was right, black mud sucked at Dan's boots and spattered his pants, and the depot building and the adjoining small traveler's hotel and restaurant seemed an impossible distance away. Brown-tainted mud flowed directly from the area of the stockyards and the air was unspeakably foul and hard to breathe. Ephraim cursed steadily and colorfully as he slogged through the mire.

"Where was she?" Dan asked Boyd.

"The Excelsior Hotel," the marshal said. "The most expensive place in town. She wasn't hiding from you boys, she was in plain sight the whole time, living high on the hog."

"We never tried that hotel," Dan said. "Why didn't you tell me about it?"

Boyd smiled and shook his head. "Because the Excelsior wouldn't let a couple of saddle tramps like you see their guest list. Hell, they wouldn't allow you past the front door. And I didn't think a woman on the run from the law would be there because it was too obvious a hideout. Lucky my spy thought otherwise."

"Who was the spy?" Dan said. He was breathing hard from the effort of plodding through clinging mud. The black dog had quickly given up and returned to firmer ground.

"His name is Gus Knott," Boyd said. "Luke Short calls him a little ferret, but he's a first-class detective. I told him he should be a Pinkerton. He was at the Excelsior earlier this morning and just missed seeing the woman leave."

"Damn, this mud is heavy going," Dan said.

"It's slowing us down," Boyd said. "Blame yesterday's rain." He consulted his watch. "We got less than fifteen minutes left." He turned to Ephraim. "How are you doing, old timer?"

"I'll make it, I reckon. It's the worry about coming back that's eating on me."

"I'd bring you a horse, Ephraim," Dan said. "But I doubt it could get through this mud."

"Nothing could but loco humans, including railroad passengers," Boyd said.

Dan lifted his feet higher as he walked into an area of deeper mud. "How did Maria von Erbach get through this?" Dan said.

"She'd more time than us and took the long way around, coming at the depot from the north," Boyd said. "It's firmer ground up that way and she was no doubt riding in the Excelsior hotel's private carriage."

"Hell, right now I wish I had a private carriage," Ephraim said.

"Ten minutes," Boyd said. "Thank God we're almost there." Then, "Keep your powder dry."

It seemed that Bully Boyd expected a gunfight, but Dan Caine fervently hoped that wouldn't happen. The odds were three to one . . . surely the woman would come quietly. She had to.

Chapter Fifty-five

Maria von Erbach was in considerable pain.

The migraine hammered at her head and the morning light streaming through the Pullman car's large window stabbed at her eyes.

Then a voice from the platform. "Hold the damn train!"

She looked out the window and saw three men, one of them Dan Caine, the man she planned to burn at the stake only to have him escape. Now he was here with two others, determined to make an end to all her carefully laid plans . . . intent on destroying her future, saving the man of blood, Cardinal Ahren von Recke, from death.

It was intolerable. Maria screamed in pain and frustration as she took the Marlin revolver from her purse. She'd kill Caine, and the others would flee. Yes, that was the answer . . . the solution to her problem.

Historians believe that Maria von Erbach's migraine was so severe, so painful, that it destroyed her ability to think logically. Certainly, what followed were not the actions of a woman in complete control of her senses.

Maria rose to her feet and walked to the middle of the

car so that she could cover both entrances. Caine was a lawman and he'd come in first. And he'd die first.

Dan Caine drew his Colt and walked up the steps into the Pullman car.

Maria von Erbach stood in the middle of the passage-way between the rows of seats, a gun in her hand. She wore a green traveling dress and a tiny boat-shaped hat with a veil that covered her eyes. The woman's beautiful face was ashen, the wolf's head on her cheek a vivid scarlet, and she leaned heavily against the back of one of the seats.

"Drop the gun," Dan said. "You're under arrest."

"Damn you. I'll see you in hell first," Maria said. Crushing pain. Flashing, dazzling lights. A misty aura around the lawman. His face a white blur. The woman aimed for the face and triggered a shot.

The bullet burned across the right side of Dan's face, just under the cheekbone, and drew blood. The wound shocked and hurt him and for a fleeting moment the lawman was out of the fight.

Bully Boyd, seeing the deputy wounded, stepped in front of Dan, revolver in hand, and yelled, "Lady, drop the gun in the name of the law!"

Ephraim Traynor stood behind the marshal and a little to his left, ready to shoot.

Women on the frontier were indeed shot, stabbed, and hanged, but those deaths were an exception to the rule. It's worthy of mention that men like Dan Caine and Bully Boyd grew up under the unwritten Western code that men offer no physical harm to the fair sex. And that was why, faced with a young woman of considerable beauty, both men hesitated to fire.

But Maria von Erbach didn't live by any code, except the law of the wolf pack, and she didn't recognize their hesitation for what it was.

In that moment as she faced the two lawmen, she knew her dreams were shattered. At the worst, she faced death from a gunshot. At best, many years in a woman's prison or even a noose. She could accept none of those alternatives, nor could she, crucified by the migraine, take on three gunmen.

As Dan Caine and Bully Boyd cautiously stepped toward her, she opened her mouth and savagely screamed her anger and despair . . . and then she placed the muzzle of the Marlin revolver against her temple and pulled the trigger.

Dan Caine was stunned. Fingers of blood ran down his cheek as he looked at Maria von Erbach's sprawled body on the floor of the car. She looked smaller, frailer somehow, as though death had diminished her.

Bully Boyd glanced at the woman and said, "She didn't have to do that. She could've surrendered without a fight."

"No, she couldn't," Dan said. "She was a she wolf, the leader of the pack."

"Huh?" Boyd said.

"It's a strange story and too long to share right now," Dan said. "But I can tell you that Maria von Erbach had to kill herself. She had the spirit of the untamed wolf that refuses to be caged, and she wouldn't have survived behind bars." Dan looked Boyd in the eye. "She was also a vicious murderer and in the end, she betrayed everyone who depended on her and held her dear."

"Ah well, it's too bad," Boyd said. "Now it's you to a doctor, Deputy Caine, and her to the undertaker. It's a pity. Apart from that thing on her cheek she was a fine-looking woman."

"And you'll need this," Ephraim Traynor said, holding up the carpetbag. "It looks like just about all the money is in here."

"Luke Short has an accountant at the White Elephant who'll count it to the penny," Boyd said. "That is after you boys take out money for a bath, shave, and the best meal Luke can provide." Dan opened his mouth to object, but the marshal said, "Look at you, all shot to pieces. Damnit, Deputy, that hick bank owes you that much."

"It sure does, sonny," Ephraim said, nodding. "Truer words was never spoke."

Dan smiled and winced when it hurt his cheek. "I'll forgo the razor," he said. "But the bath and the meal sounds crackerjack to me."

Chapter Fifty-six

Sheriff Dan Caine sat behind his desk, sharing a bottle of Old Crow with Frank James and Sam Barnes. After Sam's stalwart performance as a vigilante, Dan had decided to drop the Sly nickname.

"I went to his funeral, of course," Frank said. "Jared Wagner was a decent sort of lawman."

"Did he suffer much at the end?" Dan said.

Frank shook his head. "No. Another massive apoplexy killed him right quick." He smiled. "By the way, I got my money back from the bank. They say you returned twenty-nine thousand and eight dollars and fifteen cents. The new manager seemed pleased with that."

"And so he should be," Barnes said. "I mean, after all we went through to get it."

"And Sheriff Caine, you're going to have a nice scar on your cheek as a memento of the von Erbach woman. The Broken Back belles will love it."

"In the Pullman car she came mighty close to punching my ticket," Dan said. "She was an evil woman, but right to the end she had sand."

"A regular she wolf," Frank said.

Dan nodded. "That's what she was all right, a she wolf." He picked up some papers from his desk, shuffled through them, and then said, "I can't find it, but somewhere on this desk there's a report from the Texas Rangers, explaining away the forty or so dead females, most of them white, found on the prairie. The report says the army claims they were not women but dead Mescalero Apache warriors, 'killed as the result of intertribal warfare.' The Rangers wanted to investigate further but the word came down from Washington to leave it the hell alone, since their findings could have the potential to embarrass both the army and the government."

"How could the army lose track of all those women, huh?" Frank said. "I see how that could be an awkward question."

Sam Barnes said, "How about you, Mr. James?"

"Call me Frank. You've earned the right. What about me? Well, I'm headed back to Dallas to sell shoes. I enjoy shoes. In fact, when I take these boots off, I'll never wear their like again. Bad for the feet."

Dan filled Frank's glass and said, "What about Yolanda Butler?"

"What about her?"

"Are you taking her back to Missouri like you planned?"

"She doesn't want to go," Frank said. "So what do I do? Grab her by the hair and drag her all the way back to the family farm? It ain't gonna happen. Yolanda seems to be happy where she is, so let her enjoy her life."

"Glad to hear it," Dan said. "Hey, did you hear what happened to Ephraim Traynor?"

"Yeah, he's been invited to New York or something?" Frank said.

"He's already on his way, all expenses paid," Dan said. "He's headed for the New York Institute of Natural History to join Professor Claringbold's expedition to Outer Mongolia to hunt for dinosaurs. Seems that the professor admires Ephraim's skill as a bone hunter."

"I figured Claringbold planned on coming back to Texas," Frank said.

"He did, I guess Outer Mongolia, wherever it is, was a better option," Dan said. "Ephraim is very excited about it."

"Isn't he too old to go hunting dinosaurs?" Barnes said.

"Maybe, but Ephraim doesn't think so," Dan said.

Frank James drained his glass and rose to his feet. "I got to be going, Dan," he said. "Capture the daylight."

Dan stood, and Frank shook his hand. "Thank you for all your help," he said.

"It was an experience I'll never forget," Frank said. "I'm not one for long good-byes. So long, Sheriff Caine."

"You too, Frank. So long and good luck. And if you're ever . . ."

"I'll be sure to stop by," Frank James said.

Dan Caine got started on the mountain of paperwork that came with his promotion to sheriff. He heard the Patterson stage rattle into town and rattle out again, and a few minutes later a young woman who appeared to be in her early twenties walked into the office. She was slim and winsome, wearing a plain blue traveling dress with white collar and cuffs. Her dark hair was pulled back in a bun, but a few strands fell over her forehead and the nape of her neck. Dan thought her as pretty as a field of bluebonnets.

"What can I do for you, miss," Dan said.

The girl put her carpetbag down, glanced at the papers on Dan's desk that had been taken over by his little calico cat, and said, "I'm sorry to intrude, Sheriff."

"You're not intruding in the least," Dan said. "Now how can I help you?"

"My name is Helen Hunter and I'll be the new school-teacher here in Broken Back. I was told to report to the mayor when I got here. I just arrived by the Patterson stage."

"And now you need directions to the mayor's office," Dan said.

"Yes, I do," the girl said. Then, smiling, "What a pretty little cat. What's her name?"

"Cat," Dan said. He rose to his feet. "I'll do better than give you directions, I'll escort you there," he said. "Let me take your bag."

"You're very kind," Helen Hunter said.

Once out in the street, she took Dan's arm, and he enjoyed her closeness and the clean smell of her. "Miss Hunter . . ."

"Call me Helen."

"Helen, what do you think about wolves?" Dan said.

The woman was surprised. "I don't know. I can't say that I've ever given them any thought."

Dan smiled. "I can tell that we're going to be the best of friends," he said.

"I'd like that," Helen said.

TURN THE PAGE
FOR AN EXCITING PREVIEW!

Johnstone Country. Vigilante Justice.

**Introducing the newest good guys
in the bad Old West. A ragtag team of misfit
avengers who don't wear badges, don't follow rules,
and won't stop shooting—till justice is served . . .**

GUNS OF THE VIGILANTES

It begins with a massacre. A crime so brutal and bloody,
the local sheriff refuses to solve it. But when young
deputy Dan Caine sees the slaughter for himself—an
entire family murdered—he can't let it go. Especially
when the eldest daughter is missing. Right there and
then, Caine makes a fateful decision: throw away his
badge, form a vigilante team, and go after the killers . . .

There's one problem:
Who would be crazy enough to join him?
First up is a grizzled old tinpan named Fish Lee, who
discovered the bodies. Then there's the Kiowa, an
Indian scout with a grudge; Cooley, a washed-up
gambler; Mortimer, a whiskey-soaked newsman; and
Holt, a half-grown stock boy.
Sure, they might be crazy.
They might be inexperienced.
But one thing is certain: be it from heaven above
or hell below . . . *vengeance is coming.*

GUNS OF THE VIGILANTES
By
**NATIONAL BESTSELLING AUTHORS
WILLIAM W. JOHNSTONE
and *J.A. Johnstone***
First in a blazing new series! On sale now!
www.williamjohnstone.net

The killing haunted historians for generations and even London's *Strand Magazine,* of Sherlock Holmes fame, was intrigued enough to publish an article about the incident under the headline, "The Medusa Mystery," so-called since to look into the woman's face meant death.

But there was no mystery about Susan Stanton's demise. She was said to be a temptress, a witch, the most beautiful and dangerous woman on the Frontier, fast with a gun and a demon with a knife, and the tale of her downfall begins, as it inevitably must, with a bloody massacre . . .

In all his born days old tinpan Fish Lee had never seen the like . . . the entire Calthrop family massacred . . . and it was white men that had done it.

Fish looked around him wide-eyed, everything sharply delineated by the glaring sun.

Big, laughing Tom Calthrop had been shot several times. Nancy, his plump, pretty wife died of knife wounds and unspeakable abuse. Their ten-year-old twins Grace and Rose and sons Jacob, fifteen and Esau, thirteen, had been shot and Grace, possessed of long, flowing yellow hair, had been scalped. There was no sign of sixteen-year-old Jenny Calthrop and Fish reckoned she'd been taken.

The family dog, a friendly mutt named Ranger, lay dead in the front yard and only Sadie, the cat, had escaped the slaughter, but now mewing in piteous distress the little animal twined and untwined itself around Fish's boots like a calico snake.

All the bodies, sprawled in grotesque death poses, lay in the main room of the cabin.

The dusty, white-bearded prospector picked up the cat and held her close in one arm as he looked around him again. Part of the cabin had been scorched by a fire that had burned for a while and then gone out, and the smell of smoke still hung in the air. There was blood everywhere and amidst it all the six Calthrops lay like marble statues. It was a wonder to Fish how still were the dead . . . perfectly unmoving, their open eyes staring into infinity. The china clock on the mantel tick . . . tick . . . ticked . . . dropping small sounds into the cabin with clockwork dedication as though nothing untoward had happened.

The walls closing in on him, Fish Lee pulled down Mrs. Calthrop's skirt so that others would not see her nakedness as he had and then stepped out of the cabin. He lingered on the shady porch for a few moments and then walked into the hot, West Texas sun. The calico cat wanted down and ran back inside, tail up, where the people she loved would no longer make a fuss over her.

Fish lit his pipe and then took a pint bottle of whiskey from his burro's backpack. The little animal turned her head and stared an accusation at him.

"I know, Sophie," he said. "But this is strictly medicinal. I seen things this day that no Christian man should ever see." Around him were the tracks of horses and high-heeled boots, most of them clustered near the well, and Fish figured six or seven horses and riders, though he didn't have enough Injun in him to make an accurate count. Tom Calthrop's bay riding mare still stood in the corral in back of the ranch house, so horse theft was not the raiders' motive. But the cabin had been ransacked, so they'd been after something. But what? Cash money probably . . . what little the family had. Fish took a swig of rye and then another and pondered that answer. He shook his head. Yeah, it was most likely money, but damned if he knew. Going back two decades, Fish Lee visited the Calthrops once or twice a year and was always given a friendly welcome and dinner and a bed for the night. He knew that in recent years with cattle prices low, Tom barely scraped by as a rancher, and money was always tight. He bred good Herefords, but they were few in number because he could no longer buy additional stock and hire punchers to work them. The boys helped and did what they could, but neither of them were really interested in ranching. Fish remembered Nancy telling him, "Jacob and Esau are readers, and readers aren't much help come roundup." At the time, she'd smiled, but he'd seen bittersweet concern in her eyes.

Damn, that had been only a six-month ago. And now the Calthrops were all dead, and the young boys being readers and not riders no longer amounted to a hill of beans.

Fish Lee was short and wiry, dressed in worn-out, col-orless clothes that he'd had for a long time. His battered top hat looked as though someone had stepped on it, a pair of goggles on the brim for protection against blowing sand. He had a shovel in his pack but didn't have the strength to bury six people. He had a Bible but couldn't read the verses and he had a Henry rifle but no enemy in sight. In other words, as he stood in afternoon sunlight beside his uncaring burro he felt as useless as teats on a boar hog.

"Sophie, we'll head for Thunder Creek and let the law into what's happened here," he said. "Sheriff Chance Hurd will know what to do." He read doubt in the burro's dark eyes and said, "He will. You'll see."

After one last, lingering look at the cabin where shadows angled across the porch where the ollas hung, Fish shook his head and said, "Oh dear Lord in Heaven, what a terrible business."

He then led Sophie west toward town, walking through the bright light of day under the flawless blue arch of the Texas sky.

Chapter One

"I send you out to investigate a murder and you bring me back a cat," Sheriff Chance Hurd said.

"With all the rats we get in here, we need a cat," Deputy Sheriff Dan Caine said.

"Rodent or human?"

"Both, but mainly rodent. I saw one in the cell the other day that if you whittled down to middlin' size would still be as big as a hound dog."

"Well, I guess the cat is kinda cute at that," Hurd said, eyeing the calico that sat on his desk and studied him with fixed, glowing attention. The lawman sighed. "You feed it. Now, put the Kiowa back in his cell and make your report. The coffee is on the bile."

"We'll need the Kiowa when we go after Jenny Calthrop and the men who murdered her family," Caine said.

"The Indian is a drunk," Hurd said.

"Drunk or sober, he can follow a cold trail best I ever seen," Caine said.

"Dan, we ain't following no trails, cold or otherwise," Hurd said. He was a big man with a comfortably round belly and heavy bags under wide open, expressive and cold blue eyes that gave him a basilisk stare. He pointed a thick forefinger at his deputy. "We're city. The Calthrop spread is Concho County and always was."

Hurd's chair scraped across the jailhouse's rough pine floor as he rose and stepped to the stove. He took a couple of cups down from a shelf and poured steaming coffee into both. He handed one to Caine. "Fish says seven riders."

"He thinks there were that many. He isn't sure," Caine said. "I saw the tracks, and I'm not sure either."

"What did the Kiowa say?"

"He says seven, maybe eight."

"Too many," Hurd said.

"The Kiowa says that judging by her tracks, one of them was a woman, but I'm not sure of that either. But I read a dodger that said Clay Kyle runs with a woman," Caine said.

"Black-Eyed Susan. Yeah, I know," Hurd said. "She's named for the prairie wildflower, or so they say. And she kills like a teased rattlesnake. I heard that too. But it wasn't Clay Kyle done this crime. Get that out of your head. It's too far west for him."

"No matter. The sooner we form a posse the better," Caine said. "So why the hell are we sitting here drinking coffee?"

"Like I said, we're not going after them killers," Hurd snapped. "And, like I already told you, it ain't Clay Kyle an' them, because he never, and I say never, rides west of the Brazos. Everybody knows that."

"That's not what old Fish Lee thinks," Dan said. "Fish gets around, he talks to people, some of them lawmen and Rangers. He says there's stories about a crazy man by the name of Loco Garrett who scalps women with long, blonde hair. He makes a pastime of it, you might say, and there's a ten-thousand-dollar price on his head, dead or alive. Grace Calthrop was scalped . . . and Garrett runs with Clay Kyle."

"There's plenty of big windies told about Clay Kyle and his boys," Hurd said. "Don't believe all you hear." The sheriff studied Dan Caine for a few moments and then said, "The county sheriff is living up Paint Rock way and I already sent him a wire. It's his responsibility. Me and you, we got enough to contend with when the punchers come in on Friday nights." He smiled. "Fright night, I call it."

"Lucas Ward is nearly seventy years old," Caine said. "He delivers warrants during the day and at night pulls padlocks on locked store doors. He's not about to ride out after seven killers on a chase that could last weeks."

"And that's exactly why we're staying put," Hurd said. "If you and me was away from Main Street for weeks, Thunder Creek would become a wide-open town, and wide-open towns attract outlaws, gunmen, gamblers, fancy women, and all kinds of rannies on the make. The damned burg would fall into lawlessness and come apart at the seams."

The sheriff's statement was so absurd, so palpably false, that Caine smiled, his teeth white under his sweeping dragoon mustache. "Chance, look out the window, what do you see?"

"A town," Hurd said. He was an inch taller than Caine's lanky six feet, a heavy, joyless man with rough-cut black hair, long sideburns that flanked a spade-shaped beard, and a nose that had been broken several times, a relic of his wild, outlaw youth. He dressed like a respectable law clerk in a charcoal gray ditto suit and a wing collared shirt and blue tie. But he had none of a clerk's sallowness, his weathered face being as dark and coppery and heavy-boned as that of a Cheyenne dog soldier. On those few social occasions when he had to deal with out-of-town rowdies, he wore twin Colts carried in crossed gunbelts. It was not an affectation, but the mark of a shootist, a man to be reckoned with.

"Look at Main Street," Caine said, turning in his chair to glance out the fly-specked window. "Three fair-sized frame houses, built in a rickety hodgepodge style, but painted white and shaded by wild oaks. The houses are surrounded by outbuildings and behind them two dozen tarpaper shacks that could fold up and blow away in a good wind. There's Doan's General Store that doubles as a saloon. Ma Lester's Guest House and Restaurant for Respectable Christian Gentlemen, and Mike Sweet's blacksmith shop with its steam hammer that he claims is the eighth wonder of the world. What else? Oh yeah, a rotting church with a spire and a cross on top but no preacher, a livery barn and corral, and a windmill with iron blades bitten into by rust. And all of this overlooking a scrubby, gravelly street throwing off clouds of dust that gets into everything. Oh, I forgot the Patterson stage that brings the mail. It visits once a month . . . if we're lucky."

Caine swung back and stared at Hurd. "After the law rides out of town, do you really think all those gunmen, outlaws, gamblers, and fancy women of yours are going to beat their feet in the direction of Thunder Creek, population 97? Hell, Chance, even the town's name is a lie. It seldom thunders here, there ain't even a creek, and half the folks are as poor as lizard-eating cats."

"Poor but proud. There's enough money out there to pay your twenty-a-month," Hurd said.

"That's three months in arrears," Caine said. He waited to let that sink in, and then said, "Did I tell you about Nancy Calthrop's wedding ring?"

Hurd rose, poured himself more coffee, and sat again. "No, you didn't."

"She was very proud of it. Showed it to me one time. She said it was a rose color made from a nugget of Black Hills gold that Tom bought from a Sioux Indian one time and inside the band it said, "*forever.*""

"I'm glad she liked it . . . it being a wedding ring that was rose gold and said Forever and all," Hurd said.

"Somebody cut off Nancy's finger to get that ring, and I bet right now he's wearing it," Caine said.

"Why are you telling me this?" Hurd said.

"Because I want to go after the feller who's wearing that ring and hang him," Caine said. "And I want the animal that scalped Grace Calthrop. And I want to rescue her sister Jenny. And, Chance. I want you to authorize a posse and I want you to do it right now. Time is a-wasting."

Chance Hurd sat in silence and studied the younger man. Caine was brown-eyed, broad-shouldered, and in his early thirties. He was a good-looking man with jet black hair and eyebrows that were slightly too heavy for his lean face. He had a wide, expressive mouth and good teeth, and women, respectable and otherwise, liked him just fine. Dan Caine looked a man right in the eye, holding nothing back, and most times he had a stillness about him, a calm, but of the uncertain sort that had the brooding potential to suddenly burst into a moment of hellfire action. He seldom talked about himself, but Hurd knew that the young man had served three years in Huntsville for an attempted train robbery. He'd spent the first four months of his sentence in the penitentiary's infirmary for a bullet wound to the chest he'd taken during the hold-up. At some point during that time, probably in the spring of 1880 according to most historians, he was befriended by John Wesley Hardin. Prison life had tempered Hardin's wild ways and Wes convinced the young Caine to quit the outlaw trail and live by the law. Released early in the summer of 1882, Dan Caine drifted for a couple of years, doing whatever work he could find. He arrived in Montana in January 1884, the year the citizenry, irritated by the amount of crime in the Territory, appointed hundreds of vigilantes to enforce the law. Hard-eyed hemp posses dutifully strung up thirty-five cattle and horse thieves and an even dozen of just plain nuisances. Dan didn't think Montana a good place to loiter, and in the fall of 1885 owning only his horse, saddle, rifle, Colt revolver, and the clothes he stood up in, he rode into Thunder Creek, missing his last six meals. Chance Hurd liked the tough, confident look of the young man and gave him a job as a twenty-a-month deputy sheriff. Caine made no secret of his past, but, having ridden the owlhoot trail himself a time or three, Hurd was willing to let bygones be bygones. That was three years ago, and now it looked as though their association was about to come to an end.

"Dan, you're willing to go this alone, I can tell," Hurd said. "Why?"

"Because I liked the Calthrops," Caine said. "They were good people, kind, generous people, full of laughter and of life and the living of it. They didn't deserve to be slaughtered the way they were and their oldest daughter taken. Now they lie in cold graves, all of them, and their killers run free, warm in the sunshine."

"How the hell are you going to find a posse in Thunder Creek?" Hurd said. "You think about that?"

"Holt Peters and Frank Halder helped me bury the dead," Caine said. "They're willing to ride after the killers."

Hurd made a strange, exasperated sound in his throat, then, "Peters is an orphan stock boy at the general store and Halder is a momma's brat who wears spectacles because he can't see worth a damn. As far as I know, neither of them have shot a gun in their lives." The sheriff smiled. "That's two. Go on . . ."

"Fish Lee says he'll go, if he can find a horse," Caine said.

"An old man with the rheumatisms who's half-crazy with the gold fever," Hurd said. "That's three. Go on . . ."

Caine glanced at the railroad clock on the wall. "It's gone two thirty. Clint Cooley will be getting out of bed soon. He owes me a favor or two."

"A washed-up gambler who drinks too much and is trying to outrun a losing streak," Hurd said. "He's in Thunder Creek because his back is to the wall, and he has nowhere else to run. Maybe that's four, maybe it's not. Go on . . ."

"Cooley is good with a gun," Caine said. "That's a point in his favor."

"Sure, because he carries them fancy foreign revolvers; we heard that he's been in a dozen shooting scrapes and killed five men," Hurd said. "Only problem with that is that nobody can say where and when the killings happened. Me, I don't think he's gunned anybody. He just ain't the type."

Caine didn't push it. Cooley was a man with his own

dark secrets, and he'd never heard of him boast of killings. Wild talk always grew around lonely, unforthcoming men and meant nothing. This much Dan Caine did know . . . the ivory-handled, .44 caliber British Bulldog revolvers the gambler carried in a twin shoulder holster were worn from use. But how and when he'd used the pistols was a matter for speculation, as Hurd had just noted.

"The Kiowa makes five," Caine said. "Yeah, I know he's a drunk, and we believe he's the one who killed Lem Jones behind the saloon that time, but he's a tracker."

"I never could pin that shooting on the Kiowa," Hurd said. "It doesn't take much evidence to hang an Indian, but it was like good ol' Lem was shot by a damned ghost. No tracks, nothing."

Caine smiled. "Now he is dead, he's good ol' Lem. When he was alive, he was a mean, sorry, wife-beating excuse for a man. He needed killing and hell, I sometimes took the notion to gun him myself."

The sheriff sighed. "Lem cheated at cards and he was hell on blacks and Indians. Hated them both." Then, "All right, round up your posse, Dan, but leave your badge right there on the desk. You ain't going after them killers as a deputy sheriff of Thunder Creek."

"Why?"

"Because what you're doing is not authorized. Now put the badge on the desk like I said."

Caine removed the nickel silver shield from his dark blue shirtfront and laid it in front of Hurd. "Now what am I?" he said.

"Now what are you? As of this moment, Dan, you're no longer a lawman but a vigilante . . . and until a few minutes ago I'd have thought that as likely as hearing the word love in a Wichita whorehouse. A man can sure be wrong about some things, huh?"

Caine stepped across the floor to a shelf that held a number of Texas law books, three novels by Mr. Dickens, an unthumbed Bible, and two quarto volumes of *Webster's Dictionary of the English Language,* the late property of a preacher who'd taken over the church and died a week later of apoplexy.

Caine flicked his way through the pages until he reached V, flicked some more and then said, "Vigilante. It says what I am right here."

"Read it."

"'A member of a self-appointed group of citizens who undertake law enforcement in their community without legal authority,'" Caine said. He paused and then said, "This part is important because it explains why folks like me do what we do. It says here, '. . . without legal authority . . .'"—then louder—"'typically because the legal agencies are thought to be inadequate.'"

Hurd nodded. "Now you know what you are and what I am." He picked up the badge, opened his desk drawer, dropped it inside, and then slammed the drawer shut. "Good luck, Mr. Caine," he said. "And thanks for the cat."

Chapter Two

"Damn you, Caine! You make a habit of waking a man at the crack of dawn?" Clint Cooley yelled from behind the closed door of his cabin.

"It's almost three in the afternoon, Clint," Dan Caine said.

"Like I said, the crack of dawn," Cooley said. "I should come out there and shoot you down like a mad dog . . . like a . . . a rabid wolf."

"I need you, Clint," Caine said. "Big doings coming down."

"Then why the hell do you need me, lawman? Speak, thou apparition."

"Tom Calthrop is dead, murdered, him and his whole family and young Jenny's been took," Caine said. "And as of a few minutes ago I'm no longer a lawman."

A long pause and Cooley said, "How do you know about the Calthrops?"

"Because I buried them today," Caine said.

A bolt slammed open and a tall, well-built man, dressed only in his underwear, stood framed in the doorway. "I knew Tom Calthrop, and I liked him," Cooley said. "What do you want from me, Dan?"

"Ride with me. Help me find his killers."

"What about Hurd?"

"He won't leave Thunder Creek."

"He's afraid of his damned shadow. He has the backbone of a maggot."

Caine let that pass without comment and said, "Ten minutes, Clint. Don't wear your fancy dressed-up-for-the-poker-tables-in-New-Orleans duds. It could be a rough trail."

The gambler eyed Caine from scuffed boots to battered hat, taking in his canvas pants, blue shirt, army suspenders, and the washed-out red bandana tied loosely around his neck, a blue Colt in its holster worn high, horseman style.

"Dan Caine, when I want sartorial advice from you, and that will be never, I'll ask for it," Cooley said. "Now bring me a cup of coffee, will you?" He glanced at the blue sky and shook his head. "My God . . . the crack of dawn."

"Not for the Calthrops," Caine said.

"No," Cooley said, his handsome face suddenly serious. "Not for the Calthrops."

Dan Caine walked from Cooley's shack in the direction of the general store, smiled, and touched his hat to the local belle, Estella Sweet, the blacksmith's daughter. She was seventeen years old that year, a slender, elegant girl with wavy blonde hair that fell over her shoulders in a golden cascade. Some said, out of her father's hearing, that it was high time she was wedded and bedded, but Estella showed no inclination to partake of holy matrimony or of mattress time either. It should be mentioned here, because historians of the more sensational kind always draw attention to it, that the girl had prodigiously large breasts. But she bore them proudly, her scarlet, front-laced corset jutting aggressively ahead of her like the figurehead on a man-o'-war. Under the corset Estella wore a light gray shirt in a railroad stripe, and a front-bustled skirt of the same color fell to the top of her high-heeled ankle boots. She wore a flat-brimmed, high-crowned hat, and her blue eyes were protected from the sun by a pair of round dark glasses with a brass frame. Around her neck, poised above her cleavage, hung a small silver pocket watch with a white face and black Roman numerals.

For the cowboys who came into town on Friday nights Estella was one of the sights to see. But it was very much lookee but no touchee, because blacksmith Mike Sweet was a powerfully strong man, hard, dangerous, and profane, very protective of his pretty daughter and with no great liking for the cattlemen who provided ninety percent of his livelihood.

With an outstretched hand, Estella stopped Dan and said, "Holt Peters over to the general store told me about the Calthrops. Dan, who could've done such a terrible thing?"

"I don't know, Estella," Caine said, seeing a distorted version of himself in the girl's dark glasses. "It might have been a man called Clay Kyle and his boys, but that's far from sure. I aim to find out."

"You and Sheriff Hurd are going after them . . . the killers I mean," the girl said.

"I'm going after them," Dan said. "Sheriff Hurd doesn't want to leave the town without a lawman. Don't worry, I'll bring Jenny Calthrop back safe and sound."

"Jenny's been my friend since, well, forever . . . since we were both children," Estella said. She smiled. "And I never minded it a bit when folks said she was the prettiest girl in Concho County."

Dan grinned and said, "When it comes down to who's the prettiest gal between you and Jenny, I'd say it's a tie. You're both as pretty as a field of bluebonnets."

Estella's uncertain smile slowly faded. "Find her, Dan. Bring her home."

Dan said, "Clint Cooley, Holt Peters, and Frank Halder have all volunteered to join my posse. And maybe old Fish Lee if he can rustle up a horse. Oh, and the Kiowa."

Estella frowned as though she was about to say something, changed her mind, and said, "Then do be careful, Dan. And make sure Frank Halder remembers to wear his spectacles. He forgets them all the time."

Dan Caine's answer to that was a smile and a nod, but Estella Sweet wasn't quite done with him. "You could always get some cowboys to join you," she said. "The ranchers hereabouts set store by Tom Calthrop."

"I thought about it, but the fall gather is coming up, and the ranchers want their punchers to stick close to the home range. Besides, I don't have time. We're pulling out now while there's still a few hours of daylight. The Kiowa can track in the dark, but he's not keen on it."

"Then good luck, Dan," the girl said. She laid a slim hand on Dan's shoulder. "I think you're going to need it."

* * *

Holt Peters, an orphaned boy around sixteen years of age, and Frank Halder, short, fat, and myopic, were in Doan's General Store when Dan Caine stepped inside.

"Howdy, Dan," said Pete Doan, a middle-aged man with sunken cheeks, hollow temples, and gray eyes tired out from constant pain. "Sheriff Hurd raising his posse to run down those killers?"

"Not Hurd, just me," Dan said. He answered the question on Doan's face. "Somebody has to stay in town and look after things."

"Is that so?" the storekeeper said, not liking what he'd just heard. "I'm the mayor of this burg, and I say there isn't much to look after in Thunder Creek."

"Sheriff Hurd doesn't see it that way," Dan said. Then, "Holt and Frank, you listen up. I'm no longer a deputy, so this posse isn't legal. Sheriff Hurd says I'm a vigilante, and I guess that applies to anybody who rides with me."

"I'll stick, Mr. Caine," said Holt Peters, a tall, good-looking boy, a blue-eyed towhead who'd outgrown all his duds and was wearing Pete Doan's threadbare castoffs.

"Me too," Halder said, blinking behind his spectacles like a plump owl. He was a year older than Peters and a head shorter.

Doan looked skeptically at Dan. "Who else have you got?"

"So far, Clint Cooley and the Kiowa."

"That's it?"

"So far."

"What do you mean, so far? Where are you going to get anybody else?"

Dan Caine smiled. "How about you, Pete?"

Doan took the question in stride. "I've got a cancer growing inside me, and I haven't sat a horse in twenty years. All I'd do is slow you up."

"Pity. I'd sure like to have along a man who fought Apaches backwhen."

"When I was a Ranger, I fit the Comanche, not Apaches," Doan said. "It was a long time ago and something I wouldn't want to do ever again."

Dan nodded. "I can understand that."

"I reckon you'll understand it better if you catch up to the killers who massacred the Calthrop family," Doan said. "A sight of my bad experiences were written in blood and lead." His eyes opened and closed several times as though blinking away remembered images, then he said, "I've loaned each of these two . . . vigilantes . . . a .32-20 Winchester and a box of shells each. The rifles are old, but they still shoot. What else do you need? Supplies? You'll need supplies."

"Yeah, I do, but I'm a little short of the ready at the moment," Dan said. "I'll need to talk to you about that."

Doan, a normally sour man, managed a thin smile. "Coffee, cornmeal, dried apples, bacon, and a pan to fry it in. Tobacco? You got tobacco?"

"Truth is, I'm kinda low on the makings," Dan said.

"And tobacco. I'll sack up the stuff, and you can pay me when you get back," Doan said. "Bring back Jenny Calthrop, and you don't have to pay anything at all."

"And a cup of coffee for Clint Cooley," Dan said. "Add it to my bill, Pete."

"Coffee is on the house," Doan said. "The pot's on the stove."

Connect with

Us

Visit us online at
KensingtonBooks.com
to read more from your favorite authors, see books
by series, view reading group guides, and more.

Join us on social media
for sneak peeks, chances to win books and prize packs,
and to share your thoughts with other readers.

facebook.com/kensingtonpublishing
twitter.com/kensingtonbooks

Tell us what you think!

To share your thoughts, submit a review,
or sign up for our eNewsletters, please visit:
KensingtonBooks.com/TellUs.